O9-BTN-080

MORRIS AUTOMATED INFORMATION NETWORK
0 1029 0025672 2

THE BRITISH CROSS

ALSO BY BILL GRANGER

Fiction

The November Man

Schism

The Shattered Eye

Public Murders

Queen's Crossing

Sweeps

Time for Frankie Coolin *(as Bill Griffith)*

Nonfiction

Fighting Jane: Mayor Jane Byrne and the
Chicago Machine *(with Lori Granger)*

Chicago Pieces

THE BRITISH CROSS

A NOVEL

Bill Granger

CROWN PUBLISHERS, INC.
NEW YORK

Grateful acknowledgment is made to Michael B. Yeats, Anne Yeats,
Macmillan London Limited and Macmillan Publishing Co., Inc.
for permission to reprint lines from "Sailing to Byzantium"
from *The Collected Poems of William Butler Yeats*,
copyright 1928 by Macmillan Publishing Co., Inc.,
copyright © renewed 1956 by Georgie Yeats.

Published by Crown Publishers, Inc.,
One Park Avenue, New York, New York 10016
and simultaneously in Canada
by General Publishing Company Limited
Manufactured in the United States of America
Library of Congress Cataloging in Publication Data
Granger, Bill.
The British cross.
I. Title.
PS3557.R256B7 1983 813'.54 83-7475
ISBN 0-517-55035-0
Book design by Jane Treuhaft
10 9 8 7 6 5 4 3 2 1
First Edition

For Alec, who was there,

and sailed the Baltic Sea with me

NOTE

A very brave man named Raoul Wallenberg undertook, in the middle of the Second World War, to save Jews condemned to execution in the Nazi death camps. He was a Swedish national and an official neutral in the war; scion of a wealthy and powerful banking family that still has great influence in Sweden, Wallenberg used his many connections to aid his mission of mercy.

Wallenberg worked in Budapest. By dint of bribing, string-pulling and by issuing Swedish passports to Hungarian Jews, it is estimated he saved more than one hundred thousand lives. In several instances, he actually stopped death trains in the marshaling yards and bullied train officials into releasing their human cargoes.

Wallenberg had been persuaded to his task by the United States in secret, subtle negotiations.

In the last days of the war, the Soviet Army entered Budapest first; they arrested Wallenberg and he disappeared behind Soviet lines.

Some believed the arrest was a mistake. Others held it was part of the professional paranoia practiced in the MGB, the Soviet Intelligence service that is now called the Committee for State Security (KGB). The Soviets may have considered Wallenberg to be an American spy.

After many protests from the Wallenberg family, Sweden and the United States—though the official protests were muted, indeed—the Soviet Union issued a report that Raoul Wallenberg had died in a Soviet prison in 1947. Unfortunately, his body was destroyed and no proof of the death remained except the word of Soviet officials.

Since that Soviet report, dozens of prisoners who have been released from the Gulag Archipelago have reported seeing him still alive. It is not unusual, despite the brutalities of the Soviet prison system, for prisoners in the Gulag to serve twenty, thirty or forty years' imprisonment.

The Bulgarian Secret Police act as surrogates of the KGB in certain acts of espionage and sabotage in the West. In 1982 the Bulgarians were accused of carrying out a plot to assassinate Pope John-Paul II on behalf of the KGB. They denied it.

For fifty years, Finland has existed in delicate political balance between the Soviet Union and the West. The Soviet Union is believed in intelligence circles to have considerable influence over internal affairs in neighboring Finland.

For forty years, British intelligence has been riddled with Soviet spies and traitors. In 1982, it was revealed that the Soviets had turned an intelligence worker at the joint Anglo-American listening post and computer center at Cheltenham.

These statements are true and are reflected in this book.

An aged man is but a paltry thing,
A tattered coat upon a stick, unless
Soul clap its hands and sing, and louder sing
For every tatter in its mortal dress,

WILLIAM BUTLER YEATS

He is an Englishman!
For he himself has said it.
And it's greatly to his credit,
That he is an Englishman!

W. S. GILBERT

1

HELSINKI ✱✱✱✱✱✱✱✱✱✱✱✱✱✱✱✱✱✱✱✱✱✱✱✱✱✱✱✱✱✱

Foul, leaden clouds threatened, but it had not snowed for four days and the streets were finally clear. The bricks of the old streets seemed to glisten in the light of a weak sun, polished by the shattering cold. Cold was piled on cold; wind piled on wind, keening unexpectedly around corners, barreling into pedestrians who fought for their footing along the treacherous, ice-streaked walks. The streetcars ground noisily against metal rails as their steel bodies arched around the corner into Mannerheimintie, making sounds colder and more hurtful than the touch of warm flesh on frozen metal. Every sound in the numbing cold of the city seemed a sort of strangled scream; every sound scraped at the senses because the smothering muteness of the snow had been cleared away from the streets and piled in dirty heaps along the curbs. Pale, sullen days came and withered and they were scarcely noticed because this was the dark heart of the dark Finnish winter and the sun seemed like a dead planet in another solar system, far and distant. The nights were long and starless: gray clouds at sunset, scudding in from the choppy, shallow Gulf of Finland beyond the frozen port of the city smothered the sky and did not permit light from stars or moon.

Devereaux awoke in darkness.

He blinked once and again, but darkness remained. He held up the face of his wristwatch and perceived the hour. He awoke at the same time each morning; except morning was always night.

The room was too warm but nothing could be done about that. Devereaux lay naked on the sheets, half-covered by the comforter. A sudden burst of wind broke against the window of his room; it howled like a damned soul, seeking warmth and entry.

Seven in the morning, Devereaux thought. But to say morning in the darkness has to be an act of faith. Maybe this is the morning that the light will not return. He smiled then, mocking the darkness and his own depression. The Scandinavians called this horrible pit of long, black winter "the murky time."

Devereaux reached for the lamp at the side of the bed and flicked it on. The room was bathed in yellow incandescent light that made the sense of perpetual night much more real. He pushed himself up in bed and stared at nothing; he waited for the first red streak of morning beyond his window.

For seven weeks in Helsinki, he had moved ever more slowly each day, as though caught in a dream.

He had come to serve his time here like a prisoner. He shut down all his senses. He deprived his mind of expectation; he did not note the passing of the days or mark them on a calendar or keep track of the weeks. The miniature appearances of daylight could not be celebrated or enjoyed for fear of making the long and bitter nights unendurable; he began to understand this was part of the character of the Finns, part of the stoicism, part of the muted suffering. The streets of Helsinki were never crowded.

Seven weeks.

Devereaux stared at the night outside the hotel and still there was no morning light.

No message from Hanley, no answer to questions that had to be asked. In the fourth week—it was the fourth week, Devereaux thought, but perhaps it was not—he had requested more money. And two days later, in the mailbox behind the front desk in the lobby of the Presidentii Hotel, a small envelope waited for him. Again, no words, no messages, no admonitions, no instructions. Money and a copy of a receipt noting the money had been passed to him. At least it was contact; Devereaux had felt lightened by the anonymous touch for the rest of that day; he had nearly felt something like happiness in the way a grateful prisoner might acknowledge the end of time in isolation.

There.

He turned his eyes back to the window and was very still. He felt a curious sense of anticipation that was both pleasant and unpleasant.

Slowly, moment by moment, the blackness became purple and etched the buildings in that color beyond the hotel-room window. And then he saw the redness splitting the horizon; a chill, winter sunrise. He smiled, threw off the comforter and put his feet on the brown carpet; at least this morning was to be different. Perhaps it was the end of the isolation and waiting; in a little while, he would go to the underground mall and make the contact and perhaps that would provoke the resolution.

But he would not hope too much. Hope wounds.

He turned on the tap in the bathroom and the water drummed flatly from the shower against the molded fiberglass tub. When the water was very hot and the room was filled with steam, he stepped into the tub and let the coldness he felt in himself wash away.

On the morning it began, Devereaux was outside on the flat ground beyond the cabin, splitting firewood against the threat of snow later in the day.

He had not expected Hanley because Hanley had never come to this place in the Virginia mountains where Devereaux had his house. "Not a house exactly," Hanley had once joked to the Old Man. "More like the place where Devereaux goes to ground."

The mountain was not very high but it had the virtue of being deserted, penetrated by a single-track dirt road that steeply scaled the hill to the place where Devereaux's house was buried in the forest. From the simple cabin you could see the only approach to the mountain, up the only road, but the one who approached could not see you at all.

Devereaux had put down his ax when the black car began its slow ascent off the main highway that led to the little town of Front Royal, snug at the entrance of the Blue Ridge Mountains six miles beyond.

The car worked slowly up the snow-packed road. Once it nearly slid sideways into a shallow ravine broken with birch and pine trees. When it seemed certain that the black car would reach the summit of the mountain, Devereaux went inside the cabin. He removed the Remington double-barrel from its place on the stone-covered wall and broke it open. He shoved two red shotgun shells into the chambers and closed the piece. He took a box of similar shells from a drawer in a small pine cabinet on the wall.

Devereaux waited outside for the car grinding up the treacherous road. It stopped fifty feet from the cabin. After a moment the rear door opened. Devereaux cocked the shotgun.

It began to snow gently.

Hanley closed the rear door and made his way across the slippery ground to the cabin. He wore a black overcoat, a small black hat, a white woolen muffler and he wore black gloves. His face was pale and even the exertion of walking across the sloping, uncertain ground to the cabin did not give it color.

At ten feet, he stopped as though he saw Devereaux's shotgun for the first time. He blinked and did not speak.

Devereaux uncocked the rifle and pointed to the car.

"He's Henderson," Hanley said, understanding the silent question. "He hasn't the faintest idea what this is all about."

"And me?"

"No. He doesn't know it's even you. If I had known about that road, I would have insisted you meet me in Front Royal. Why don't you improve it? A car can barely make it."

"That's the idea."

"So this is where you come to ground."

Devereaux said nothing. They stood beneath the shelter of

a wooden porch roof on the bare, frozen ground. Hanley slapped his gloved hands together. "Are you going to invite me inside?"

Devereaux said nothing. He had worked for Hanley in R Section for nearly twenty years. The time had not softened Devereaux's contempt for his control; nor softened Hanley's perplexed distrust of the agent he ran. They existed in a symbiotic balance that teetered back and forth on a thin wire, suspended above a black gorge without a net.

"Then should we stand out here and freeze to death?"

Hanley attempted to force a smile as he said it, but Devereaux did not respond for a moment. Then he said: "Why did you come here?"

"It must have been important." Hanley said it with a note of sarcasm. The mountain was winter silent in the falling snow; the larger animals were asleep or dead; the deer had gone to lower ground; the bears snored in filthy dens; the birds were gone; only the ground squirrels and the possums, still foraging for food, left tracks in the mountain snow.

Devereaux decided. He held the shotgun loosely in his right hand. He pushed against the rough wood door. Hanley followed. The room was lit at each end by two small lamps and illuminated by a fireplace where logs spit and crackled and the flames licked at the edge of the stones.

Devereaux turned and waited while Hanley carefully removed his gloves and took off his hat and coat. He folded the coat precisely and laid it across a table behind the large red couch that faced the fire. Devereaux stood at the stone wall and put the shotgun back on the wall. He turned to a small kitchen-bar and poured a glass of vodka.

Hanley was thin, precise, small. His hands were calm and white, like ivory sculptures. His fingers were very long. When he spoke, his flat Nebraska voice surged without emphasis, as though there could be no depressions or elevations coming from the man. He was a winter pond, flat and still.

"We've had a probe from someone in the Opposition."

Devereaux did not speak. He sipped the Polish vodka from the glass; the bottle had been cold an hour before but it had warmed while he had worked outside. The vodka warmed him.

"One of their boys," Hanley said. He did not sit down because Devereaux stood. "One of their boys wants to become one of ours."

Devereaux put down the glass. He was in his mid-forties but his body was still large, still strong, still carried a sense of power. His face was hard, his eyes were gray and flat and unrevealing. His face was not handsome because it was lined and because of the hardness in it; and yet there was something compelling in it. His hair was mostly gray, as it had been since he was twenty. His fingers were flat and his hands were wide. He did not speak very often because all of his life was part of a deceit and speech betrayed a person too often to be trusted. When he spoke, his words cut like glass; they were remorseless.

He spoke now. "Why did you come here?"

"Because we have a little matter."

"Asia," Devereaux said. "You remember that little matter?"

"In time. Everything in time. It's working."

"Is it?"

"I haven't forgotten my promise."

The promise had come at the time of the Mitterand business. Quid pro quo; Hanley owed him and in his position of acting director of R Section, he had been able to pay his debt to Devereaux.

Devereaux had been an old Asian hand in the beginning; Devereaux had been recruited out of Asian Studies at Columbia University in New York; Devereaux had served in Asia during the Vietnam War until he made a mistake in 1968. He told the truth about the coming Tet Offensive and it was understood that his usefulness was over. He had been sent home and cast adrift in the Western world he despised. Only Asia had been home to him; only the warm jungle nights and the chattering of people in a dozen dialects and languages; only the elaborate courtesy that masked an elaborate deceit which in turn finally revealed simple truths—and he had been exiled from that world for fifteen years. Until the Mitterand matter when Hanley had finally been in a position to promise him that the exile was over; that he could go back to the only world he had ever wanted as home.

Hanley had promised. Hanley said he had not forgotten the promise.

"I don't care about your probe from the Russians," Devereaux said slowly. "We made a little bargain between us."

"It's not quite that simple," Hanley said, and they both knew then that it was a lie.

Devereaux did not speak.

"The Russian business," Hanley said.

For a long moment, there was silence. What did it matter if Hanley had promised? Or that he lied now? Or that Devereaux could not go back to Asia? The Section had trapped them both in time. Hanley was trapped as his control and Devereaux was trapped as an agent; twenty years and they could only share a lie. Perhaps it was enough. Devereaux stared at the white-faced man with thinning hair and long, pale hands and realized he felt pity for him.

Or perhaps it was for himself.

"The defector. Does he want an assignment?"

Hanley shook his head. "He wants to come out of the closet."

"Is he in a position to dictate the terms?"

"Not really," Hanley said. "But we are curious."

"Why?"

"There are unusual aspects to the matter."

"Where is he?"

"Inside," Hanley said.

"What is the problem?"

Hanley had not said there was a problem but it was implied in everything from the shallow lie he told Devereaux to the unusual trek to Devereaux's retreat in the Blue Ridge Mountains.

"We would like to be certain. Of his intentions."

Devereaux reached for the bottle of Polish vodka and poured another long drink. He did not offer the bottle to Hanley; neither man sat down.

"Nothing is certain."

"Langley was burned last August on that fellow. You know the one."

"The alleged Soviet cipher clerk."

"Very clumsy. It exposed a mole of theirs working inside the Central Committee apparatus."

"Yes," Devereaux said. The CIA mole had been murdered in his cell by two KGB interrogators who were subsequently reprimanded for their overzealous examination of the prisoner. "It was too bad."

"Too bad," Hanley agreed with matching insincerity. "Langley can get away with mistakes like that but we can't. I don't have to tell you the Section lives too close to the edge. These are perilous times for all of us."

"Yes, you don't have to tell me."

Hanley frowned. "That's sarcasm," he said pedantically. "We want to minimize the risk in contact."

"For the Section," Devereaux said.

Hanley looked surprised. "Of course for the Section."

Devereaux waited.

"This is a delicate business."

For the first time, Devereaux smiled. The smile was without comfort. Hanley was chief operations officer for the Section, which meant he had never been on an operation; operations were actions and all actions in the bureaucratic establishment were fraught with peril and political liabilities. Hanley would prefer to do nothing, to not have been contacted by this Soviet defector; but the single action made a response necessary, if only to ensure that nothing would result and nothing would be done.

In the shadows of the dim-lit room, with the fire making dancing lights on the walls, Hanley did not see the smile. "We will minimize risk at contact. He isn't the sort who is expected to turn, you see. I want you to see what he is like, take his measure; we need some input to make a decision."

"You sound like a corporate recruiter."

"Yes," Hanley said, suddenly pleased. "I suppose we are in a way."

"What do you want?"

"Our defector-in-waiting comes from a sensitive area inside the apparatus of the Opposition. But not one that is of particular interest to us. So two things come to mind: Why does he want out? Why does he want to come out through the Section?"

"Because Langley would be leery of another defector so soon after being burned last August," Devereaux replied.

"Exactly. The Opposition has been neglecting us. Perhaps the Section would be so eager for a small coup that we would not be careful when checking his *bona fides*."

"And that might mean he is a triple."

"The thought crossed my mind."

Devereaux put down the empty glass and went to the fire. He picked up a black poker and shoved a large piece of oak back into the grating. The gesture exposed unburned wood and the fire leaped in the stone fireplace.

"Where does he come from?"

"Leningrad. He's very high in the Gulag."

Devereaux turned from the fireplace with the poker in his hand. His eyes betrayed interest for the first time. "That's odd," he said.

"Yes, isn't it? Obviously, we can't ignore him. But who cares about the Gulag Archipelago?"

"Don't let the human-rights groups hear that."

"If they had an interest in my opinion, I would tell them," Hanley said stiffly. "There are no secrets in the Gulag, not secrets worth having. We proved that prisoners worked on the gas pipeline, we fed the information to every agency, we created a propaganda front in Europe . . . to what effect?" There was an edge to his voice. "Nothing. The Soviet Union has slaves and prisoners and no one is concerned; and once we have learned about the prisoners, what more is there to say? There is no profit in the knowledge."

Devereaux stared at Hanley a moment and then put down the poker. "Why has this one sought us out?"

"That's the question, isn't it? The one you have to answer."

"Do I go into black?" Black was undercover, illegal.

"No." Hanley crossed to the fire and held out his hands to the flames though he felt perfectly at home with the cold in the cabin. In the bowels of the Department of Agriculture building on 14 Street in Washington, Hanley kept his office at sixty degrees Farenheit, summer and winter. The flames gave color to his pale features.

"You agree to the operation?" Hanley asked softly.

"No. Not at all." Devereaux said the words flatly. "But there is no choice, is there?"

No, Hanley thought. There is no choice at all. There never was.

"His name is Tartakoff. They accord him a degree of confidence, which means a degree of freedom. That bothers us as well. He received a rapid elevation after Andropov took over. That bothers us, too. He's only forty-six. Far too young for those people."

"You know a lot already."

"Too much. Everything is so delicate." Hanley frowned. "He makes a shopping trip next week to Helsinki."

"From Leningrad."

Hanley nodded. "You can meet him at Stockmann's. Were you ever in Helsinki?"

"Going back. Once. To Vietnam. It was 1966." Devereaux seemed to recall the memory involuntarily. The words were as flat as computer-generated speech. "There was business in Copenhagen; it had a connection to that business at Da Nang. Do you remember?"

"Vaguely."

"I took Japan Lines back across the Soviet Union."

"That was risky."

"I was an accredited journalist."

"But they knew what you were."

"It didn't matter. I spent a long night in Helsinki."

"He has a wife but he does not mention her in the matter. He's buying her some trinkets at Stockmann's. He likes to get out of the Soviet Union. He spent two years in Paris in the early seventies."

"KGB."

"Of course."

"What does he have to sell?"

"Himself at the moment. It's not enough. I want you to lead him, find out what he can put together for us."

"What do I tell him?"

Hanley stared at the fire as though hypnotized by it. He had been a child in Omaha so long ago that it seemed remembered as a fragment of someone else's dream. A fire in a fireplace and the Nebraska winter raging outside. He saw ships colliding in the fire; the ships were the logs, the flames the death. He could hear men crying as they fell into the sea.

"Anything you wish to tell him. Promise anything because it doesn't matter. Take the time to see what he is worth to us."

"Only promises after all?"

Hanley blinked and tore his eyes reluctantly from the flames. He could see the cold, mocking face clearly despite the shadows. He felt the chill of the gray eyes resting on him.

"I have to get back," Hanley said. "This seemed the best way. I thought if I called you to Washington, it would be under false colors. I mean the Asian business. It's difficult to arrange, Devereaux."

"You're a liar, Hanley."

Hanley did not speak for a moment. When he found his voice, it was sure and flat, the bureaucrat who has always prepared an answer. "Examine Tartakoff. If he promises us nothing, we have no use for him. There must be a middle ground between too much and too little."

"Until then, he's trapped."

"Yes. It's the only comforting part of the whole matter."

"He can't get out without us."

"He wouldn't be alive by the time he got to Paris."

"How long does he dangle?"

Hanley shrugged. "As long as it takes. As long as we need."

Seven weeks and there had been three meetings with the Soviet defector named Tartakoff and there had been no message from the Section.

Devereaux would buy the new English-language papers in the afternoon at the red granite Helsinki train station. He would savor the newspapers, not daring to read them too quickly like a child who saves parts of his candy bar against a time when he will want them more. He walked the streets of the city until he could remember all the street names. He walked down to the frozen harbor where the vegetable market was held in the open in the warm weather. A squat cathedral in the Russian style sat on a hill above the harbor and brooded over the silence and the ice stretching into the Baltic waters. Channels were cut in the ice for some ships and the Silja Line ferry left on time each evening for Stockholm fifteen hours to the west.

The city was less than two hundred kilometers from the western border of the Soviet Union. Soviet television filled one drab channel on the set in Devereaux's room at the Presidentii. Sometimes, driven by boredom, he would sit and watch the channel and watch endless propaganda films about heroic Soviet workers or endless panel discussions. The signal was distorted on the station, jammed by Finland; but still Devereaux would watch until the very drabness of the life portrayed on the Soviet screen could make him bear another long Helsinki winter night.

Across the street from the hotel, from the window on the fourth floor, Devereaux could see the frozen remains of an open construction pit dug during the summer. Winter had stopped construction. The walls of the pit were revealed to be rock on rock.

He would drink Finlandia vodka in the bare, cold lobby bar or in one of the raucous taverns at the edges of the main shopping district along Mannerheimintie.

In the basement of the hotel were a sauna and a small pool. He would rent trunks and then swim back and forth in the small pool until exhaustion plucked at his muscles. Then he would sit in the sauna alone and let the heat fill him. He would close his eyes and remember when he had not been an exile in the cold, sterile West; he would remember Asia and its blood-red suns, the farmers squatting in the fields between watery rows, bent to ancient tasks. But the heat of the sauna would become too great in time and then he would stop his dream and plunge back into the cold pool and swim again until his strength was finally gone and he could sleep.

Four reports to Hanley and a final conclusion.

And still, Hanley did not answer.

Devereaux had found comfort always in the isolation of the cabin in Virginia. He had not needed words or companionship or human contact of any kind. But now he did not feel isolated by choice; he felt imprisoned, shut in, kept away, held in silent chains.

So he understood much later why he accepted the invitation of the prostitute who had approached him around midnight one Friday in the lobby bar of the Presidentii. Her name was Natali and she said she was part Russian and part Swedish. Her hair was black and her eyes were a sort of lazy blue. She said she thought Devereaux was English.

Of course it could have been a trap. He understood that at

the time and much later. But he had yearned to speak to her and when he led her to his room, he had touched her gently and he had slept next to her and he had cupped his body next to her so that he could touch and feel her nakedness beneath the sheets and become lost in her. He kissed her because she wanted to kiss him. But he held her as a child holds to a promise.

Natali had arched her back and he could feel the bones beneath the pale, milky skin when he held her. He had kissed the nipples of her breasts. When he had made love to her, he held her so tightly that she thought she could not breathe.

"Who are you?" she had asked once and he had thought of a name. When she had left him in the morning, he realized he had slept and he had not felt the perpetual chill in him that had nothing to do with winter.

He stepped from the shower on the fifty-first morning of the winter he had spent here. It was seven-fifteen. He shaved slowly but not carefully. He still saw Natali in his mind's eye. And saw the image of Tartakoff—a now-frantic Tartakoff—who would meet him in two hours in the vast underground shopping mall that extends from the train terminal to the shopping district.

Who are you?

Devereaux stared at himself and carefully drew the single-edge razor down across his throat and then rinsed it in the hot water in the sink. It doesn't matter, he had told Natali at first. And then he had given her a name plucked from a memory of stolen names.

Tartakoff had been left to dangle.

Devereaux would cut the string this morning. There was no point to this. He would end it because it had to be ended by someone.

Morning broke reluctantly at last. The red sky at dawn had become pale at midmorning. A sickly yellow flooded the sky. Bundled men and women from the suburbs arrived in the city at the bus terminal across from the hotel. The buses belched and blew black smoke against each other.

At the entrance of the train station, heroic figures were

carved into the soft red granite of the walls. Devereaux entered the terminal from the side and slowly passed the newsstand where the *Times of London* sat side by side with *Pravda.* He crossed to the steps that led to the subterranean shopping plaza that had been carved out of the rocks beneath the Helsinki streets.

The underground was a Finnish solution to winter. Lights were low in the low ceiling but all was bright. People in heavy furs and wool coats shuffled past with dark, scowling faces. There was a perpetual smell of roasting coffee coming from a dozen shops.

Devereaux stood for a long moment in front of the designated shop and looked at the faces of those inside.

Satisfied, he crossed and took a seat at the counter. He ordered coffee using one of the hundred or so Finnish words and phrases he had taught himself.

The coffee was black and bitter but welcome. Those around him wore heavy coats. One man with a red face and small, black eyes was actually sweating in the steamy atmosphere of the shop but he did not open his jacket as he poured black coffee down his throat. There were slabs of black bread smeared with soft cheese on the counters. The smells of the shop were earthy, full of sweat and breath, of dark foods and dark coffee.

Devereaux saw him then but made no sign.

Tartakoff was dressed well, in a black fur cap and a black fur coat. He was tall and large-boned; his face was wide. He stared without expression across the crowded shop at Devereaux at the counter. He stared until he was certain that Devereaux had seen him. And then he turned and left the shop as though he had decided it was too crowded.

Devereaux left a ten-markka note on the counter and the waitress scooped it up as though she had been waiting for it. He pushed through the first door of the shop and turned to the left, going around the shop to the side hallway, following the retreating figure of the Russian.

They were suddenly in an empty corridor that led to the

rear entrance of a department store that was not yet open for the day. The corridor was quiet but beyond was the murmur of a thousand people speaking, the shuffle of a thousand feet pushing along over the slush-streaked tiles.

"What is the answer?" the Russian asked in his thick voice. He spoke English well but with a burring accent, as though the words were caught in a web in his throat before they emerged.

"There is no answer."

"Damn you, Messenger."

Devereaux had told him from the beginning that he was Messenger. The name implied a certain powerlessness and implied that any decision would come from beyond Devereaux and this place.

"They must have their cautions," Devereaux said.

"I know why you hesitate. Because of that cipher clerk." Tartakoff smiled. "I knew about that."

"Then you know why we must be cautious."

"I will go to the British—"

"You will not go to the British," Devereaux said calmly.

"Why not, Messenger?"

"Because British Intelligence is a sieve. You'd be killed in London before a week was out."

Tartakoff's face turned an ugly shade of red. He bunched his bare fists but made no other move.

"Yes, Messenger. That is right. That is what would happen to me."

The two men were silent.

"Every time I make contact, I am at risk."

"I have no instructions."

"But what must I do to make them decide?"

"I don't know," Devereaux said.

"Messenger. Yes. That is what you are."

Devereaux stared at him without emotion, as though he waited for the Russian to understand, to see that nothing would be done at all.

"I am in danger all the time," Tartakoff said. A slight note of pleading entered his voice.

Devereaux waited. Tartakoff was not stupid but he refused to understand. Hanley by silence had decided. It was a matter of breaking off the matter.

"What do you want from me?"

"Tartakoff," Devereaux began. "Don't you see?"

"Yes, Messenger. But I cannot accept—" For a moment, Tartakoff seemed unable to speak. "If you do not trust me, say that."

But he did not speak.

"What must I do? What must I give you?"

Devereaux turned away and stared at the bare walls behind him. The tiles were fastened to the rocks in the cold earth that bound the city. It was ugly and too bright in the tunnel and yet the light gave succor that the sun refused to give.

"Messenger."

Devereaux turned. His gray eyes fixed the Russian coldly. Nothing could be done; he felt no pity for the Russian, no pity for himself. They were both dangling and now it was time to cut both of them down.

"Tomas Crohan."

Devereaux was very still. The name did not mean anything to him but it was so odd to hear the Russian state the Irish name that it frightened him in that second.

Tartakoff had decided something. His eyes were set and hard. "He is in Leningrad. Under my jurisdiction. You tell them that. You tell those people who will not answer me. Tell them that I have Tomas Crohan."

"Who is he?"

"You do not know? You thought he was dead, all of you. Officially dead. Yes, you would like this fellow to come out. Yes. But you must take Tartakoff as well. And then I will bring you Tomas Crohan."

Tartakoff touched Devereaux on the sleeve and his hand was heavy. "You tell them, Messenger." He said the last word with contempt. "Tell them that I can give them a dowry after all. Tell them that Tomas Crohan is alive and I will give him and that is the bargain that we will have between us."

"Why will we want him?"

"Not you, Messenger. You are not important to this. But they will want him very much. I must have contact made on Monday and you must accept. I cannot come again to Helsinki; it is too many times." He still held Devereaux's arm in a tight grip.

"Who is Tomas Crohan?"

Tartakoff laughed then and dropped his hand.

Devereaux waited.

"A man," Tartakoff said. "A prisoner for a long time." He was smiling. "Come back from the dead."

2

CHELTENHAM, ENGLAND

"Enter." The voice was clear and sure of itself. Mowbrey pushed the door open timidly. He had never been in Wickham's office. He didn't know anyone who had.

Wickham looked up from his Queen Anne desk at the far end of the large room with the expression of a good-natured man interrupted at his labors. In fact, he was neither good-natured nor one who worked excessively.

"Yes, Mowbrey?"

"Mr. Wickham. I thought it best to come to see you on this matter—"

"Matter?"

"Some of the special monitoring we've been doing . . ." Mowbrey mumbled.

The good nature on the broad, ruddy face faded. "Are you on special monitor? I don't recall your name sent in for positive vetting."

"Yes, sir. Since first of the year." Mowbrey had a thin, uncolored face of high cheekbones and a nose that took a slight twist as it descended his face.

"Well." Wickham pushed his papers aside as though clearing his desk for whatever matter Mowbrey was to bring him.. In fact, like all of his gestures, it concealed another careful fraud. Wickham was a shrewd, arrogant and lazy man whose rise inside Auntie had been less a tribute to his talents than to his name. He was the second son of the ninth earl of Bellefair.

"Sir. We've been working a cross-monitor. You know. Taking some routine Russian radio traffic and comparing it on the computer with routine American traffic—"

"That is not to be spoken of. Not even in this room," Wickham warned.

"Sir." Mowbrey stood his ground though he felt terrified in the presence of the other man. He vaguely noticed that there was a print by Monet on a far wall in lieu of a window. A window would not have been practical in any case because all the rooms at this level were twenty-seven feet below the surface of the green, pleasant pastureland above. Cows grazed still in this suburb of Cheltenham. Below them lay the home of the North Atlantic Treaty Organization's second most sophisticated listening post and computer espionage center.

"Sir," Mowbrey began again. "This is the first time that we've had any sort of a connector. Single name in this case."

"All right, Mowbrey; what are you talking about?"

The question was delivered a little shortly, but that also masked the fact that Wickham, in all likelihood, did not have much of an idea of what Special Section was actually trying to do. It had been set up in a hurry after the latest spy scandal involving the Cheltenham post, the one that had not been publicized in the news media for the simple reason that the double agent had escaped back to the Soviet Union before British Intelligence could catch up with him.

Wickham was in nominal charge of the section, and that was why Mowbrey had thought to go to him with his information. Mowbrey was as ambitious as Wickham was arrogant.

"Sir. Yankee signal from Delta Z—"

"Mowbrey, God gave us the English language to make matters clear, not to obscure the mundane."

"I'm sorry. The Americans received a signal from their special posting in Stockholm yesterday inquiring on a name. Tomas Crohan."

"So?"

"Struck me funny, sir, at first when we picked up the American signal. Just buzzing around these last weeks, making certain the apparatus was functioning—"

"Yes, yes."

"Tomas Crohan. Name struck me because it was so odd. Spelling and all. Mick name in Stockholm? It didn't seem right. So I bought five minutes in Seeker and—"

"Seeker?"

"Ministry record computer, sir. New nomenclature came down at Christmas, sir, you must have the memorandum—" It was beginning to dawn on Mowbrey that Wickham was a fatuous incompetent.

"Yes, I did. Damned names keep changing. All this razzle to impress the Americans that we're quite certain we know what we're doing. Not certain it works at all."

"Sir, Seeker sent me a query in return. The name was under wraps and Seeker wanted my identity and all, very hush-hush. I was bowled over. Tomas Crohan was in an old file but it was still protected under War Secrets Act, even for me. I've got a Thirteen-grade classification. . . ."

"When was your last vetting?"

"Six months ago, sir, when I applied for transfer here. They were cautious, I can tell you, especially after the Prine matter and all the other—"

"Yes. We don't have to keep dwelling on it. What aroused your curiosity again?"

"Sir. Here was a signal from the Yanks in Stockholm, carrying just a name, making an inquiry. I never heard of it, have you, sir?"

"Can't say I have."

"And when I run it through Seeker, I get this rude note from the computer questioning my identity, my need-to-know, all sorts of stuff. I shouldn't be surprised if a couple of men from Internal Security come round and ask me questions. That's why I came to you, sir. Internal Security has no need-to-know on what Special Section is up to. But if I start answering their questions, I'm going to have to bring in the American signal we picked up from Stockholm and that could lead to all sorts of complications."

Wickham tapped a pencil against his lip as he contemplated the neat problem for a moment. It was a characteristic habit. He also chewed pencils and pen caps in moments of stress and his desk was littered with their remains, like the small bodies of dead animals.

"What paperwork do you have on this?"

"Sir." Mowbrey handed over three sheets, including the original code of the American signal from Stockholm received Saturday, the code breakdown and the classification of the code. It was Aram One, one of the simpler American codes, indicating the inquiry was at a low level of security. Because of the notorious insecurity of the telephone systems in Scandinavia, the American signal might have had its origins anywhere: the Russians, Danes, Norwegians, Finns, Swedes and the Americans had so many line taps operating in the vast sweep of Scandinavia from the Arctic to the Baltic that frequently a single telephone line would carry two or more taps from competing intelligence organizations.

The second sheet contained Mowbrey's routine search request to Seeker. The third sheet contained the computer's chilling response.

Yes, Wickham thought. High-level stuff and mighty strange. This was really out of Mowbrey's hands now.

He glanced up at the younger man and managed a smile. The avuncular Wickham was back on stage after a momentary lapse.

"An interesting business, don't you think?"

"Yes, sir, I do and that's why I brought it straight to you, sir."

"Now what about Miss Ramsey?"

Violet Ramsey was operations officer, American section, Special Section, and the likely superior that Mowbrey should have spoken to about the matter in the first place.

"Sir, I took it right to you, and Miss Ramsey didn't have need-to-know. This was an experiment with our machines, sir. Special Section hasn't even tapped into Stockholm yet. I did that, sir."

"Did you?"

Mowbrey managed a grin that he intended to convey a sense of modesty. Unfortunately, two blackened teeth to the right-center of his mouth dampened the effect.

"So no one in Special knows about this signal?"

"No, sir. Only you, sir, and Seeker, of course."

"I'll take care of Seeker," Wickham said. Though a lazy man, he saw something vaguely important in the business that Mowbrey had brought to him. Perhaps a chance for promotion; perhaps a chance to take on a good foreign posting inside Auntie. "How did you answer Seeker?"

"Didn't, sir. Figured it was better to tell you and shut down Seeker at my terminal."

"All right, Mowbrey. Leave these papers here and I'll inquire into this for you. I'm sure we can find something about this and why all this mysterious business about . . . what was his name? Kelly . . ."

"Crohan, sir. Tomas Crohan."

"Yes."

Three hours later, Wickham had managed to duplicate the original inquiry about the identity of Tomas Crohan and feed it into Seeker. Scarcely twenty minutes later, the computer repeated the questions that it had asked of Mowbrey but this time Wickham identified himself, his position, and his grade number and demanded to know why he could not inquire further into the matter of Tomas Crohan.

Seeker did not answer.

The business frustrated Wickham to the point where he circumvented the computer entirely.

It was just after four and the cows above had long been driven to their barns. Darkness poked at the edges of the sky.

Wickham had locked the door of his office. He had taken the blue telephone out of the locked box at the bottom of his desk. He had not dialed a number; he merely picked up the receiver and waited.

"Yes." A woman's thin voice with a London accent.

"George, please."

"One moment." A buzz on the line and another voice. This one was a man.

"Who is it?"

"Bluebird," Wickham said.

"Yes. I expected as much. I was just going to get around to you." The voice of "George" was as thick as a heavy gravel walk in Kew Gardens.

"You were?" Wickham was truly surprised and his voice conveyed that impression.

"Was this something of your Special Section?"

"What are you talking about?"

"Crohan, man. You made two inquiries in the last five hours to Seeker. Why didn't you identify yourself the first time? Could have saved us half a morning running around."

"I-I had no idea."

"Not the first time you've ever said that, I'll wager."

Silence.

"Well, Bluebird, why did you tumble to a name like that? After all these years."

"Sir, this is the highest level—"

"Yes, damn you. What are you raving about? I am Security, there is no level above my level."

"I'm sorry, George."

"Where did you pick this up?"

Wickham was completely shaken. He felt trapped in his own ambition. Why hadn't he left the whole business to Miss Ramsey? Damn that Mowbrey. Now he had gotten in on it and he would have to see it through.

"Signal, sir. Bit of an experiment in Section. I thought I would take some of their . . . spaghetti—"

Spaghetti was listening-post slang for the millions and millions of pieces of cable, secret and radio chatter picked up every day in places like Cheltenham. There were so many conversations, orders, messages and sometimes real secrets that it was a losing battle on the part of listeners inside Auntie to actually sift through all the material and isolate those bits that were truly significant. It was an enormous plate of spaghetti and by digging away at it diligently each day, bits and pieces of worth were found . . . while other worthwhile bits were never discovered at all because of the sheer amount of material that had to be sifted.

"American spaghetti, was it?"

"Yes, sir. How did you know?"

"What the hell is Special Section supposed to be working on if not tapping the Yanks?"

Wickham was shocked to hear George state it so baldly. After all, it was a safe phone but no one ever spoke of the project inside Special Section. The Americans were allies, after all; American liaison offices actually worked in the public buildings aboveground in Cheltenham with their British counterparts. Auntie—the nickname everyone used for the Ministry for External Affairs (Extraordinary)—was an open secret at Cheltenham, but Special Section was a secret buried within a secret and the probe of American intelligence security was the last secret of all, so sacred that none spoke of it.

"Where was it, Bluebird?"

"Stockholm, sir."

"Stockholm?"

"Yes, sir."

"I don't like this at all."

"What, sir?"

"Nothing, Bluebird. Are you absolutely certain you handled this strictly on your own?"

Wickham lied without compunction. He had done so all his life. "Yes, sir."

"Good. Now I want you to forget the whole business."

"Forget it?"

"Exactly what I said," the gravel voice rumbled. "If you've made notes for yourself, destroy them. Everything. And don't breathe a word about this if you value your neck."

"Sir—"

"Good night, Bluebird."

The connection was broken.

The car was waiting and the motor was running. Puffs of white smoke from the rear of the Jaguar danced in the light evening wind. The lights were trained on the entrance of the modest two-story office building set in the middle of a pastureland off the main road to Cheltenham town center.

There were six entrances to the underground complex used by Auntie and by the Auntie listening post where the man called Bluebird worked. Under new security procedures, the work force rotated in sections each month using different entrances and exits. It was vastly confusing to all involved and no one would have been surprised that Wickham had helped devise the system and that Wickham routinely flaunted it. In fact, he had left by exactly the same entry way each night for two years.

"Damned Rogers," he said as he emerged from the darkened entry and was temporarily blinded by the lights of the Jaguar. Rogers was his driver and usually reliable but he had been late this evening because of motor trouble on the M4. And to cap it off, he had turned on the brights of the headlamps and it was more light than Wickham needed. He blinked and shielded his eyes as he walked across the crisp snow to the car.

He opened the rear door and slid inside.

The automobile was comfortably warm.

"Have to hurry along tonight. Maggie is expecting guests at eight—"

Rogers nodded and put the heavy car into gear.

Wickham sighed, picked up his unread *Telegraph* on the seat next to him and flicked on the rear reading lamp. The Jaguar also had a small bar tucked discreetly into the back of the front seat where Rogers drove.

The car purred onto the B highway and turned north. Maggie had finally found something suitable after an unsatisfactory six months in lodgings in Cheltenham itself. The house was not convenient but it was exactly what Maggie expected for people of their station. Maggie had greater expectations than Wickham—but that was to be expected. Wickham's brother was in line to become earl and he was a vigorous, healthy man of fifty and it seemed quite unlikely—given the longevity of the various family members—that Wickham would ever receive the coronet. But life was not uncomfortable for him and if he would tell the truth, he found the tedious life inside the listening-post section of Auntie to be rather fulfilling in a mild way. He was an important man, by anyone's lights, and not one of these posturing upper-class twists who couldn't make a career on his own. Given the privileges of life he inherited with the privileges he had earned, Wickham was a contented man.

"Careful," Wickham said absently as the car slipped around a curve. He always said that; the car always slipped in winter on the same curve. And Rogers always replied that it looked like more ice tonight.

Funny.

Wickham rattled the thin pages of the *Telegraph*.

Funny.

"Rogers," he said.

There was no reply. He blinked in the thin light in the back of the large car and noticed that Rogers's hair was growing a bit long. All the chauffeurs fancied a bizarre sense of personal hygiene. Their cars were cleaner than they were. That is what he had once told Maggie after they had to sack Tulliver.

"Rogers?"

"Yes, sir?"

The chauffeur glanced at him in the rear-view mirror.

Well, Wickham thought. You see. It was Rogers. What had crossed your mind, old boy?

Wickham smiled. "Thought you'd say we'd get a bit more ice tonight."

"Yes, sir, I expect we will."

"Suppose." The subject did not interest him. He glanced at the murder story on page three. Trust the *Telegraph*, good and gray, to have a nice murder story each day on page three. Wickham found the occasional peek into life in the London underworld fascinating, even if he never told Maggie about it. Too brutal, she would have said. Too vulgar.

And then the car stopped.

Still. On the middle of the deserted roadway.

"Rogers?"

"Sir." The chauffeur turned.

"Why have we stopped?"

"Something's wrong with the motor, sir."

"Damn. Thought you had it fixed this afternoon."

"So did I, sir."

"Seems to be running."

"No, sir. Something wrong. Let me take a look."

Wickham turned back to his paper in annoyance. Woman on the Portobello Road had been raped, trussed up and then slashed to death. Particularly brutal.

"Sir."

Again, Wickham put down his paper. He glanced at Rogers standing outside the car with the left front door open.

"What is it?"

"Sorry, sir. You weren't the worst. I was fond of you. But you have to understand, sir."

"Understand?"

"Sir, I wish it would never have come to this."

"Understand what?"

"You and the Mrs. were really quite nice," Rogers said in an uncomfortable voice.

Wickham blinked. "What are you talking about? Close the door."

"Can't, sir."

"Can't?"

"Would you come this way, sir?"

Wickham flushed. He really was becoming quite angry. "See here—"

"Sir."

And then he saw the gray pistol in Rogers's hand.

Slowly, as in a dream, he opened the rear door and climbed out of the Jaguar still rumbling in the middle of the deserted roadway. And then he saw the lights flash a hundred yards away.

"Over there, sir."

He allowed himself to be pushed along. It had not snowed for six days but it had been freezing cold and the snow crunched under his feet. He thought absurdly that he would ruin his shoes walking across this frozen field of snow. Why was he doing it? He felt the pistol at his back.

"Nothing will happen, sir," Rogers said unhappily.

"What is the meaning of this?" But the question did not carry conviction. He asked it like a man who knew the answer.

The other car, hidden in darkness, was black. Rogers opened the rear door.

Two foreigners were inside. Their clothes did not suit their builds. One wore a gray hat that was not fashionable. Wickham noticed these things. He was pushed into the back and sat down heavily on the vinyl seat which felt cold through the layers of his clothing. He hated a cold automobile. He always insisted that the car be properly warmed before he would enter it, even if he was in a hurry.

"Goodbye, sir."

Rogers was already crossing the field back to the Jaguar. What would he say? What would he tell Maggie? What could he expect?

"See here. What is this? Do you know who I am?"

The man at the wheel turned. His features were flat. His eyes were small black coals that had never burned. His tie was knotted too tightly at his thick throat.

"Certainly, Mr. Wickham." The accent was harsh, Slavic. "We know who you are very well."

And the other man smiled.

3

AMSTERDAM

The two men sat at the curving end of the little bar off the lobby inside the Victoria Hotel. Beyond the windows, the storm that had blown in from the North Sea that morning was now ebbing with the afternoon light. Along Damrak, the street that separated the hotel from the canal, the snow had been pushed into little mountains of slush. The red streetcars were silenced by the snowfall and moved dreamlike along the bright, straight tracks. There were no boats in the canal and the streets were empty.

"What is the business?"

"In a little, Antonio." The second man was round and pleasant like a Rubens cavalier. In fact, he was not Dutch but a Bulgarian in charge of the obscure Bulgarian travel service in Amsterdam, where hardly anyone ever wanted to go to Bulgaria on holiday. It did not matter. He had other jobs.

"If we have so much time, why did I have to run like hell from Paris all the way up here? In a goddamn snowstorm."

"The express train was late."

"Obviously."

The first man drank more Heineken from his heavy tulip-shaped glass. He was as unpleasant in appearance as he was in tone of voice. His face was dark and his cheeks were hollow. He had black eyes set deeply into his dark features. Nothing in his appearance spoke of aggression or prominence—Antonio had a weak chin and his lips were thin. Yet it was not a weak face, merely one of stony silence and of secrets.

"The job, Penev."

"Have another drink."

"What is the job?"

"It's a complicated business, comrade."

The implied familiarity of "comrade" annoyed Antonio but he said nothing. He rapped on the bar with the stem of the glass to summon the bartender who was in another room. The windows of the bar rattled in the wind.

"I can take care of it."

"That's why we sent for you."

Antonio smiled. "Something kinky in it?"

"Perhaps. Perhaps it will be in time."

"Where's the damned barman?" Antonio rapped the glass on the wood again. He was called Antonio but that was not his name. He had once been baptized and given a name that had been placed on a parish register in the city of Reggio Calabria where he had been born. But that book had long been stolen and the name had been expunged from the Italian records kept in Rome and now he was Antonio to all who dealt with him. A sweet name, one of his girls had said. Like the sweet smell of flowers at funeral.

The bartender—short and dark and sullen—appeared in a doorway and again Antonio rapped his glass on the wood. The bartender made a face and walked slowly behind the counter.

"Do you want another?" he asked in Dutch, though both men had been speaking English.

Penev glanced up sharply, understood the reprimand in the change of language, and replied in Dutch.

"Another then," the barman said to Antonio, switching back to English.

"What do you think I want in a place like this? Unless you have girls."

"That is rude," the Dutchman said with typical Amsterdam bluntness. For a moment, Antonio merely stared at him as though he were a gray mouse who had blundered into a warm room. Antonio's black eyes chilled. The barman turned away, picked up a green bottle beneath the counter, placed it on the bar and opened it. He stared back at Antonio.

"What are you waiting for? A tip? Just put it on my bill."

In a moment, they were in the room alone again.

"What is the business then, Penev?"

"Two matters, one simple, the other more complicated."

"Where?"

"The first hit is in Dublin. In the next two days. Definitely before Thursday. Do you understand?"

"How does it happen?"

"Accident. If possible. Very much an accident." The Rubens figure of Penev smacked his lips over a gin-and-tonic in front of him. He sipped. "The target is not a player, it shouldn't be too difficult."

"And the other?"

"Very much a player. In Helsinki. You do the Dublin business first and then Helsinki."

"You couldn't have picked someplace warm, could you?"

Penev did not smile. Despite his girth and external pleasantness, he had no sense of irony or sarcasm. He was a station agent for the Bulgarian Secret Police (External), and the principal northern European contractor for special jobs that called for free-lance help. Antonio was a free-lance assassin and terrorist who had proved reliable in other matters. The Bulgarian Secret Police was the choice assassination tool used by the Soviet Committee for State Security, the KGB.

"Are the matters linked?"

"That is my understanding, but I have not been told too much. It is not necessary for you to know too much."

"I'll decide that, Penev," Antonio said. "What is the Dublin target?"

"Nonplayer. A priest. About seventy years old. Everything is in the file."

"How do I kill him?"

"The method is yours. There won't be enough time to set-up anything elaborate. The umbrella trick might be—"

"No. I don't want to get that close. I'll think of something."

"The player in Helsinki. . . ."

"Good. What about him?"

"Make that any way you want."

"Who is he?"

"Middle-aged. Professional player."

"Not on contract?"

"An organization man." Penev sipped again at the gin.

"I could cut off his balls and put them in his mouth." Antonio smiled and Penev blanched. "I did that once in Marseilles. Not your business then. I was hitting for the Mafia; they wanted to kill an informer. It's slang, you don't understand, but it would be hard to translate. The bird sings, the informer sings. Well, the worst part was finding the bird. They wanted it done fast and I said, 'Well, I don't have the time to go and get a bird and kill it and then keep it around just to put in this guy's mouth when I hit him.' So I thought I'd just put his balls in his mouth. It worked out."

"Nothing like that."

"Well, I could just garrot him. Or do a cutting."

"I do not need to know the details."

"At the embassy?"

"No. Presidentii Hotel. His photograph is in the second envelope. When you're finished going over the material, get rid of them."

"Of course."

"Standard contract—"

"Expenses."

"Yes. The whole thing should not take more than a week."

Again, the windows rattled in reminder of the storm still beating outside. The city seemed poised between light and dark. In a little while, in the tangle of streets near the Nieuwmarkt and off the Zee dijk across the canal from the old Victoria, the whores would be waking up and having their meager breakfasts in small, drafty rooms, explaining matters to their pimps and protectors. The bars would be open, waiting for the girls of the district—and the boys who served the same purposes for some—and for the customers, culled from half-a-hundred countries who knew what they wanted to buy in Amsterdam. For all its culture and art museums, it was still the old port city on a hard, gray, perpetually angry sea where the sailors had always taken their pleasures roughly. A sort of bitter melancholy lingered in the city, frozen between the maritime past of great Dutch empires and the empty present of life in a beautiful city that had lost its sense of joy beyond existing another night in the red-light districts, beyond surviving a few small pleasures of purchased touch, warmth, whispers.

"Why is it connected?"

"Why do you want to know, Antonio?"

"Because it's my skin, isn't it? Because I've played you fair in the past but I don't always trust you, you know?"

Penev did not speak.

"The Turk did the hit on the pope for your people—"

"That is not proven."

"And I'm not a lawyer." Antonio sneered. "I wouldn't have taken a job like that."

"Would you be afraid?"

"Yes."

"Of your soul?" Penev smiled.

"What? To kill a pope? That wouldn't mean much. It was done all wrong. The Turk was a fool to trap himself in St. Peter's Square. And I wouldn't have trusted you people. Not on a hit that was so large. You were going to kill him if he escaped."

"We keep our word."

"A Bulgarian has no honor."

"And you? What are you?"

"How is this connected?"

"There won't be any problem in Dublin. If it works out, you might have to go back to Ireland in two weeks to finish . . . some matters."

"And I don't see why you don't take care of the Helsinki business yourself. You must have a hundred Soviet agents in that city."

"I have my orders. We want an independent contract with a free lance."

"All right." Antonio took the two envelopes from the counter and shoved them in the pocket of his black coat. He drained the last of the beer. "Penev, I want a woman tonight. Arrange it."

"I'm not a pimp—"

"Don't tell me what you are."

"You could go too far."

"I have gone too far. Don't warn me. Not ever. You can send one of your agents if she's not ugly. I won't tell her any secrets." Antonio smiled and got up from his barstool. "I might want to hurt her a little bit, but she'll be all right."

"What kind of a man are you?"

"I told you in Paris I wanted some cocaine. I've had problems getting—"

"Yes. It's in the first envelope. I'm not a pimp—"

"I know exactly what you are; you are just like me, Penev." Antonio slipped both hands into his pockets. "I'm tired. The train was late. I want to take a litttle nap now. Send up a woman, you know the room. Someone young. Not one of your old Bulgarian sows. Tell her it will be for all night, okay?"

4

LONDON

Ely paused a moment before he trudged up the worn stone steps to the entrance of the Georgian graystone at the far side of the square off Pall Mall. There were just seven stone steps to the glass door but the effort to mount them always seemed to the agent to be out of proportion to the task.

He climbed the stairs heavily and rang the bell. A buzzer sounded and he pushed the locked door and was in a cold entry hall which was covered with a soiled red carpet. At the end of the dim hall was a young man behind a standard wooden government-issue desk. He looked like every hotel clerk Ely had ever known.

He glanced up and Ely produced the required bit of plastic with his photograph embalmed on a card. Ely. How long had he been Ely? What was his name, anyway?

He smiled at the earnest young man who gave the card careful scrutiny before returning it. Ely had once been Gemstone and before that 0047 in the early days when the service decreed everyone in Auntie had a number. But it wasn't even called Auntie then, was it? Codes on codes, names on names, and the identity of all men is buried beneath the rubble of their own histories.

"The identity of all men is buried beneath the rubble of their own histories," Ely said to the clerk.

"I beg your pardon?"

"Nothing. Doesn't matter."

"You're to get a new card at the end of the month, sir."

"More security? Or merely to keep the printers employed?"

"I couldn't say, sir."

"No. I suppose you couldn't. Perhaps none of us could."

Silence. Ely felt saddened but he had been a part of sadness for so long that there was something familiar about it, like an old friend who drinks too much or talks too much or insists on reciting poetry at awkward moments; an old friend such as Ely would be if he could afford the trivial nature of friendships.

"I'm supposed to see Q this morning."

"Should I ring you up?"

"I know the way."

"You can't take the lift, I'm afraid, it's out of repair."

"Of course," Ely said gently. "Or it would be a work-to-rule job action by the lift operators. Or perhaps a new measure to cut government costs."

The clerk nodded again absently like a hotel clerk who cannot pay attention to the foreign guest.

Ely sighed and went to the stairs. They were covered with the same hideous red carpet that covered the worn floor in the front hall. The building was very old and in need of repair; the ceiling in files leaked, for example, something Ely had discovered on his first day in the assignment. Poor old England, he had thought then.

Poor old England, he thought now, stepping on the first step, pulling himself up to the second, to the third, to the fourth. . . .

Q was on the fourth floor in the second building. All the buildings on the south side of the little square off Pall Mall were attached and walls had been opened between them. So the establishment of Auntie was quite large, though it appeared deceptively small at first.

Ely paused for breath at the second landing.

He had thin hands that gripped the oak banisters with casual strength. He was nearly fifty, which was very old for an agent still in the field, very old for an agent who yearned to stay in the field. His shoulders drooped and his face had a wasted look, as though he had recently undergone surgery. His youthful vanity was maintained in the bright ginger mustache with fierce Guardsman's curls that belied the stricken look of his face. Something mocking was always present in his blue, clear eyes. His voice was reedy and some would mistake him, in appearance and speech, for a beloved Mr. Chips of a professor.

In fact, he was called the Fixer inside the upper ranks of Auntie. He fixed things that were broken. He put the pieces back together. Should that be in the past tense? He had been a fixer. Sometimes, when he killed, the job description was strained to match the event. Ely would have said that a fixer who has to kill in the end has merely failed. Perhaps that explained it; he had merely failed.

"He's expecting you." The woman was not yet twenty-five and Ely noticed that she had already begun to ruin her once-fair English country complexion with hideous amounts of cheap makeup in the current style. Her name was Mary and she was not terribly bright, a quality that suited Q who did not believe in surrounding himself with bright and ambitious people. "I want people who will do as they're told," he once said to Ely in pointed reference. Ely knew exactly what Q would like from him.

"Thank you, Mary." Politely, without emphasis, gently; the old, honored employee showing courtesy in the course of a day's work.

"Good morning," he said when he entered the room.

In fact, it was not. Blustery winter banged at the windows. There was rain in the gray, brooding clouds covering the old city. The room was chill—all the rooms inside Auntie were too cold or too hot or leaky or carried some permanent defect—and Q had a small gas fire blazing in a corner. He sat very near the fire behind a Queen Anne period desk. There was one other chair in the bare room and it was in front of the desk and away from the fire. It was not pleasant, on a cold day, to be interviewed by Q.

"Take a pew," Q said.

Ely sat down.

"We need a fixer," Q said.

Ely was surprised. He had botched the matter two years before in Vienna, botched it badly. Tompkins, who was Q's Number One, had gotten him off the hook but not without cost. Tompkins had pulled him back to headquarters and put him under Miss Marple in Record Retrieval. It was a purgatory but at least it was not expulsion. Tompkins had been his friend; Tompkins had explained that Ely had botched the matter because of bad luck. Ely knew that it was a lie, even if Tompkins did not. Ely had failed because his nerve had failed. He had dishonored himself for the first time. He had failed to act when an action would have saved the business. Not to mention the lives of six people.

He showed no emotion as he listened to Q.

"Two days ago, one of our men in Cheltenham disappeared."

Ely did not speak. He saw the purgatory opening. He was going back. And yet he still felt the chill of his failure in Austria two years before.

"He was working on Special Section. I don't have to go into the thing too deeply, the Section I mean. But he had made an inquiry to Seeker before he disappeared. Strange inquiry, it seems." Q was wearing a gray cardigan sweater. He had intense blue eyes and was clean-shaven. His white hair was parted in the middle in an old-fashioned cut. His eyes were framed by rimless glasses. There was something so cold about the man that Ely felt the chill of the room was more than an accident of the season.

"I don't know what Seeker is, sir."

"Really? I thought you had been cleared—"

"Perhaps I have but I haven't had training in it."

"Well, this damned security really turns on itself, doesn't it? We begin by not trusting the enemy, work our way to not trusting the Americans, and now we don't trust ourselves."

"Yes, sir." Ely agreed quietly because it seemed agreement was called for. He rarely understood what the Old Man was saying when he entered into a flight of philosophy.

"Seeker is the highest-level record keeper. Computer. Been on-line, as they say, for two years, goes all the way back now to Crimea . . . really marvelous, space efficient . . ."

"Yes."

"Name of Wickham."

"Who, sir?"

Q frowned. He was annoyed. "Damn it. The man who disappeared."

"But what was his inquiry?"

"Tomas Crohan. Wanted to know what we had on Tomas Crohan."

"Why?"

"Didn't explain. He talked to George but George thought he was lying. George was going to get to the bottom of it when he disappeared. That very night. Chauffeur came along to pick him up at the usual time and he wasn't there. Chauffeur waited for an hour, called his wife, great hue and cry, and that's all we know."

"Well, you know something more."

"I do?"

"Tomas Crohan. What was it about?"

"I told you that George—"

"Yes. But why was George so interested?" Ely spoke gently, almost diffidently. George was the code counterpart of Q who ran the electronics retrieval division of Auntie. Q was nominal superior to George but because Q didn't understand in the slightest what electronics were and how computers operated, George ran his division with some measure of independence.

Q frowned again. "I don't think I can tell you that right now, Ely. The point is not merely that Wickham has disappeared but that this morning we picked up a routine message from our Dublin stationkeeper. Same name pops in."

"Tomas Crohan? In what context?"

"I don't know. Damned Parker."

"Penny Parker?"

"Yes, him. Run across him?"

"We were in Czechoslovakia doing a black job ten years ago. Penny Parker is in Dublin?"

"Yes. Listening post. A week ago he justified an expense accounting by sighting a Soviet T-class submarine off the Blaskets."

"Island?"

"Yes. About five miles from Great Blasket."

"Justified his expenses?"

"Talking out of shop, I suppose. The trouble with agents in the field is that they become so accustomed to pulling the wool over the eyes of the Opposition that they come to think we are the Opposition as well."

"You don't believe him." Again, gently.

"It doesn't matter what I believe. There's hardly any secret that the Soviet navy is operating in the northern Atlantic, even off our dear cousins' island. What matters is why Parker was in Blasket in some godforsaken part of that country when he should have been attending to duties in Dublin."

"And what connection is there between his sighting and Tomas Crohan."

Q swiveled in his chair and regarded the weak, hissing fire behind him. With his back to Ely—a characteristic act of rudeness—he continued in his thin voice.

"It would appear none at all. But there are coincidences inside coincidences. Wickham picked up his name through a test of penetration of American radio traffic. In Scandinavia."

Ely understood suddenly, understood that a great problem was looming and understood that Q wanted to wash his hands of it. Q did him no favor now; Q wanted something swept under a rug in a room far away.

Still Q ruminated aloud, facing the fireplace, avoiding both the necessity of seeing Ely's reactions to his words and hiding his face from the agent.

"Our stationkeeper in Stockholm is looking into the matter

there, has been since we first got notice that the Yanks have sent someone special to Helsinki."

"I don't quite understand the connections," Ely said, raising his voice slightly in the event that lack of visual contact between the men had rendered them both somewhat deaf.

"No. Neither does anyone. Even George is puzzled. Imagine puzzling George." He paused as though he had not considered it before. "This is all a load of rubbish about some . . . some name out of the past and—"

"Who is Tomas Crohan?"

"Who *was* Tomas Crohan is more likely."

"Who was he, then?"

"Irish national, fiercely pro-Nazi before the war. The Americans somehow got to him, used his country's neutrality which was really pro-Nazi, sent him into Vienna. Your old bailiwick."

Q turned rapidly and faced Ely again. He wanted to see if he had scored by mentioning Vienna.

Ely did not respond. If he felt pain over the failure, the pain had burrowed its way inside him. It lived like a tapeworm in his body; it fed on him and wasted his features. But outwardly, Ely was still the professional, still the Fixer. His eyes did not waver. His fierce mustache seemed fiercer still.

"What happened?" Ely inquired in the same even, soft voice.

"Red Army marched into Vienna before Crohan got out. They arrested him, hinting he was an anti-Soviet American spy. Well, he was an American agent of some sort, that's clear. But the Americans kept saying he was on a humanitarian mission—"

"Like Wallenberg."

"Yes. Like Wallenberg. There were similarities, I suppose. In any event, he died in Soviet captivity. Nineteen forty-six."

"And now his name comes up again."

"Yes. American agents in Helsinki, Penny Parker blathering in Dublin, and this damnable business with Wickham. He was positively vetted just six months ago."

"And?"

"Nothing. No mistress in Pimlico, no penchants to become a raging queen in Soho. Just a good, dull, sober chap, the sort the service could use more of."

Again, the implied reprimand; again, Ely did not respond. His blue eyes fixed themselves on the glare of the rimless spectacles that framed the old man's cold glare. Outside, it began to snow, a brittle, mean snow of mixed sleet and rain, a snow that knocked on windows like a cat scratching its way inside a house.

"I understand the Crohan name in the context of Wickham. But how did Penny Parker send his?"

"Very mysterious, which is typical of Parker, which is the reason I had him posted to Dublin in the first place. The Irish love a conspirator and Parker is one of them. He wasn't completely clear but it involved a priest, someone who had information on this Crohan fellow."

"Q?"

"What is it?"

"What do you want done?"

"Information. I don't know, but we need information."

"Can I see our files on Crohan? I mean, this was the request Wickham made, wasn't it?"

"George has charge of them—"

"Will he show me the files?"

There was a long silence which implied the answer. Ely waited, nonetheless.

"They are under fifty-year seal."

"I am hardly a representative of the *Daily Express*," Ely replied.

"I've given you the essential story. You can get the rest from our routine reference-and-search."

"Q, why are we interested?"

"Is this necessary? Suffice we are interested. Terribly. Not so much in Crohan but in why his name suddenly pops up with alarming frequency and why the Yanks are so bloody interested all of a sudden. And just why the hell did Wickham disappear after he made his inquiry."

"I'll go to Dublin first. To see Parker," Ely said.

"Yes." The director of Auntie leaned forward with his hands folded on his desk in front of him in a gesture of sincerity. The gesture was so obvious that Ely was certain the old man intended to lie to him.

"We are not terribly interested in this Crohan fellow. It's history. We are interested in attempting to discover who is playing a game with us. Americans? The Opposition? Even the Irish, though I should doubt strongly they have the requisite intelligence to penetrate our system."

"Penetration of our security hasn't been so very difficult in the past few years," Ely said. Again, said gently but with some of the razor's edge his words used to carry before the business in Vienna had shipwrecked him.

"Ely, I'm giving you a chance. I won't bring up the Vienna business again. You have your friend Tompkins to thank for saving your hide when that blew up. I'm convinced my confidence will not be misplaced."

Ely said nothing.

"Good luck, then."

Ely got up. He stared at the old man who was Q for a moment and then decided to speak. "You want silence, isn't that it?"

"What do you mean?"

"I mean you really don't want to get to the bottom of anything. You merely want this matter brushed away."

Q regarded him through the rimless glasses and placed the tips of his fingers together in a tent in front of his lips. He thought a long moment before he replied.

"You've put it crudely, Ely."

"Yes. I'm afraid I have to be blunt. I have to know."

"Of course you do. The fixer has to know what the job is." Another pause. "Fix it, Ely. Something is broken. Fix it, make it quiet again."

"And if it can't be fixed."

Q managed a frosty smile. "Then sweep it away into the dustbin. Broken things are always thrown away in the end, aren't they?"

5

DUBLIN

The Aer Lingus 747 named *St. Brendan* swept low over the brown winter fields of County Wicklow and began the final approach to Dublin airport. The transatlantic flight had been typically tiring and Rita Macklin yawned now and stretched as the gray morning light of Ireland coated the windows of the immense, half-empty plane.

The night had been restless though the journey in the darkness had been smooth as usual. Because the plane was half-empty, she had slept across three seats but she had awakened again and again with fragments of bad dreams prodding her conscious mind.

Rita Macklin rubbed her green eyes and shook out her medium-length red hair and rubbed color into her cheeks. She looked younger than she was—she would be thirty in the fall—but there was a curious tough quality to her strong, angled face that made the judgment of her actual age not very important to most people. She was not beautiful by any common convention because her jaw was too strong and the slight overbite of her teeth made her seem too aggressive to be conventionally attractive; all the defects in her face and lean figure combined to make her seem quite beautiful to men who were not afraid of such women.

Like Devereaux.

"Damn," she said to herself in a whisper and she reached for her purse tucked beneath the seat and fumbled it open for a brush.

Devereaux had been part of the bad dreams of the long night's journey for no reason at all. He was not remotely involved in her present assignment; she had not seen him for nearly three years since he had brushed her off.

"Damn," she said again for no reason, and a passing green-clad stewardess with a motherly figure and the face of a nun stopped and asked Rita if anything was wrong.

"No, I'm just thinking aloud," she said and the stewardess went down the aisle to the back of the plane.

Why had she dreamed about Devereaux a half-dozen times? In one dream, she had slept with him as she had slept with him the first time in the motel room in Clearwater Beach, Florida, three years ago. She had thought he was a fellow journalist; before the dreadful night she was chased across the beach by two killers and she found out Devereaux was an Intelligence agent using her to get the secret journal of an old priest named Leo Tunney.

That was it.

Spies and priests and it was all tied in intricate memory to the present assignment—to interview an old Irish priest in Dublin who might know something about a man named Tomas Crohan.

Devereaux. Damn him.

She realized she was angry. She pushed the brush roughly through her hair until she made tears in her eyes.

In the end, after she had known what Devereaux was, it had not mattered to her. But he wouldn't speak to her, even though she was certain he had fallen in love with her. He had pushed her away at the last minute and she had cured herself of him in three years by working hard and by not mooning over him and by avoiding the temptation to wonder about him. After all, she worked in the same town he worked in and she was a magazine reporter with a lot of resources; she could have discovered his whereabouts anytime she wanted.

And he could have discovered hers as well. If he had wanted her. Priests and spies, she thought, dropping the brush back into her purse. The plane's wheels locked down and tiny Dublin airport stretched into view on the north side of the old city below. Priests and spies and bad dreams on a long night's crossing.

As soon as she passed through customs at Dublin airport, Rita Macklin changed money and found a pay telephone and put in a call to the priest she had come three thousand miles to interview.

Father Cunningham was retired now and lived in a room in St. Adrian's rectory on the south side of Dublin, beyond the Ring Road.

A housekeeper answered and gave the telephone receiver to another priest who had a suspicious voice. No one ever called old Father Cunningham, he explained; was she a relative from America?

"Yes," Rita lied easily. The phone was put down with a thump and there were background noises and then an old, quarrelsome Irish voice came on the line.

"Who be ye then?"

"Rita Macklin."

"I've no such relation."

"But Mrs. Fitzroy from Chicago wrote to you."

"She did, did she?"

"She wanted me to come to see you."

"She did, did she? And why d'ye come from America in the dead of winter to see an old man?"

"Because of her cousin. She says you can help her find her cousin."

"Find Tomas Crohan, is it? Ye'll find him with the angels. Or the devil."

"Do you think he's dead?" Rita asked calmly. Mrs. Fitzroy had said he would be difficult to get around.

"I'm an old man, Miss Macklin, and I don't know a thing anymore and that's the truth. Alive or dead it don't matter; in a little while, I'll be able to tell for meself."

Rita bit her underlip and stared hard at the green telephone box in front of her. She wouldn't take no from the old man; there was no question of that, but she hoped it would be easier to get to him. The story had grown and grown in her own mind since the day Mrs. Fitzroy sat down with her in the interview room at the magazine in Washington and began to tell her the long and fantastic story about her Irish cousin, Tomas Crohan.

"Father," she began, softening the word like a respectful Catholic girl, "I'm a journalist in America. In Washington. You know Mrs. Fitzroy came to see me. She wrote you a letter, I have a copy of it. I tried to reach you a dozen times by phone but you wouldn't speak to me."

"And why do you suppose I'll speak to ye now?"

"Because I'm here. I've come across an ocean to see you."

"Is it that important to ye, Miss Macklin?"

"Yes. Important enough. Important to Mrs. Fitzroy—"

"Ah, Catherine Guilhoolie—that's Mrs. Fitzroy to ye. A stubborn girl, always was, stubborn as a donkey blocking the creamery road and ye with a full load to get in before noon." The pastoral reference went past Rita but she understood the sentiment.

"Miss Macklin, ye must be able to find all ye want to know about Tomas Crohan from ye own resources in yer own country. I don't want to be bothered—"

"But you wrote Mrs. Fitzroy a half-dozen times in the past six months about Tomas, about what hapened to him—"

"I'm getting old, Miss Macklin; the past is more comfortable to me than the thought of the present. Even a priest is terrified of eternity when he stands close enough to touch it, as it were. Are ye Catholic?"

"I am," she said.

"Ah, American Catholics aren't all the same, not at all. I've met them in my time, I can tell ye." His voice trailed off. "Where was I? Ah. Ye can learn all ye need to know about Tomas Crohan from yer own people—"

"You mean the Central Intelligence Agency."

"I do indeed. Didn't I say that to Mrs. Fitzroy?"

"I went to the CIA under the Freedom of Information Act to find the files on Tomas Crohan and they wouldn't show them to me. Files that are forty years old—"

The old voice laughed on the line. "And why d'ye suppose that might be?"

"Because the CIA is hiding something."

"Bright girl, ye are."

"If you'd let me talk to you."

"There's nothing to be talking about."

"You said in your last letter an Englishman in Dublin had been after you to tell him about Tomas Crohan."

"I said that, did I?"

"I've got a copy of the letter."

"So Mrs. Fitzroy has told ye everything then?"

"An Englishman named Parker. He sounds like a spy."

"Does he now, girl? And ye no doubt have had wide experience of spies?

"I know spies," she said.

"And ye are a brave journalist after this story to make it a sensation in yer newspaper or on the telly."

"I want to know what happened to Tomas Crohan and I have to start somewhere. I want to start with you." Her voice rose slightly; her cheeks flushed; her green eyes grew deeper in color as her anger rose. "I'm going to find out what happened to him whether you tell me or not. If this is a wild goose chase, then I'll go to square one and start over but I'm going to find out, you just bet on that."

There was a long silence so that Rita thought Father Cunningham might have severed the connection.

"God rest his soul," the old man said at last.

"You think he's dead."

"I'm nearly certain of it. During the war . . . It was so long ago and yet to me it was yesterday. That's the problem of age, Miss Macklin, when the long ago is closer than what ye did an hour before breakfast."

She waited. She felt the door opening. She pushed now slowly, with softer words, for fear of cracking the door.

"What happened during the war?"

"Terrible things, Miss Macklin. Terrible and dreadful acts and not just on the field of battle. Tomas Crohan was not loved by the English, I can tell ye; but I tell ye true few would weep at his wake in the old De Valera government either. A firebrand, he was, a bloody atheist, but that was to be accounted for by his age . . . we all pass through a period of not believing. Ah, but a patriot true and not a public-house singer, either; if he had been old enough at the rising in 'sixteen, he would have led them into the bloody post office himself, he would," the priest said with some pride, recalling the Easter rebellion against British rule in Ireland. "Mark me, he was no fool, but he was blinded by his own ambition and impatience. The Devil might have feared dealing with him for fear of losing Hell; shrewd, he was, and ruthless too, and the Americans were no different. They couldn't leave us alone all during the war, never saw the sense of Ireland stayin' neutral. Never saw the English had used us too long to fight their bloody wars for them; sure, hadn't we bled enough in our red coats for the British? Aye. But Tomas was a boyo. . . . I never knew how he had dealt with everyone until now. . . ."

"You were in the De Valera government—"

"Before I took the cloth," the priest said. He sighed. "I knew them all. I knew Crohan. I knew Catherine Guilhoolie. All of them gone now. I knew too much—"

"You were in the Intelligence branch—"

"I might have been."

"Mrs. Fitzroy is certain you were."

"And what would a woman be after knowing about it?"

"All these years, she's certain that Tomas Crohan was still alive and now you write her these letters, hinting about what you know. . . . We need leverage, Father, to use on the American government, to find out what happened to Crohan, to clear it up."

"And what leverage would ye be after using with the Reds then?"

"You think he is a prisoner in the Soviet Union?"

"I didn't say a word," the old man said. "Where are ye after staying in Dublin?"

"The Buswell Hotel—"

"Ah, good enough, good enough. I have in mind an outing for meself. I'm after thinking of a nice luncheon at the Shelbourne. D'ye know the Shelbourne?"

"No, I don't know this city—"

"Durty Dublin," the priest said. "Well, it's a grand place just a block from your rooms, across from the Green, Stephen's Green, y'see. I'll be taking a table there I think about noon. And I'll be looking for a lass with red hair and green eyes to be taking tea with me or something a bit stronger—"

"Then you were going to see me?"

"I'm an old man and I must be humored," the voice said. "Ye can't be too certain who yer talkin' to these days. This Parker fellow. I know he's a damned English spy, I can smell him. At noon, then."

And they broke the connection but Rita stood for a moment with the green receiver in her hand. She had pried open the door but the other side of the door was still dark and it was up to the old man to make a light. There was so much she didn't know; the story had unfolded like an endless series of dark rooms, each with enough light to lead on to another dark room.

She replaced the receiver and picked up her overnight bag and started across the terminal toward the taxi line. It was just 9 A.M.

Three years before, Rita Macklin had broken a story linking the secret journal of a missionary priest long thought dead in Asian jungles with the buildup of a Soviet missile ring in Asia aimed at China. The sensational story had prompted several job offers from newspapers and television.

Rita Macklin had fallen in love with an American Intelligence agent named Devereaux and during the days of indecision that followed the completion of the assignment on the missile story, she had tried to make him understand that she loved him. In the end, he had turned her away; Rita still thought that he had returned her feeling for him but there was a cold, black reservoir of bitterness in him that smothered all emotions, all feelings except the will to survive.

She had taken a job with the magazine at last for the mundane reason that it paid well. She had buried herself in work because that was the sort of reporter she had always been; naturally, following the story of the old priest named Tunney who had revealed the secret missile bases in Asia, she had been inundated for months with tips on stories involving other missing old men, on conspiracies involving the Church and the Communists, on stories about secret journals. They were no good and she knew it; journalists are always forced to fight through such "tips" and "off-the-record scoops"; in time, the stories faded and dried up and Rita Macklin went on to do other investigative pieces for the magazine, far removed from the world of espionage and international plots.

Until an elderly woman named Catherine Fitzroy of Chicago was escorted into her cubicle at the magazine one afternoon by Mac. Mac was the managing editor/news of the magazine, a gentle and laconic soul who was a sharp contrast to Kaiser, the man who had first brought Rita to Washington to work for his small, grubby news service. Mac was a graduate of Yale which everyone knew but which Mac never talked about; he had an accent that might have been Maine and might have been southern Virginia; he had become Rita's rabbi in the intricate political organization of the magazine for no other reason than he thought she was the best reporter he had ever known.

"I want you to meet Mrs. Fitzroy," Mac had begun on that day nearly six weeks ago. "She wants to tell you a story about a fellow who might or might not be dead. At least he's been among the missing for forty years. Mrs. Fitzroy, this is Rita Macklin—"

"I wanted to see you," Mrs. Fitzroy had said and grasped her hand with a strong grip. "I know about your work. You found the priest who had the secret journal. Three years ago, I remember the story was in all the newspapers in Chicago."

"Thank you," she had said, holding the grip but giving Mac one of those "who the hell is this" looks.

"Mrs. Fitzroy is a friend of Mr. Camper," said Mac, explaining and introducing at the same time. Carlton Camper was the publisher of the magazine. "Mrs. Fitzroy said that she wanted to talk to you and so Mr. Camper thought it was a good idea and so do I, Rita."

"Oh, Miss Macklin, I know this is all dirty politics and clout," Mrs. Fitzroy said suddenly, "I realize you think I'm an old lady who's going to tell you some fantastic story, and I am. But you just listen to me and if you don't think it is worth doing anything with, you can just tell me to get back on the plane for Chicago and I'll leave you alone."

Rita had smiled then, suddenly and genuinely, and she had taken Mrs. Fitzroy to the interview room and sat fascinated for two hours as the old woman brought out her family photographs and old clippings about her cousin in Ireland who had disappeared suddenly in 1944 while on a mission for the Office of Strategic Services—the OSS that preceded the creation of the Central Intelligence Agency.

The story had been intriguing enough for Rita to follow up with a request to review CIA archives on the matter under the Freedom of Information Act. The file would be forty years old.

That is when she met Mr. Wallace, a junior officer in the CIA who met her in Langley, Virginia, at CIA headquarters one bright winter afternoon, bought her coffee in the cafeteria, led her to a windowless and soundproof interview room and then explained for four minutes why she couldn't see the files.

"I want to be perfectly honest with you, Miss Macklin."

"No. I think that's exactly what you don't want to be with me. This case is forty years old, it's got mold on it. I'm asking to see historical documents related to the war. Even the British release their war stories after a forty-year wait."

"But there's really nothing to release."

"Then release it and let me judge that."

"Why are you interested in this story, Miss Macklin?"

"Why are you interested in covering it up?"

And so it had gone.

A search of the clippings morgue at the *Washington Post* turned up not a word about Tomas Crohan because the file had been stripped. By tediously going through public library copies of the paper from the critical months in 1944 and 1945, Rita Macklin was able to find out that Tomas Crohan was believed to have been arrested by Soviet authorites when they entered Vienna in 1945. But why was he there? And what was the American connection to it? And why was it important forty years later to keep the matter buttoned up at Langley?

A clipping in the thin file at the magazine showed the Russians admitted capturing Crohan but that he had died in prison in 1946. The magazine had called Crohan "a prewar Irish hothead who had strong ties of friendship to the Nazi gang around der Führer" and who "championed Irish neutrality in the critical days of the war."

Bits of clippings and, of course, the extraordinary letters hinting at dark involvement of the Americans with Crohan sent to Mrs. Fitzroy by her childhood friend, Father Cunningham.

It became intriguing enough to involve Rita's attention day and night and when she had asked Mac for permission to pursue the story with Cunningham in Ireland, he really had no choice. He had smiled and said, "This is blackmail, isn't it? Just because it's a Camper Request, I'll have to do it."

"Ireland is hardly a pleasure spot in winter."

"True. But some get their kicks out of masochism."

* * *

"Wrap yerself, ye'll catch yer death," said the housekeeper Mrs. Ryan who bustled around old Father Cunningham like a mother wrapping up a schoolboy for his daily trek to school.

The old priest muttered and allowed her to fuss with his buttons and scarf and then gently pushed her away.

"I'll be back by two," he said.

"See that ye are," Mrs. Ryan said, standing with her hands on hips. "And why couldn't ye see this person here, I want to know?"

"Ah, and would I get a better meal here than at the Shelbourne Hotel? And her to pay for it? Besides, she's probably a pretty thing and I don't want ye after scaring her out of her wits."

So they ragged at each other in loud voices to the front door of St. Adrian's rectory. Mrs. Ryan opened it, held it and slammed it behind the old man who went down the cold, glistening stone steps slowly, his gloved hand on the railing.

It had started raining and the rain blew gustily down the narrow, drab Dublin street. It began to glaze the walks with traces of ice.

The old priest took a step off the curb between two cars and paused at the street, looking both ways though it was a one-way street. By nature, he was a cautious man.

He stepped into the street and a small, black Ford Escort, which had been waiting for him in a double-park lane, suddenly bolted forward. The old man saw it out of the corner of his eye.

He turned and stared at the car and realized what was going to happen to him; curiously, he did not feel panic; it was as though he had expected this from the moment he had decided to write the first letter to Catherine Fitzroy after all these years of silence.

In that instant, he prayed for the soul of Tomas Crohan because he was certain that Crohan was dead. And then he realized, with something like calm relief, that he would see Crohan in a moment.

He did not even feel the impact of the car.

He felt he was flying; he felt removed from laws of gravity and chains of mortality.

In fact, he was literally flying from the impact across the narrow street even as the car was beyond him. The driver had not stopped or braked. The priest's body crashed heavily through the window of the fishmonger across the way, cut by a hundred shards of plate glass that ripped his ancient flesh and clothing even though he was dead enough. He was dead before his bones crumpled on the white tile of the fish store.

At the far corner, Antonio braked, looked left and swung into the main street.

In thirty-one minutes, he was inside the terminal of the Dublin airport. He boarded the plane for Kastrup Airport in Copenhagen about the moment the police removed the body of Father Cunningham from the fishmonger's and about the time Rita Macklin learned from a sobbing housekeeper named Mrs. Ryan that Father Cunningham had been killed on his way to meet her.

It was purely an accident, a dreadful thing, Mrs. Ryan told Rita Macklin when she called on the telephone.

But Rita Macklin did not answer because she felt a heavy chill descend over her; she suddenly felt tired; she suddenly, for the first time since the time of the other priest three years before, felt afraid.

She said nothing to Mrs. Ryan because there was nothing to say.

Except that it had not been an accident at all.

6

HELSINKI ✦✦✦✦✦✦✦✦✦✦✦✦✦✦✦✦✦✦✦✦✦✦✦✦✦✦✦✦✦✦✦✦✦✦✦

Kulak stared at the body half buried in the snow of the construction pit. There had been too many policemen and he had chased half of them away and used the few left to screen the site.

He bent down and lifted the blanket that covered her.

She was absolutely white, absolutely frozen in a position of death. Her arms were sprawled like the arms of a broken doll. Her eyes were open, her mouth lolled open. She had been drained of blood.

The cut had crossed between her breasts and driven down through her belly to her sex organ. She was naked.

"Where was she killed?" Kulak said, still staring at the face.

"We don't know."

"How many places could there be? Look at the blood. Hardly a trace."

"He had wrapped her in plastic."

"Who was she?"

"Natali Kkonhn. A prostitute. We knew about her."

"Where did she work?"

"The nice hotels. She wasn't so bad."

Kulak replaced the blanket and stood up. "Not so bad? You had her?"

"I didn't mean that." The face of Ahakn was sullen, thin, and his black eyes never met Kulak's when Kulak spoke to him. Kulak did not like him very much; Ahakn was ambitious, which made him a bad policeman.

"Where was she working last night?"

"Her usual spot was the Presidentii."

"Who did she work with?"

"She had a pimp but she got rid of him. She was a lesbian. Her friend is in Stockholm; she had letters from her."

"They're all lesbians. A lesbian isn't going to do that to her."

"Is that right?" Ahakn said. A trace of a smile drew his dark face into a grimace.

"Yes, Ahakn, that's right," Kulak said with tiredness in his flat voice. "Get her to the institute and let's start working the hotel. Check the register, talk to the manager. Be discreet for a change if you think that is possible. This is a very important hotel, important to Helsinki, and I do not want any complaints from the management about a stupid policeman arousing the guests."

Ahakn thought to speak but clenched his fists instead. Kulak was built like a bull with thick neck, thick arms, thick hands. His face was curiously sensitive and even placid. His eyes rarely showed any emotion except contempt. He seemed like a man perpetually angry about something that did not involve those he was working with. He had been a chief inspector for twenty-one years.

Natali. What a stupid waste. His mind addressed the corpse frozen in death under the blanket, on the snow at the floor of the construction pit. Are you the beginning or the end of something? Was it your pimp or one of your customers? What a stupid thing to do, Natali, to get killed like that. Stupid.

He felt a smoldering anger in that moment directed at the dead woman but also at himself, as though he had caused her death by failing in some duty. It was nonsense and, on one level, he accepted that; but in his guts, he felt immensely guilty and he knew that he could not put the feeling of guilt away. Not even if they had found the one who had done this.

He looked up at Ahakn who was staring at him.

"Well, should I make a written invitation for you? Or do you think you could find the hotel by yourself?"

Ahakn made a face in response and turned.

He knew better than to speak now. Kulak was angry, really mad; Ahakn could never understand why the death scenes affected him this way. Fortunately for himself, he never thought to ask Kulak either.

Devereaux sat on the far side of the square-shaped bar off the lobby of the Presidentii. There were no windows here and no sense of the winter beyond the walls. The bar was nearly empty except for the man in a gray suit who had taken up a place across from Devereaux a half-hour before and had been watching him when not pretending to be reading a day-old copy of the *Times.*

Contact was inevitable. Devereaux knew all the signs. He wondered what story the other man would tell him—whether it would be plausible on the face of it or so ridiculous that the deceit would barely have any credence.

It was four days since he had seen Tartakoff. Nothing had happened and yet he had a sense that he was at the dead calm center of a great storm building somewhere over the defection.

The name Tomas Crohan had been met with utter silence in Washington, a silence so frozen and complete that it was a profound answer in itself, like the silence that follows prayers.

Hanley and the Section had not responded; Tartakoff had not sent any signal.

Devereaux picked up his glass of vodka and tasted it again. Out of the corner of his eye, he saw the other man rise.

Devereaux waited while the other man held his gaze and came around the bar with the drink in his hand. Like an American, Devereaux noted; but he did not resemble an American. His face was thin. His clothes too fussy in their evening neatness. He dressed formally which was odd to Devereaux, considering the late hour of the afternoon and the deserted place they found themselves in. It was as though the other man hoped to make a good impression.

"Beg pardon. I've seen you in here before. American? My name is Sims."

Devereaux did not speak. He stared at the other man in a silence that seemed as calm as an ice field.

"Do you mind if I sit down?"

"No."

"Sims. With British-Suomi Exports. I'm here on my annual winter holiday."

"So am I," Devereaux said.

The thin man frowned. What had he expected, Devereaux thought.

"Didn't mean to intrude," Sims said.

"No. Are you staying at the hotel?"

"Actually, I am this time. That's why I saw you. Talk to bloody Finns all day, I was looking for someone of my own kind."

"American," Devereaux said.

"Well, so. Cousins under the skin," Sims said, moving quickly as though the threads of the conversation might be recalled at any moment. "Are you here on business?"

"Pleasure."

Sims stared at him and then managed a smile. "Scant pleasures in winter in Helsinki."

"I like cold weather."

"Ski?"

"No. Just the cold. It makes it easy to get ice for the vodka."

"I see." The smile faded.

"What do you export?"

"Arabia dinnerware, glasses. Marimekko cloth. Quite a market, a nice little enterprise."

"You have an office here?"

"No. Actually, we deal directly with the makers. Offices in Kensington Mews in London. Do you know London?"

"From time to time."

"You're in business?"

"Everyone is in business."

The faintest frown. "Didn't mean to pry."

"Of course you did."

"Beg your pardon."

"You followed me from the hotel this morning when I went to the train station. I took a walk to Upsala and you were behind me."

The other man darkened suddenly. His color might have meant danger but Devereaux did not stir as he talked. He did not look at Sims. He stared at the glass of Finlandia vodka on the wooden bartop in front of him.

"You're not very good," Devereaux said at last.

"What do you mean?"

"This. The shadow this morning. You're not very good. They must not consider this very important if they sent you. Unless you're supposed to be bad. At the job, I mean."

"Yanks have a gift for giving insult," Sims said.

"And the English have the gift for coming back again and again for more of the same," Devereaux said.

Sims rose abruptly but Devereaux held his sleeve. The bartender, wiping glasses at the far end, turned to observe.

"Just being here has told me more," Devereaux said. "I never saw you before yesterday."

"Not terribly observant of you then," Sims hissed. "I've had you watched for a week."

"Why?"

"Because we know who you are."

"Who am I?"

"Amnesia? Or merely perplexed."

"Tell your master to send someone a little more expert the next time."

"Let go of my sleeve."

"Sure." Devereaux dropped his hand. "Tell them it doesn't pay to send up someone dressed like a French pimp. He stands out."

"You might regret that."

"I doubt it."

The Englishman mustered some dignity and took his drink to the far end of the bar again and deposited it on the bartop. He pushed a five-mark note across the bar as a tip and turned and walked up the three steps to the lobby level where a middle-aged couple were playing the slot machines.

Devereaux stared after him but the Englishman pushed through the front doors and left the hotel. Absurd, Devereaux thought. He's wearing a suitcoat and it must be zero outside. He smiled for the first time.

"Trouble, sir?" asked the barman.

Devereaux looked at him. "A queer."

"Really?"

"Really."

The barman frowned and looked away but stayed near Devereaux, polishing glasses that had been polished a moment before. Devereaux noticed this but there was nothing to do about it. Contact had been made; Hanley could not have expected to wait seven weeks and not have someone tumble to the fact that a special agent was in Helsinki. Even a clod like Sims.

Good, he thought. Time to get out. Time to let Hanley know the game was over.

He suddenly felt released as he had not felt for seven weeks.

The game was in the open.

If the British knew about him, everyone would know about him. Tartakoff could not get out now. Tomas Crohan, whoever he was, would stay a prisoner in the Gulag.

"I'd like another vodka," Devereaux said. The barman picked up the empty glass and replaced it with another.

Time to let Hanley know that it was blown, that he was not the man for the job anymore. If they wanted to delude themselves, they could send someone else in.

Hanley must have known seven weeks was too long in an exposed place like Helsinki. Hanley must have known.

And then, with a sudden chill that capped his mood, Devereaux realized that Hanley had known all along.

The old man lay beneath the thin covers and felt the coldness in the ward press against his exposed face. For a moment, he closed his eyes as though the utter darkness would warm him; he tried to think of the old dreams that always had sustained him. But the wind howled against the windows of the old hospital wing and the wind insisted on winter, insisted on penetrating his subconscious so that there would be no place left for pleasant dreams.

The old man opened his eyes. He shivered and wrapped the blankets tighter against his thin frame.

A single light shone in the hall that was outside the ward of the prison hospital. He stared at the light until he saw the halos around the light, shimmering and dancing like rings of a distant planet.

He heard the moans of the sleepless in the darkness around him. The old man was waiting for the pill to take its effect, to remove him from the ward, from the moans of the others, from the howling wind pressing against the rattling windows, to lead him to the long dreams that occupied half his existence, that made the real part of his existence endurable.

What did he dream? He could not even tell anyone, for fear the dreams would dry up and then there would be nothing left to make the other existence—the real existence—bearable for him.

He could fall into the dreams unexpectedly, even during the day. These reveries would always protect him. Once, when they were building a barracks in the dead of winter in Siberia—it was so cold that wood shattered like glass—he was warmed for days by a dream that led him day and night. He never spoke during the days of the dream; he was scarcely aware of the horror and cold around him during the dream. The dream had been the only thing that was real.

Now, because he was old and because he had lived with the dreams so long, he felt like an aged suitor who must court the dreams gently for fear they will fly to another. He had bribed the nurse for an extra pill tonight and the pill would eventually let him sleep and the sleep would—if all went well—lead to the dreams that were warm and bright and full of beautiful forms. He never had nightmares; the nightmares only came during the day in his other existence. The dreams were always beautiful visitations.

Was he mad, as mad as the others?

He closed his eyes. It was a question to ask himself tomorrow. After the dreams came.

He felt himself falling, slowly, in the darkness of his mind and he did not struggle against the falling.

And after a while, the howling winter wind outside the prison hospital in Leningrad could not be heard anymore by the old man.

7

WASHINGTON, D.C.

"What do you know about a man named Tomas Crohan?"

The question had first been asked that morning. It was repeated now to commence the conversation.

"You mean, Hanley, what does Tinkertoy know?"

Hanley made a face that was half grimace, half acceptance of Mrs. Neumann's games with him.

Mrs. Neumann ran computer search in R Section. She was the memory of the Section and, in some ways, the conscience of the operation when it required such. Computers provided Hanley data, past and present; Mrs. Neumann told him what the data meant.

They sat at a table near the window in the special cafeteria provided on the third floor of the Department of Agriculture building on 14 Street.

The day was bright and cold beyond the heroic windows. Inside the drab, government-green cafeteria, the food was usual and not very good, served up from stainless-steel steam tables with much banging of plates and plastic serving trays. Hanley regretted being here. He never missed lunch at the old-fashioned bar-and-grill north on 14—he always ate exactly one cheeseburger (without onions) and drank exactly one straight-up dry martini—but the circumstances were unusual today and called for a luncheon meeting with Mrs. Neumann. And Mrs. Neumann, in her way as much a creature of habit as Hanley, could never be persuaded to leave the environs of the old building before quitting time.

"The stew isn't so bad," she said with the dedicated air of one who has to justify her eating habits. She speared a fork into the greasy brown mixture on her plate and retrieved a dried chunk resembling meat from the sea of carrots and potatoes.

Hanley poked at the salad in front of him. His stomach rumbled. He had not touched his food. His stomach did not understand that the pleasures of the single cheeseburger and straight-up martini would have to be foregone today. Hanley felt sorry for his digestive tract, as though it were an old friend fallen on hard times.

"Yes, Mrs. Neumann. As you say. What does Tinkertoy say about Tomas Crohan?"

"Actually, we shouldn't eat this much meat. Not every day. Leo is on a diet now where he skips eating entirely every other day."

"I'm happy to hear it."

"You wouldn't be if you had to live with him." She put down her fork and called up Leo in her mind's eye. "Leo is a sweet man but I'm going to have to convince him that this diet won't work. It will ruin his stomach or ruin me. He sits around on the foodless nights and rumbles at me. In the living room. His stomach makes these terrible noises just as yours did now. I realize he can't help it any more than you, but it is distracting. Especially when the foodless day falls on Saturday. We had people over to the house and Leo rumbles at them."

"Mrs. Neumann, I find the subject of your husband's digestion amazingly interesting."

"All right, Hanley." She put down her fork. "Let's cut the small talk then." Her voice had the rasp of an awl on old wood. She was very hoarse and never so much stated as whispered or rasped or seemed in a hurry to speak. Lydia Neumann was a middle-aged, handsome woman of big bones and large gestures who favored print cotton dresses. Her short, black hair was cut in spiky clumps at intervals by her husband, Leo, not because it saved money but because it created an intimacy between them that reminded them of when they had been young and very much in love. Both would be surprised now to hear that their friends thought they were still in love as they had been twenty-five years before. Leo vaguely suspected that his wife had an important role in an agency he knew very little about; he had treated her in a fatherly way about her job until the Paris matter two years before when she had been kidnapped right out of the agency. The incident had awed him and made him vow to lose forty pounds; the two matters were linked but difficult to explain to anyone who did not know the Neumanns. She was chief of Computer Analysis or Comp An in the slang of the trade.

Tinkertoy was her pet, her primary computer.

"Tinkertoy makes a cross reference of Crohan to the Competition."

"Langley?"

"Yes. Archives section where they stored the trash before they went into business in 1947. All the old OSS stuff and some of Wild Bill Donovan's meanderings before that. I rang up my opposite number over there."

"At Langley? Was that wise?"

She glanced at him sharply. "You said this was routine, Hanley. Strictly routine. We do cooperate from time to time, you know. It is the same government."

"I'm not all that certain CIA is convinced, let alone NSA or the defense boys."

"I know what you mean. Remember the Hamburg busienss six months ago when Langley bollixed it?"

"It's still on my desk," Hanley said, one bureaucrat explaining to another by a simple phrase showing how tedious it had become. "I can't shake it off on anyone."

"Well, the interesting thing, Hanley, is that they claim to have absolutely nothing on the business. I didn't talk with Mrs. Carruthers, though. She's normally the one I talk to. She was off. Terrible speller. Isn't that funny? She runs one hundred fifty people and two hundred machines and couldn't spell her way out of a paper bag."

"Mrs. Neumann," Hanley interrupted.

"His name was Wallace, said he was filling in. He wanted to know why we wanted to know."

"About Crohan?"

"Of course."

"What did you tell him?"

Mrs. Neumann swallowed a bit of carrot in gravy and smiled. "What the hell do you think I told him, Hanley?"

"I don't understand this," Hanley said, almost to himself. It was not the first time he had said it or thought it since he sent Devereaux to Helsinki.

"Eat up, man. You're the one who insisted on lunch," Mrs. Neumann said. She was in good humor because she saw Hanley's confusion.

"I was hungry," Hanley said with petulance.

"So I see."

Hanley shoved his unfinished plate aside. "Inedible."

"The lot of the civil servant," Mrs. Neuman said. She reached for Hanley's salad and pulled it toward her. "I thought he was very interested in our business."

"Wallace."

"Yes."

"Did you demand the file under Rule thirty-eight?"

"No." Mrs. Neumann was silent for a moment. She held her fork against the remains of the stew as though contemplating either the act of eating or what she would tell Hanley next.

She looked up. "There's something funny going on, Hanley. With the Competition at Langley, I mean. I told this Wallace the name had come up in a routine cross reference and we had no file. It didn't satisfy him, but he can go to hell. What could he make of it? For that matter, what do I make of it?"

"Exactly."

"You haven't told me anything," she said.

"I know." He had the secrets but he did not understand them and was reluctant to let them go until he knew what they really meant. Each secret was an unfired gun and when it was triggered, it demanded action. Hanley was frozen in the matter.

"This is some business lunch," she said.

"I should tell you."

"Suit yourself, Hanley. It seems to be your pickle."

Mrs. Neumann was the only person in headquarters who addressed him flatly by his last name, save the Old Man himself. Mrs. Neumann meant no disrespect; she called any man by his last name and would not have been offended to be plain old Neumann in return.

"We received a message from one of ours in Helsinki nearly a week ago. It came in the middle of a routine matter. It was not expected." The words fell reluctantly and slowly. "It pointed to the existence of Tomas Crohan, still held by the Soviets in the Gulag."

"Who is Tomas Crohan?"

"I remembered. Vaguely. Just after the war, when I came in, there was talk about an operation in Nazi Austria . . . some of the older hands at OSS. Then it was disbanded and we were all floating around from one establishment to another until Truman put the CIA together."

"Fascinating history of American Intelligence."

Hanley looked up sharply. "Damn it, Mrs. Neumann. I want to explain to you."

"Explain."

"I checked with some of our retired people after I ran his name through a routine comp search—"

"You could have told me about it."

"Mrs. Neumann. You are in charge of a vast division inside the Section. It hardly seemed worthwhile to tell you about it. Not at the time."

"What did the retired spooks tell you?"

"Enough to make it a puzzle."

She waited. Her plate was clean.

"Crohan. He was Irish, suspected of being behind the continued existence of the Irish Republican Army in the late 1930s. Viciously anti-British and the bad feelings were returned. Also a bit of a Nazi."

"Sounds like a lovely fellow."

"Well, it was explained to me that the parts were all tied in to his absolute hatred of the British. Ireland came up neutral in the war—the Irish Free State—and the Nazis were all over Dublin. They curried favor with the De Valera regime and they were using the country as a listening post on our operations in the Atlantic. Not that we weren't there as well, to do our bit. We worked on the Irish, pointed out our ties, and all that. This was the State Department, I mean, and the OSS. It was a delicate game. At the same time we were dealing separately with the Irish, holding off the Nazis in Ireland, we had to hold off the British. They were absolutely rabid when it came to the subject of Irish cooperation with the Americans. They kept thinking we were cooking up deals behind their backs for American support for Irish unity after the war."

"Were we?"

"I haven't the faintest idea. Though I should think we were promising them anything under duress."

"And how did Crohan fit in?"

"He was a perfect man. Irish neutral with valid visas to Nazi-occupied Europe. He could become our agent."

"How? When?"

"I don't know. Memories of old men just fade at that point. I hoped there would be something in Tinkertoy. And then I hoped you could somehow wring the information out of Langley since they have charge of all the old OSS files. It distresses me that this . . . this problem has come up, that nothing has come of your research."

Mrs. Neumann narrowed her shrewd eyes. "That's the point, isn't it, Hanley? Something did come of it. Absolutely nothing."

"I don't want to be left in the dark on this," Hanley said. Annoyance scratched at his plain Nebraska voice. Both were from the Midwest, different states at different times, and both had an annoying directness in their speech that offended others and attracted them to each other inside R Section, despite their separate temperaments. In that moment, Mrs. Neumann instinctively understood the lostness Hanley felt.

"What happened to Crohan?" she said in a raspy whisper.

"He was in Vienna when the Soviets marched in. He was trapped in the city but he wasn't terribly concerned. After all, we were all on the same side. The Russians just arrested him and he disappeared. After a year or so, they acknowledged they had him but said he had died, too bad."

"Wallenberg."

"There are similarities," Hanley admitted. "But what was his mission? And why does Langley want to play games about a file that is forty years old?"

"How did his name come up?"

"During a routine assignment in Helsinki. We got a flutter from our man that Crohan is still alive and that he can come out now."

"Is it valid?"

"If it isn't, I don't think we're at risk in the matter. But I just don't like it."

"Why not?"

"It is so unexpected."

"Life is full of surprises," Mrs. Neumann said.

"No, Mrs. Neumann, it is not. It is terribly predictable." He placed his forearms on either side of his coffee cup and leaned forward across the soiled plates and bowls. "When the unexpected happens, it is always a nasty shock. That is why I did not expect Crohan. Now I know that it presages something bad."

"You're a pessimist."

"A realist, Mrs. Neumann, and a careful one. There is the smell of a trap in all this."

"A trap for who? For your agent? For the Section?"

"I don't know. Why this reluctance at the Competition? The OSS file is their responsibility only insofar as they have it. Langley has no reason to obfuscate—"

"It's the nature of the beast, Hanley, you know that."

"I never expected anything out of Helsinki." Hanley bit his lower lip and chewed on it a moment like a schoolboy faced with a difficult mathematical puzzle in an examination. Mrs. Neumann studied him not unkindly. Something in her dark brown eyes suggested amusement at his problem.

"I sent November there," he said at last.

For the first time, Mrs. Neumann appeared startled. She knew the identity of "November." In fact, some of the code names were a bit of a joke inside the Section because of the way they had come about. All the prime functioning agents and stationmasters in the field had been coded by name after months, days of the week and other elements of time. There was a Winter, a Summer, a March, a Twilight. After the system was in place and working, it was discovered that the GS-11 inside the Section who had provided all the new nomenclature was a practicing astrologist and had consulted charts and dates before matching the code name with the real agent. He explained that such names would "augur good vibrations for the Section." In any case, there was no money that fiscal year to change the system and then a sort of indolence set in. November remained November because no one thought it worthwile to change anything again.

"What was he supposed to do there?"

"Nothing, Mrs. Neumann. We had a flutter a few months before that a KGB sort wanted to come to our side. I thought there might be something wrong with it. Langley was burned last year, you know. I told November to check his *bona fides.*"

"Nonsense," Mrs. Neumann said harshly. "You could have sent anyone from the Scandinavian station. That fellow in Copenhagen, he's competent for a job like that."

"It was a legitimate mission. I wanted evaluation."

"Not for November."

Hanley flushed. "Yes, damn it. I wanted to get him out of the way."

She was startled. "What on earth for?"

"Out of harm's way."

"How touching of you," she said. "What were you afraid of?"

"I'm not afraid of anything," he said.

"You wanted to get Devereaux out of the way," she said, breaking security by uttering his real name in a public place. The cafeteria was rapidly clearing out. Plates were being scraped noisily at the serving counter and banged into dishwashers. Nine-to-five official Washington was finishing lunch.

"I put him on ice as far away as I could. Some of the headhunters can't forget that Devereaux cleaned up that business in Paris last year despite Galloway and that Galloway lost his job because of it."

Galloway was Rear Admiral Galloway who had been the Old Man at R Section until he stubbed his toe on the business of the Paris terrorists and the plot to subvert the computers inside the Section.

"Who wants to get him?"

"The New Man for one. I stashed Devereaux in Jamaica for a year to watch the new government. Devereaux was a good man once, but the ambition has gone out of him."

"This doesn't sound right," she said.

"All right, Mrs. Neumann. I'll give you another story. He wants an Asian posting."

"So?"

"The New Man says no."

"Why?"

"He wants Devereaux to quit."

"Why?"

"Because Devereaux is what he is. He is dangerous."

"Nonsense. We're not running a day camp."

"I put him in Helsinki because I had to put him someplace."

"You put him in Helsinki so that nothing would happen and eventually Devereaux would realize that he was never getting out."

"Never is a long time."

"You were his rabbi; you were supposed to take care of him."

"What was I supposed to do?"

"Cover your ass," Mrs. Neumann said. Hanley appeared shocked for a moment but it passed.

"Now this Crohan business. It needs an answer."

"No, that's not it. You're afraid Devereaux is going to act without an answer."

"Yes."

"All right. Pull him back. Have a heart-to-heart. Lay out the feelings of the New Man. He can ride it out, he's a big boy. Send in Solstice from Copenhagen to relieve him and tell Solstice not to do a damned thing."

"Solstice is out of pocket," Hanley said, slipping into more slang. "He went deep cover on that Soviet matter at Nordkapp. For all I know, he's in the black now, in Russia. I can't alert Norwegian Intelligence about it without alerting everyone else up there, including the Swedes."

"The Swedes couldn't find their ass with a flashlight and a map," Mrs. Neumann snorted in her rough voice. "The Soviets practically ground submarines on their beaches and they can't see them."

"They see what they want to see," Hanley said mildly to counterpoint her raspy whisper.

"So you're stuck with Devereaux for now."

"For the moment. I just don't want him to do anything."

"Tell him."

"No. Then he will know it has all been for nothing. Besides, there's a trap working here. I can feel it."

"Your bones? It's merely old age, Hanley."

"No. First the defector. Then he offers a gift and when we start poking at the gift, it begins to smell. There is a trap working here. I can smell it."

"So what are you going to do then?"

"Nothing, Mrs. Neumann. Nothing at all." It was all he could think to say.

8

HELSINKI

Nothing.

Devereaux waited in a doorway across the wide plaza near the bus depot. He was watching the entry of the state Alko store across the way. In the afternoon, the Finns, numbed by winter and the dark days, pushed into the stark large store and bought inexpensive vodka that was still too costly. In the evening blackness, they could numb their minds as their bodies had been numbed by cold. The windows of the store carried posters warning of the dangers of alcohol abuse. The posters were to salve the conscience of the state that derived vast revenues from controlling the liquor trade. State taxes made the alcohol so costly that few Finns could afford to drink their own famous Finlandia vodka, which was mostly exported. The vodka they consumed was not made for taste but for effect.

An hour had passed and still there was nothing.

If there was contact, it would be signaled here in front of the Alko store—contact from either Tartakoff or Hanley. Instead, for the eighth day, there was silence.

Not for the first time in the past two months, Devereaux felt trapped in a state that was neither certain nor real. The quality of a dream infected his waking moments in the frozen city; perhaps it was a nightmare. Sometimes, after a night of dreams that tormented him with memories of dead men and nightmares survived in his past, Devereaux would awake and think he was still sleeping.

He had noted contact with an agent in his last message to Hanley, posted the day before. He guessed the agent was British but he didn't know. He told Hanley in the note that his cover had been blown but still there was silence.

Four P.M. The city was growing dark. The lights were flicked on in the streets but they seemed pale. People began to leave the stores and offices along the main shopping thoroughfares. In a little while, the center of Helsinki would be wrapped in silence.

Contact with Hanley was complicated by official Washington's distrust of both the Swedes and Finns. It was assumed all telephone lines were routinely tapped. The usual routing of messages was by mail, anonymous drop, to the safe house in Copenhagen. The mail normally took a day. From Copenhagen it could be sent to the States by pouch or by scrambled radio signal.

He had done one other thing. He had addressed Hanley in a separate open telegram sent to the address in Fairfax, Virginia, that was the last desperate expedient of desperate agents needing to contact the Section through extraordinary means. The addressee was "Mr. Dougherty" who lived in a seedy rooming house in that Washington suburb.

MR. DOUGHERTY. NEED IMMEDIATE DECISION ON ARABIA PURCHASE FOR CALIFORNIA STORE. DIXON.

The California store was the place in Santa Barbara where defectors were "stored" after the first debriefings in Maryland, before they were given new identities and scattered to safe sites throughout the United States. "Arabia" was the trade name for the Finnish glass-and-dinnerware company and the message sounded sufficiently like a business inquiry that Devereaux thought it would escape the special study of the Finnish censors.

Darkness at 4:15.

Devereaux gave it up for the day. He bent his head into the face of the perpetual wind that howled off the plaza between the Presidentii Hotel and the office complex across the way. If there had been contact by the Russians, the signal was to purchase a bottle of Finlandia vodka in the Alko store between three and four in the afternoon and then leave the bottle on the walk in front of the store. It had not happened.

He pushed through the front doors into the vast square lobby of the dark modern hotel. He felt cold. He alway felt cold now, as though a perpetual chill had taken root in his bones.

He walked to the left of the elevator bank and took the stairs down to the sauna rooms.

Behind the wooden desk, a pregnant woman nodded to him in greeting. She was dark and her eyes were a very dark blue; she wore thick glasses as did many of the women in Helsinki.

She handed him blue bathing trunks and a locker key and towel.

"Cold today, Mr. Dixon?"

"No. Warm. People were wearing bathing trunks outside," he said. She smiled because the exchange was ritual and he had developed an odd fondness for the pregnant woman whose name was Ulla. It was the only warm contact in Helsinki for him and he maintained it with the care of a man who blows on a small flame to keep it from dying in a frozen camp.

The sauna was usually empty at this time.

He found comfort in the ritual as much as in the physical warmth of the basement rooms. He would sit in the sauna and become lost in the luxury of the heat as it soaked into his cold bones; when he was sweating, he would go into the next room and plunge into the small swimming pool and swim himself into exhaustion. And then he would return to the sauna and fall asleep and invariably he would be refreshed at the end of the ritual.

He undressed and pulled on the blue trunks in the changing room and then padded across the floor in bare feet to the shower room that led to the sauna. There were bloody prints of feet on the floor.

He stood still for a long moment.

The prints were prints of shoes and what appeared to be a bare foot. The shoe prints led to an outside door that in turn led to a hall. He opened the door to the hall. The bloody shoe prints continued for six feet and then stopped. The blood had dried on the shoes. The shoes belonged to the killer.

Devereaux knew it was a killing.

He turned on a shower in the shower room and the water beat down harshly against the tile wall in the open stall.

Devereaux then opened the door of the sauna.

It smelled of warm blood.

A single light lit the wooden room. Warm blood—it reminded Devereaux of a battlefield in Vietnam a long time ago—warm, sickly sweet smell of blood.

The wooden walls were splattered with blood that still ran on the wood.

Propped on a bench above the heater, facing the door like a macabre butler, was the naked body of the Englishman called Sims who had made contact with Devereaux the night before.

From nipple to bladder, the chest had been opened. All the blood was draining from the body. Gray guts were splattered on the bench.

Devereaux stared at the dead features. The eyes were open, the mouth lolled open. A pail of water was next to the body; it was tinted red by the blood that had spilled into it.

Devereaux looked for the weapon but it was not there. He leaned across the body and pulled a locker key from a pair of swimming trunks cast aside on the bloody bench. Locker 112.

Devereaux stepped out of the sauna. He was sweating but he felt cold. He stepped into the running shower and bathed the blood from his legs. He stepped out of the shower and let the water keep running. He went into the changing room and pulled his towel from the locker and dried himself while he considered the possibilities.

The pregnant woman named Ulla at the front desk had seen him enter. Was it the only way in or out of the sauna? Had she seen the killer? But he knew that sometimes Ulla worked sorting clothes in a back room behind the desk where she dispensed towels and bathing garments and, oddly, beer from a tap. The killer could have slipped in and out without being seen if he was willing to take the chance.

Ulla had seen him. She would have to tell that to the police. Was Devereaux intended to be trapped by this? Was the dead man a British agent? Had he been set up to be killed here, in this time and place, because of Devereaux's habit of using the sauna in the afternoon?

Which would mean that someone had an interest in Devereaux enough to follow him every day, until his routine was established.

Devereaux put down the towel and used the key found in the sauna to open locker 112.

Trousers, shirt, sweater. No outer jacket. He had stayed in the hotel. Devereaux fished through the pockets for identification. None. Three hundred-markka notes, some Finnish change, a single British ten-shilling piece. And a key to Room 612.

He dressed quickly. After seven weeks of inaction, the discovery of the body of the dead Englishman had curiously energized him. He felt no horror. He had seen such dead men before. It was a peculiar sort of professional killing, used by some hired hands in the Mediterranean area.

He put the key to Room 612 in his pocket. He threw his outer coat over his arm and carried along his dripping trunks and the towel he had taken from the locker of the dead man. He left his own towel at the entrance to the sauna, on the sopping floor where the shower still played against the tiles.

He went down the hall.

Ulla was looking at a glossy Swedish magazine. It had a lurid cover and the headlines were bright red.

"Mr. Dixon. You are finished already?"

"No, Ulla," Devereaux said gently. "There is a dead man in the sauna."

Her face paled. "I will go to him, perhaps he is not dead, I can resuscitate."

"No. It's not that. He was killed. Murdered. No, sit down."

"But I must go to him."

"You must not. Did anyone else come into the sauna this afternoon besides me?"

"No. Except Mr. Sims."

"Yes. That's who's dead. Anyone else?"

"No. I was in the laundry room for a while."

"It's all right," he said. Again, the flat cold words carried an edge of gentleness to them. She was not involved in this, he thought. He would not involve her to get out of it.

"Are you sure he's dead?"

"Yes."

"My duty is to go back."

"No. Don't do that. You're pregnant; think about that. Just call the police."

"I will—" She reached for the phone but Devereaux put his hand over it. He needed time but he did not want to leave the woman alone in case she did investigate and saw the body.

"We'll go upstairs. I want you to call from the lobby. We can lock the door on the way up, can't we?"

"Yes."

"I don't want to leave you alone down here."

She followed him reluctantly up the stairs and they locked the door at the lobby level. "Use the phone at the front desk."

"Where are you going, Mr. Dixon?"

"I don't feel well. I have to go to my room for a moment. I'll be down."

He left her as she was crossing the lobby. Just a little time, time to call, time to explain to the front desk what happened, time to summon the police, time to unlock the door and go back to the basement sauna. Just a few minutes of extra time, but enough to go to Room 612.

Devereaux pushed open the door. There was a small piece of Scotch tape at the bottom of the door which broke as he pushed it open. A simple device to see if your room had been disturbed.

The radio was on, playing American rock songs.

Devereaux looked around the room. The window drapes were open on the frozen building site acros the street that was Devereaux's own view of Helsinki and where it was said the body of a dead woman had been found two nights before.

Devereaux opened the clothes bureau. There was a leather bag on the top shelf. Devereaux opened the bag and felt along the seam inside the bag until he came to what he wanted. He opened the seam with his finger and pulled out the wafer-thin wallet. Inside were Bank of England notes in large denominations totaling two thousand pounds. He put the notes in his pocket. He opened the wallet. A face was on a card.

Anthony Sims. Trade representative. British-Suomi Export Ltd.

He put the card in his pocket.

Another card was below the first. It was shaped like a credit card but it lacked printing or raised numbers. The card was gray. Devereaux knew what it was used for. When it was slipped into a machine like a transfer punch, the card came to life and put a message on a screen. The message was the identity of the British Intelligence agent.

Auntie. An agent from British Intelligence had tried to make contact with him. Why? Why had he been killed less than twenty-four hours later? And why would suspicion fall on Devereaux?

And silence. Why was there no response from Hanley? A defector namd Tartakoff wanted to bring out a man who was supposed to be dead named Tomas Crohan. And now the British were probing the matter as well.

Devereaux suddenly felt intensely foolish, as though he had become so careless that he had allowed the numbing routine of the past weeks of inaction to make him an easy setup for a trap. He had been intended to find the body and he had been so careless that he had been followed. Not only by Sims but by the man who had killed Sims.

Why didn't Tartakoff make contact? Why didn't Hanley answer?

Devereaux turned and left the room quietly. He walked along the deserted corridor to the soft-drink machine in the middle of the hall. He fished out the two identification cards he had taken from the body as well as the wallet full of British pounds. He put the cards in the wallet and then tipped back the edge of the heavy soda machine and slipped the wallet beneath it. He took the stairs next to the ice machine to the fifth floor and his own room. Down another empty corridor. The hotel was always silent, always seemed empty, even though it was usually full of business travelers. The silences were intentional: the hotel was built with heavy simplicity, heavy walls and doors and thick-paned windows.

He turned the key in the lock of his own door and opened it.

There was someone in the room.

For two weeks, he had not even carried his pistol with him. The routine had numbed him as surely as the weather.

The room was dark but there was someone in the faint shadows cast by the perpetual light on the clock at the bedside.

Would it be a knife?

He felt awkward in that moment, painted in outline against the lights of the corridor. He saw in his mind's eye the disemboweled body of Sims in the sauna.

"Mr. Dixon?"

"Who are you?"

"Or should I call you Mr. Devereaux?"

"Who are you?"

"I will turn on the lights."

Devereaux said nothing. The lights went on. Devereaux blinked. In front of him was a short man with a bull's neck and thick fingers extending from a thick palm. He wore a dark coat that might have been blue. His face was flat and his eyes were small like unburned coals.

He held a pistol in his hand. It was a Walther PPK automatic and he held it at the level of Devereaux's belly.

"What is your real name then? Dixon? Or Devereaux?"

"Who are you?"

"You have to tell me eventually, you know. That's the rules of the game." His English was not without accent but it had an ironic note to it that implied a deep understanding of the language.

Devereaux waited.

"My name is Kulak," the thick man said. "I am the police, Mr. Dixon or Mr. Devereaux. Do you see?"

And slowly, without a word, Devereaux came across the room until he stood near the other man. They stared at each other but the policeman named Kulak did not lower the barrel of the deadly black pistol held loosely in his massive hand.

9

LONDON

Wickham awoke, felt the beard on his face as though feeling the fur of an unexpected animal. How long had it been? But there was no time in this place. There were no windows, no passage of day to night, no passage of weeks. He slept, he awoke, he slept in no order at all. He felt his life ebbing away from him in his sleeps. He was dying because he slept; and so he struggled to stay awake but the utter boredom drove him to sleep again as a refuge. Perhaps that would be death, he thought suddenly; a sleep accepted at the end and even yearned for.

The single door in the windowless, shallow room opened and Wickham turned but he could not rise because he was handcuffed by one wrist to the edge of the steel cot.

The man was Victor. He knew their names. They never actually told him names but he had to give them names so that he could distinguish between them. Victor was the harsh one. Victor had beaten him the first night. Yes. It had been night, it was dark, Rogers stopped the automobile, Rogers got out. . . .

"Wickham. Get up and come over to the table."

Victor uncuffed his wrist. He felt the blood tingle back into the hand. He went to the table and sat down. He was naked except for the undershorts he had been permitted to keep but not to change.

He looked at Victor but did not speak.

Victor put the photographs in his briefcase on the table. He stared at Wickham. Wickham looked at the photographs.

Vile things.

In the first, Wickham was in a lavatory stall. He was performing fellatio on a young man. The identity of the young man could not be seen but it was clearly a lavatory and the young man was seated on a toilet. The picture was not clear but Wickham could make out the figures well enough.

The second photograph was equally unspeakable.

Wickham looked at Victor.

"I didn't do those things."

"Of course you did."

"No one will believe those photographs. Photographs lie."

"Do you remember everything you've done?"

"I would remember. . . ." He paused. Of course he would remember.

"The photographs were sent this morning to the *Sun*."

"They'll never print those photographs."

"Of course not," Victor agreed.

"What is the purpose of these photographs?"

"I wanted you to see them. Before you were shown them."

"Why did you do those things?"

"Your clothes are in the closet there. Get dressed. We have to take you home."

"What?"

"We have to take you home," Victor said.

Relief mingled with fear. The two emotions commingled chilled him.

"Why . . ."

"Your clothing, Mr. Wickham."

He dressed slowly, carefully. He felt tired and dirty. He did not understand. They meant to kill him, didn't they?

"Good. Now Mr. Wickham, here is a blindfold. I will take you down myself."

"Where are we?"

"Cooperate."

"But what about those photographs?"

"Nothing about them. They speak for themselves."

They speak for themselves.

Wickham accepted the blindfold almost gratefully. Victor led him out of the room. He was on stairs. He bumped his shin on the banister at the top of the flight.

"Careful," Victor said.

But of course his name was probably not Victor at all.

10

LENINGRAD

A light always burned in the night in the corridor outside Ward 7 of the ninth section of the KGB psychiatric hospital attached to the grounds of the Kresty Prison complex in the city, off the River Neva and not five hundred meters from the Finland Station where the statue of Lenin held the plaza ground. The light was oddly reassuring as though the inmates were children who feared the ghosts hidden in the darkness beyond.

The night in the ward was never silent. There were sounds of inmates wrestling with dreams that would not be silenced. They groaned in the darkness and sometimes they screamed. There were snores of those without dreams. There were other unexplained screams that came from other wards and penetrated the thick plaster walls. The screams from far away always seemed more frightening. Sometimes, some of the inmates would wake suddenly in the middle of the night and begin to cry. Some of the others would try to silence the crying ones with muttered threats that made the noise even worse. If it had not been for the comfort of the single light in the corridor, the prisoner who lay awake now and contemplated the noisy chaos around him thought he might have gone mad.

Even the screams could be ignored in the light. Even sleep could come because of the comforting, mothering light.

They had brought him here one year and six days before. He was very good at remembering time.

Was he mentally ill?

Tomas Crohan lay on his bed and considered the question he had posed to himself. Mentally ill?

Perhaps. They had discovered in the camp in Siberia that the commandant was mentally ill. They had discovered it quite by accident one afternoon when they visited the camp and saw the prisoners working in the snow naked. The commandant had explained to the visiting commissar that the coldness brought the best efforts of the men and that nakedness made them docile. The camp is Siberia had not been visited for a long time but when the visitors, who were from Kiev, noted the conditions of the camp with their own eyes, they ordered the prisoners to go inside their sheds. Tomas Crohan had watched from the window and been pleased with the way the visitors from Kiev had dealt with the mental illness of the commandant of the camp.

That was certainly mental illness, Crohan thought, staring at the blackness pierced by a single naked bulb hanging in the corridor.

There was a sound of crying in that moment and then the muttered threats. With what could you threaten a man who cried in the night because he awoke and found himself inside the Kresty Prison, so close to the city of Leningrad and yet so removed from it that he would never see it unless he had a job in the cardboard factory on the grounds and could peer at the beautiful towers from the window?

There was nothing to threaten.

The Jews, of course, presented a singular problem to the authorities in the treatment of their particular aberrations.

They thought they were Jews. That was the explanation of Kronenbourg who was another old prisoner like Crohan. Kronenbourg was from the Alsace-Lorraine which he claimed was German but which Crohan had shown him was actually in France. He had wept for days to think he might be French and then Crohan, in his mercy, had relented and allowed Kronenbourg to believe that he was German and that he had not been on the wrong side in the war.

So few remembered the war anymore. There were almost no survivors. It was just as well to let Kronenbourg have his delusions.

Crohan smiled to himself in the darkness. He was a thin man; most of the older ones were thin. If you were going to survive at all, it was best to be thin. It was a theory of Crohan's that he lectured about when he was asked to do so. His face was a mask. His skull pushed at the folds of the mask. His forehead was high because most of his hair was gone. Oddly, his skin was able to support enormous patches of tough whiskers that required great diligence in shaving each morning. The hospital provided the luxury of shaving facilities and shaving time. He had not been so fortunate in the Siberian camp where the commandant was demonstrably mentally ill.

The Jews. He was thinking about the Jews.

What had Kronenbourg said? Well, much of what he said could be put down to his anti-Semitism in any case. He wanted to be a good Nazi as he thought he had not been in the war. He had been captured, after all, on the eastern front in 1944.

The Jews. The Jews. What was the line?

Crohan frowned in concentration. It was easier to concentrate at night like this, lying in the comfortable darkness and relative warmth of the ward while the Russian winter beat beyond the walls. Snow and snow and snow; it never ceased to snow. And yet the life was not too bad. He should have become mentally unfit many years earlier.

But then, he had nothing to say about his mental status.

The Jews thought they were Jews and that was proof of their mental aberration. Who would be a Jew except a madman?

That was it.

Crohan smiled again. Kronenbourg had put it neatly.

"What if I told you I was a Jew?"

"But you aren't. You're Irish."

"All right. What if I told you I wasn't Irish?"

"But you are," Kronenbourg had said. "Anyone can see that."

"What if I told you I was English?"

"But that's impossible. If you were English, you could get out of here. You wouldn't be what you said you had been.

Besides, we would be enemies then, wouldn't we?" Kronenbourg had smiled in a superior way that irritated Crohan but he had long ceased to show his irritation with the peculiarities of others. Prisoners or camp commandants.

"You were on our side in the war. That's why you're in here," Kronenbourg had said after an uncomfortable silence.

"What if I told you I was an American?"

"An American? But then they would have segregated you, with the other Americans."

"What if I told you I was a Swede?"

"Like Wallenberg? I have heard about him but he must be dead."

"All right. What if I told you I was a German?"

Kronenbourg had frowned at that, wrinkling his dark forehead and smoothing his dry remains of hair like a farmer spreading dry hay over the frosty ground. "You could not be German. Don't be annoyed. You are my friend, Tomas. But if you were German, then you would never have denied it. Who does not want to be a German?"

"A Jew," said Tomas Crohan and they had laughed at that though the joke was slightly beyond Kronenbourg's understanding.

Now there's a mental problem, Crohan thought. Kronenbourg was not a bad fellow but he had definitely lost his mind. He was good at small things. He folded the boxes in the cardboard factory. It was the lowest sort of work.

The Jews would not admit they were mentally unstable.

That is the problem, Natasha Gulonov had told him once. She was the medical assistant who gave them their pills each morning. The pills were a reward and a punishment. The pills enabled one to make it through the day but they made the night unendurable and there were no pills given for night. The night was faced naked. Like prisoners working the snow of a camp run by a madman. Definitely mad. His name had been Fodoroff. Mad as a hatter.

Hatter. What an interesting image. Where had that come from?

Crohan turned in his cot and faced the light beyond the rows of cots containing restless, sleeping men.

Natasha Gulonov said the Soviet Union had many peoples, many tongues. Only the Jews appeared mad, she said.

"Baptists," Crohan had replied.

"What did you say?"

"Jews. And Baptists. The three fellows we had at Number 19 in Kiev about six years ago. Baptists. They baptized me three times in the barracks."

"Madness," Natasha Gulonov had said.

"It was a way to get a bath," Crohan had replied. "They saved the rain water and they would not drink it. They baptized all the prisoners before they died. I was baptized three times."

"You should not make a joke of religion," she had said.

"Why? Do you think God will be angry with me?"

"There is no God."

"Of course not. So there is no reason to think he will become angry with me."

"But it is not good for you, Tomas."

"Doctor—"

"I am not a doctor. Yet."

"The Jews are mad," he had said. "Because they wish to be Jews?"

"No. Because they do not accept the State."

"Is everyone mad who does not accept the State?"

"No. Some are traitors." She talked to him as though he were a child. Tomas Crohan had become her pet. Sometimes she allowed him to give pills to the prisoners. Once she gave him a small cache of extra pills which he could sell for cigarettes.

"I accept the State," Tomas Crohan had said.

"Yes, I know."

"How can I still be mad?"

She had turned away from him that morning. "Don't speak of such things. Go away, Tomas, you make me angry."

The Jews, at least, had an instinct for survival inside the camps. Crohan could not understand how some of the others would just give up suddenly. Take the Finn. What was his name? Unpronounceable in any case. He had been brought to Novo Gordunov, what was it? ten years ago?—and he had raged so greatly they nearly shot him right away just in self-defense. That would have satisfied the Finn. He wanted it over with. But when they didn't shoot him, he became indifferent, even to food. Naturally, the other prisoners stole his food. And his clothing. If the fellow wasn't going to make a protest, then it was too bad for him. The Finn died in the summer. Hardly anyone at Novo Gordunov died until October came and the first snow. The Finn did not have an instinct for survival, Crohan realized. But the Jews always did. Once you are willing to die gladly at the hands of the guards, then you are dead already.

An instinct for survival was not such a common thing. And it was not simple. Crohan could lecture on the subject and did from time to time, to fill the restless days. For example, resistance was useless and therefore counterproductive. Do not resist; survive. A very thin line, a fine point, wouldn't you agree?

Darkness.

Crohan blinked; the restless night ward was suddenly still.

Crohan blinked again but he could not bring back the light. And then he saw the two men at the door of the ward blocking the light. He turned in his cot to stare at them. The ward was deathly silent; all tears, all screams had ceased. Night visitors, and they always brought bad luck with them. Sometimes they took prisoners away and the prisoners were never seen again. Sometimes they gave patients midnight examinations, as they were called. A day or two days later, the exhausted patient would be returned to the ward, covered with bruises, his face hideously reshaped by the pounding blows of the examiners.

They had paused at the door and now one of them, at the direction of the night nursing guard, had started to walk through the tangle of beds in the ward.

Crohan closed his eyes. It was always best not to be too curious. It was best to pretend the matter of the night visitors was a bad dream and that when one opened one's eyes, the dream would be ended.

"Crohan." The voice was harsh, low.

My God, he thought and shivered and held his eyes tight. It was just a dream.

He felt the rough warm hand on his shoulder. He was being pulled up. He opened his eyes and saw the flat face before him. The night visitor had steel teeth that glittered in his mouth in the thin light from the single bulb in the corridor.

"Come," he said.

"What have I done?"

"Come," he said.

And Crohan's feet somehow found the cold floor. In a moment, he was out of the ward, in the light of the corridor. He blinked because of the light, because of the fear that wrapped itself around him. From the dark womb of the ward came the sounds of night again, so comforting and so beyond his reach now: screams and the familiar sounds of men crying in the darkness.

11

DUBLIN

On the same night that Tomas Crohan was taken from his ward in the Kresty Prison psychiatric hospital in Leningrad and a man named Sims was murdered in a sauna in Helsinki, Rita Macklin finished her work at the rectory of St. Adrian's parish and began the long trek to Baggot Street to find a cab to take her back to her room.

It had not been difficult at all.

Father Cunningham had no family left anywhere in Ireland and only a vague reference to "a family friend" who might live in Chicago in America. Rita Macklin assured the priests at St. Adrian's that she was the family friend. The deceit was never questioned because there was nothing to be gained from the old man's possessions.

Indeed, there was no wealth among them.

Rita Macklin was not looking for money, however. She catalogued the possessions meticulously, including his clothing.

Her presence in the rectory for four days upset the housekeeper, Mrs. Ryan, but did not seem to displease the priests. If Rita Macklin was pretty, it was the sort of fresh-faced beauty that is not dispensed in creams or lotions but comes from genes and good health.

"Priests again," the M.E. had laughed when she called him.

Even Rita Macklin, despite the painful memories, had smiled during the transatlantic telephone conversation. Priests again. Nearly three years before, she had worked on the story of the old priest named Leo Tunney who had come out of the Asian jungles after twenty years and had a dreadful secret to tell someone. He eventually told Rita, before he died, and put Rita's life in peril. But that could never happen again in any case; the matter of priests was just a coincidence, she thought.

"I'm sorting through his things, I'm trying to get some clue—"

"I think I told you to be careful," Mac said and his voice was so lazy and calm that she could imagine him now leaning back in his leather swivel chair with the phone cupped in the crook of his shoulder, with his hands folded on the back of his graying head.

"I am careful."

"Watching both ways when you cross the street?"

"You think he was killed. I mean, deliberately?"

"What do you think?"

"I don't know." She thought she did know.

"There aren't too many coincidences in the real world," Mac said.

"Except for priests," she replied and she evoked another chuckle that sailed over the phone lines three thousand miles.

"Find anything?"

"Yes. And a big no."

"What's the yes?"

"Note on a meeting two weeks ago. With a man named Parker who lived in Dublin. That's all it says, just Parker. He thinks Parker is a British agent. That sounds a little fantastic, doesn't it?"

"You mean secret agent, spies, booga-booga? Just the thing we're looking for, Rita."

"Yes. Do you know how many Parkers there are in the Dublin phone directory? And what if the spy wasn't even listed?"

Again, Mac chuckled. "What are you going to do?"

"When I get done, I'm going to the British Embassy and ask for him."

"Do you think that's a good idea?"

"It's the only idea I have. Flush him out. Never hesitate, as Kaiser used to tell me." Kaiser had been her first editor in Washington; he had been her father and mentor and her cynical conscience.

"You might not want to flush him."

"Oh, I'm not afraid of a British secret agent. Unless he happens to be a Russian double agent."

"Half of them seem to be," Mac said. "So all this is tied to this Tomas Crohan?"

"I don't know but I think so. I guess I believe in coincidences more than you do. I mean, I think they mean something, that they connect things that shouldn't be connected. I went to Dublin airport and ran down every plane that left within two hours after Father Cunningham was killed. I eliminated the flights to Shannon because it seemed unlikely he was doubling back to another airport in the country. I think the killer wanted to get out of the country. Well, there was supposed to be a flight for Belfast twenty minutes after the killing. That's a possibility. And there was a plane for Amsterdam at noon. And one other international flight—for Copenhagen at twelve thirty-five. That would be perfect."

"Copenhagen? I don't understand any of this."

"Father Cunningham wrote that he had a visitor a year ago and it must have started him thinking about the whole business again. A man named O'Donnell, retired in the Irish government, he had been part of the De Valera government in the 'forties, during the war. He had known Cunningham then. Well, apparently they just had a get-together, a chat, but at one point, Cunningham brought up Crohan. He said he had known Crohan as a child and he had just received this letter about Crohan from his cousin, Mrs. Fitzroy, who lived in America. He told O'Donnell that Mrs. Fitzroy was convinced that Crohan was still alive in the Soviet Gulag."

"So?"

"Well, you know how you need legs of a tripod to make the camera stand steady? Up to now, I've had two legs: Mrs. Fitzroy and the letter that Father Cunningham sent to her. Now I think I've got the third leg, except there's a problem with it."

"Rita, you're talking me in circles again."

She realized she was breathless, speaking too quickly into the ancient telephone receiver provided in a booth off the bare lobby in the little Buswell Hotel. The connection faded at times and it seemed Mac's voice rose and fell like ocean waves.

"This fellow O'Donnell, who is dead now—he died six months ago of cancer—this fellow O'Donnell, he said he wasn't all that certain that Mrs. Fitzroy wasn't right. He said that he learned that Crohan was being held in some prison hospital or something in Leningrad."

"Did he just divine this or did it come as a stroke of lightning from on high?"

She smiled. "Well, that's the part that gets interesting and frustrating at the same time—that's the part I can't understand.

It seems there was some sort of connection between British Intelligence and the Irish special branch or whatever it is. This O'Donnell was a liaison. Cunningham was writing all this out, almost like a term paper, he was going over it over and over again as though he didn't understand it any more than I do. But this is what I think it means: Somehow, the British know that Crohan is alive in the Soviet Union. And somehow, they weren't unhappy to let the Irish government know, too. For all I know, the CIA knows it too, which is why they've been playing hard-to-get with me from the beginning."

There was a pause so long that Rita thought for a moment they had been disconnected.

Finally, Mac spoke slowly. "Why? Why, Rita, would they all know this and keep it a secret?"

"Why do birds fly? Why do Swedes have trouble finding Soviet submarines in their waters? Why do we cancel grain sales and then renew them when nothing has changed? Why a lot of things?"

"Because it is not profitable to acknowledge that Crohan is alive."

"That's part of it. The Swedes didn't exactly kill themselves trying to get Wallenberg out of the Soviet Union right after the war. The Swedes had to learn to get along with the Russians, even if they didn't want to. And Wallenberg came from a big important family, a helluva lot more important than Tomas Crohan."

"I don't see where any of this is going to lead," Mac said.

"Neither do I."

"Fortunately, you have the time. We are a wealthy magazine and quite given to flights of fancy that consume both time and money. So what are you going to do?"

"Go to Leningrad," Rita said.

"The direct approach," Mac said.

"That's the way Kaiser taught me," she replied.

"Well, your Kaiser did a good job."

Kaiser had done a good job on her. She hurried along Adrian Lane to Shelbourne where she could take a shortcut across the Kingwell Crescent to Baggot Street and find a taxi. It was bitterly cold as all the days became as they sank into early evening. She huddled in her wool navy coat, her head turned away from the direction of the wind. Rita wore an Irish wool cap on her head, pulled down over her ears.

There was nothing more to be gained from going through Father Cunningham's possessions. *Requiescat in pace.*

Kaiser.

The thought of the old sausage of an editor had come back to her again and again while she sifted through the life of Father Cunningham contained in a few notes, a diary and bits of memorabilia. Kaiser had no scruples but to get the story. There had been one photograph that finally struck her: Cunningham, a woman, a man. The woman must have been Mrs. Fitzroy, taken probably in the late 1930s. They were very young, probably teens or just into their twenties.

They were identified on the back of the snapshot by nicknames. "Toby" was Mrs. Fitzroy and the other identifiable figure was "Danny." It must have been Cunningham. But who was "Sarsfield"?

Crohan. It must be Crohan. Wasn't Sarsfield the name of an Irish rebel?

Kaiser would not have wanted her to wait. "Get the story out, little Rita." But Rita would have to wait. There was a story here that kept growing and growing the longer she waited.

There was a tour out of Helsinki to Leningrad they had suggested at the American Express office on Grafton Street. It might be the quickest way to get into the Soviet Union. She would risk it and risk spending a couple of idle days in Helsinki waiting for the tour.

One of the flights after Cunningham's death had been for Copenhagen. Had the killer gone back to Russia through the northern door as well? Was he a Russian?

Nothing is what it seems.

Damn, she thought. She had been haunted by the thought of Kaiser all day, Kaiser who had killed himself during the business with the other priest. And now she had to think of Devereaux again, even though he had been buried out of her thoughts for nearly three years. Devereaux had said nothing good could happen if they had remained together; Devereaux had frozen her out at last and now she even wondered if he was still alive.

She realized she was crying. The tears warmed her cheeks and then froze in the stinging wind.

Damn, she thought. I don't want to remember him. But now the memory was dominant. Devereaux had been an Intelligence man; she never really understood everything about him, but she had known at last that she had loved him. And he had denied it. "Nothing is what it seems," he had said and he had turned away from her. "Even Intelligence agents get married, you know, or have women, live-in," she had said, half in jest and half in anger on that last day together. And he had looked at her so sadly: "What do you see, Rita? A lover? Protector? Kindness incarnate? Do you see a good life?"

She was running now in the howling wind, crossing the Crescent, fleeing the thoughts that still unreeled slowly in her mind.

"I see you, that's all."

"No. Not me. You see what you want to see," he had replied and he could not explain it anymore. He had left her alone in that place in the mountains and she had waited for him for six days and she realized he was not coming back and she had driven back to Washington and picked up threads of her life that she had been willing to sever for him.

She saw the taxi turning the corner at Baggot Street and she waved and the cab came down the lane toward her. She threw open the back door and slid inside, out of breath and out of tears. Damn, she thought again, damn the thoughts of Kaiser and the dead priest and him.

"Buswell Hotel," she said and the driver turned.

He was a middle-aged man with bright blue eyes and a fierce ginger mustache like a Guardsman. "Very well," he said and started the engine and Rita could have sworn he had an English accent.

12

HELSINKI

Devereaux sat quietly on the chair next to the window. It was snowing again and flakes clung to the glass like survivors until they melted to nothing.

The policeman sat in a straight chair next to the built-in walnut desk. He stared at Devereaux again. Periodically, during the long interrogation, the policeman had lapsed into a moody silence, as though he were contemplating thoughts that began far from this hotel room.

"A commercial traveler who has spent two months in Helsinki and has done no business."

"Times are hard," Devereaux said.

"You discover a dead man in the sauna. Everything about you is very mysterious, Mr. Dixon or Mr. Devereaux or whatever your name is."

"I hate to be a mystery."

"No telephone calls. You never make phone calls. But two days ago, you send a telegram to someone named Derr . . . derr—"

"Dougherty," Devereaux said.

The policeman named Kulak merely stared again. "Yes. You mention Arabia glassware."

"This is where they make it, isn't it?"

"This is a murder, not a joke. Why did it take you so long to make a business arrangement? And when we check with the glassware people, they will not have heard of you, do you know that? I am certain of it."

"I don't have the authorization yet to make an offer."

"Why do you not make any telephone calls? I know you are lonely. You brought a prostitute up to your room. I know all about you."

"Were you peeking?"

"Don't make jokes, Mr. Devereaux. I think I will call you that. I think that is what your name really is."

"All right."

"Two murders."

"Two?"

"Come on, Mr. Devereaux. You killed the prostitute. Natali."

"I don't know what you're talking about."

"You cut her open like a butcher. You left her body down in the construction pit across the street."

"When did I do this?"

"You know, Devereaux. And now you killed this man in a sauna. This Mr. Sims, another man I do not understand. Are you a maniac?"

"Are you a fool?"

Kulak clenched his fists and his neck seemed to swell. His hard eyes went flat and hot, like rocks in a desert sun.

"I arrange to enter the sauna, see Ulla at the desk and kill Sims. Then, without getting a drop of blood on my clothes, I come back and inform Ulla that there is a dead man in the sauna. I do this because two days before, I have killed a prostitute named Natali in exactly the same way and I know that everyone in the hotel will tell you that Natali had dated an American named Dixon who has been in the hotel for seven weeks."

Kulak slowly subsided but he still clenched his fists. "You are not what you seem," he said at last.

"Nothing is," Devereaux agreed.

"You might be mad."

"Anything is possible."

"I searched your room."

"I suppose you did."

"You have a weapon. This is not permitted in Suomi," Kulak said, pronouncing the Finnish name for his country "Why do you have a pistol?"

"Enemies."

"Enemies?"

"A businessman always has enemies. He can be robbed. You have already pointed out to me that Helsinki is a dangerous place."

"I don't take this lightly, not murder," Kulak said slowly. "I think I will have to arrest you for a while and see what you are made of. I think perhaps you can tell me more things when you have been in prison for a while."

"I think you are making a mistake," Devereaux said. "I think I want to speak to Mr. Cleaver at the American Embassy."

"Oh, you know someone at the American Embassy? How nice."

"I think you will want to call Mr. Cleaver."

"And who is he?"

"Third assistant."

"Well, what would you say if I told you I knew exactly what Mr. Cleaver really was? What would you say? Would you say that a dumb Helsinki policeman is a little smarter than I gave him credit for?"

"He's a third assistant in the embassy," Devereaux said, watching the words carefully, watching the box that Kulak was opening for him.

"He is a goddamn spy," Kulak said.

"I didn't know that."

"I think you might be a goddamn spy, too," Kulak said.

"First I'm a double murderer and now I'm an agent."

"You could be both things. I don't understand this business, not about you, not about Sims, not about poor Natali."

Devereaux did not blink, did not show emotion. She had been a prostitute who had felt warm against him in the night, who had reminded him of a time when there was no death and cold and bleakness. He could love a whore because he could not love anyone else.

"The long winter nights have addled you," Devereaux said calmly.

"I could lose you for a long time in prison," Kulak said.

"My embassy would protest."

"We have heard protests. What is a protest? We fought two wars against the Soviet Union and we won them. So don't tell me about protests, like pieces of paper."

"Are you certain you won?"

"Damn you, Mr. Devereaux. I think you are coming with me."

"I want to call the embassy."

"Maybe in a few days. Or a few weeks. Maybe when I have talked to you some more—"

"Now."

"No, not now. I don't want murders, I don't want spies thinking they can defile my city."

"Now," Devereaux said.

"No, Mr. Devereaux. Now you are the prisoner, now you are not the keeper of time. I am the keeper, Mr. Devereaux, when I found this gun in your room. Do you think your protest would mean very much when I show them this gun?"

"I don't own that gun."

"You said you did. I found it in the room."

"I said nothing," Devereaux lied evenly. "You planted that gun. You are going to cause yourself harm."

"I don't think so, no—"

And the telephone rang. The rings were short and sharp. Kulak picked up the receiver.

He listened for a long moment and his eyes narrowed and the veins in his neck began to bulge.

"Yes," he said in Finnish. "Yes." And then he spoke a string of words so quickly that Devereaux could not follow them. And then he slammed down the receiver.

Kulak stared at him again. And spoke: "This is only a game, isn't it, Mr. Devereaux."

"What do you mean?"

"No." Kulak rose. He took Devereaux's pistol out of his pocket and placed it on the desk. He seemed suddenly weary, suddenly sad. "A young woman is killed in the most vicious way. Cut open. And a man named Sims is cut the same way. Murder, Mr. Devereaux. Real deaths. Do you know that those two people were alive and now they are dead. They walked, they breathed, they talked, they laughed . . ." He paused and stared at Devereaux. "And you sit there and you know about death, don't you? I have seen your eyes. You have killed people, Mr. Devereaux, I can smell death all around you."

"What are you going to do?"

"Nothing. I can do nothing. You know that. You know that I must obey my orders."

For the first time, Devereaux was startled. He had expected everything but this. "What do you mean?"

"When I am told to leave someone alone, I obey. I am a policeman and I have a good job and I do the best that I can. And sometimes, someone will tell me: Do nothing. And so I will obey."

"I don't understand this."

"No, Mr. Devereaux. Neither do I." Kulak walked to the door and opened it and turned back to Devereaux who sat perfectly still at the window weeping with streaks of snow. "But you, Mr. Devereaux, you are playing a game and I tell you that I am not."

"But who told you?"

"It doesn't matter. It is not for me to tell you."

13

LONDON

Wickham had wandered into the house three hours before like a wounded animal. Except he had no wounds that were visible.

He had been gone nine days. Maggie had met him at the door of the estate house. She was a small woman, chiseled like a marble statue, with sharp ears and sharp eyes that reminded Wickham of a fox. She was quite beautiful in a small and distant way. The first thing he had asked her was where Rogers was.

Maggie had been too shocked to answer. Wickham smelled like a beast and his eyes looked hunted; he had lost weight in nine days and his cheeks were hollow. His hair, normally so neat that one never gave it a thought, was wild and shaggy and he had a thin coating of beard on his face.

"Rogers is gone," Maggie had managed to say as Wickham staggered into the two-story entry hall. She shrank from him as though he were a stranger.

"Of course he's gone, he'd have to be gone."

"I dismissed him," she said.

"You what?"

"The police. Your disappearance. I thought it was terrible, I couldn't stand to see—"

Wickham laughed and went into the drawing room and found the brandy on the cart and poured it into a glass. He took a strong drink.

Outside, sleet came down in driving sheets. It coated the brick walls of the estate house like silver leeches.

He seemed mad to her.

"Where have you been?"

"I don't know. I don't even know how long I've been gone—"

"Nine days."

"My God," he said to himself and poured another glass of Hennessey and drank it too quickly. Color returned to his frozen face. His clothes were sopping wet; they dripped onto the yellow Oriental carpet in the drawing room.

"Get out of those clothes, get into something warm—"

"Yes. I must call George—"

"George? Do we know a George?"

"Maggie, for God's sake, get out of here a moment and let me call—"

She had retreated facing him, had nearly stumbled at the door, and closed it. He made a telephone call but she could hear very little. Then he opened the door to the drawing room and began to tear at his clothing. "Warm," he mumbled. "Bath. Clean clothing. For George . . ."

Three hours later, a black Rover prowled up the gravel drive from the road to the front door of the Georgian estate house and two men climbed out of the rear seat. A third man stayed inside the car, behind the driver's wheel; he kept the motor rumbling for warmth but doused the headlamps.

Some normalcy had returned to the house. Wickham had bathed and changed and shaved. Maggie had prepared him eggs because it was the cook's night out.

The eggs had nourished him at least and another large brandy had made him feel not so cold. Victor had released him from his car two miles from the house. It had been a cold, wet two-mile walk down a narrow road bereft of traffic.

In the tub, Wickham had considered every option and decided he would tell George the truth this time, no matter the consequences.

He even had the photographs in his pocket. He had not shown them to Maggie.

George and the second man waited for him in the library which was across the entry hall from the drawing room. The room was filled with books on shelves that reached to the ceiling. The rug was a deep-red Oriental pattern that was cousin to the yellow rug in the drawing room. There were the requisite leather side chairs, armchairs and leather-topped desk in burnished rosewood. The fireplace was lit and crackling and throwing out small patches of color into the dark, warm room.

Wickham came into the room and smiled wanly but no smile greeted him in return. He started to speak and thought better of it. He closed the door.

"Will you have a drink?" he began.

George stared at him. He was not tall but he had large shoulders and a large head with large blue eyes and white eyebrows that curled fiercely above his eyes. His eyes seemed to glare into the soul of Wickham standing before him like a truant schoolboy caught at last. George had his hands behind his back, revealing a large belly and a bright red wool waistcoat.

"What happened to you, Bluebird?"

"I was kidnapped, of course."

"You were?"

"Of course," Wickham began. "I didn't even know how long I was held, the place had no windows—"

"And they returned you to your home and hearth?"

"Yes."

"Ransom?"

"No."

"Why do it?"

"Beg pardon?"

"Why kidnap you, Bluebird?"

"Political."

"Ah."

The second man who had come with George came around the desk to stand by the fire. He, too, held his hands behind him as though warming them at the fire. He, too, held Wickham with glaring eyes. He was taller than the man called George and he had a harder face. He was clean-shaven, his eyes were soft brown, his hair was cut unfashionably close to his head. He did not speak but the movement to the fire had interrupted the dialogue between George and Bluebird for a moment.

"Can I get you a drink?" Wickham asked a second time.

"Certainly. Scotch'll do."

"With ice?"

"No."

"And you?" Wickham said turning to the other man.

He merely shook his head.

Wickham realized his hands were shaking when he poured the drinks, a brandy for himself and scotch for George.

When he turned back to the room from the brandy cart, George was seated on the edge of his desk. He handed George the glass and turned again to find a chair.

"Sit down, Bluebird," George said, as though he were the master of the house.

Wickham sat.

He stared at both men and then sipped the brandy.

"Now why don't you begin at the beginning?" George said. And slowly, reluctantly, Wickham began to tell them the truth, from the moment Mowbrey came into his office nine days before with a signal intercepted from the American station at Stockholm.

George handed over the photographs to the man who stood at the fireplace. Three-quarters of an hour had elapsed since Wickham began his story. He had interrupted himself once to pour himself another brandy. George had not moved or spoken, except to prod the other man with a sharp question to aid the narrative. The man at the fire had merely watched Wickham throughout without speaking.

"Well, Bluebird, that's a pretty story," George said, his voice like coal poured into a scuttle from a metal chute. "Pretty."

"It's absolutely true," Wickham said.

"And your wife dismissed the chauffeur."

"He would have been gone in any case. If they were going to release me."

"The *Sun* has these photographs?"

"That's what Victor told me."

"His name was Victor?"

"Not actually." Wickham blushed. "I gave them names. There were two of them."

"Yes. Well, we can show you some photos, of course, and see if you can pick them out."

"Anything I can do."

"We questioned Rogers, naturally, after the police talked to him."

"You must have known he was lying."

George grunted. "It crossed our minds. We're not completely daft, you know. We also questioned people in Special Section, Bluebird. Including Mowbrey. I'm glad you've decided to tell the truth for a change about who intercepted the American signal from Stockholm. About this Tomas Crohan."

"It was a misunderstanding, George. I had access to you, I thought it was important, I was intending to mention—"

"No more lies, Wickham," George said at last, using his real name for the first time. He stood up. "You've put us in a pretty mess, my boy. Neatly done on their part." George nearly smiled but thought better of it.

"What can I do?"

George looked at him as though it was the last question that would have crossed his mind. "Do? Do? What do you mean?"

"What can I do?"

"There's nothing to do. Not for you, in any case."

Wickham only stared at him until George, realizing he had not made himself clear, turned to face him full, his back to the man at the fireplace.

"You've been through a bad shock, but a lot of it was of your own making. You hired Rogers without getting positive vetting through Auntie and clearance."

"He was only a chauffeur—"

"No, Wickham, I believe you can see he was more than that."

Wickham dropped the glass of brandy on the red carpet. It did not make a sound. He was so entranced by George he was not even aware the glass had slipped from his hand. The brandy spilled from the glass and stained the red carpet in an irregular, circular pattern. Wickham sat very still.

"Now these nasty photographs have been sent to the *Sun*. No doubt we shall get a call from one of Murdoch's people in a little while suggesting that the *Sun* is too much of a patriotic paper to publish such unless, of course, it happens to be true. . . ."

"But it isn't true. My God, it would kill Maggie if—"

"My dear Wickham, don't be an ass. Will the *Sun* publish the photographs? Not at all. They're obscene, old fellow. But we will have to slap them with a D Notice on the whole matter and that is tedious. It tends to give the press the feeling that we're trying to hide something when, in fact, we're trying to save your skin."

"I'm grateful, believe me, George—"

George rumbled, "You lied to me, Wickham. Bluebird is dead. You have no more status. I should remind you of the Official Secrets Act you signed when you joined the Service . . . in the event you decide to publish your memoirs in your retirement."

"Retirement?"

"Of course. What do you suppose I was talking about?"

"But I've done nothing—"

"You're a leak, Wickham, you're dangerous to us. You have to be rendered harmless, inoperative. You lied to me about Mowbrey's finding of the American signal. You were picked up by the Opposition and they worked a crude frame against you. They knew it was crude; they told you so. The problem is, you present too much of a security risk to us. They know that. They know the Americans are terribly interested in our inability to keep our own security in the service without every second man turning out to be a poof or a bloody traitor. My God, we can't even keep Buckingham Palace secure, let alone the Queen." George made a face. "You could do us harm, Wickham, and so we are defusing you. Over the next few days, we expect your cooperation. Photographs to look at and we would appreciate a full report. We've done a background check on you, and you won't do badly in retirement. There's your government pension plus a one-time payout plus your wife's inheritance and your own money from the estate of your father. You'll be as comfortable as you are now."

Wickham was merely stunned. He could not speak.

The second man with brown hair and brown eyes and a face without expression continued to stare at him over George's shoulder.

"Of course you will receive recommendations should you seek further employment outside the Service. Just one note of caution, besides reminding you that you have signed the act; check with us before you get into another line of work, will you? In case it is one of our sensitive areas and we don't want you muddling up."

"Please, George—"

"All right, I think that's it. We're off, Wickham. You may tell your wife as much of this as you wish but she is also under the act, you realize. It will be in your best interest to say as little as possible. Don't return to Cheltenham; your goods have been boxed and will be returned to you in a few days. Your office is sealed and your pass is invalid."

"George, for God's sake, George, after what I've been through—"

"Yes, old man," George said with irony. "After what you've been through, there's still more for us. You and your damned messages to George; you were sucking up and now you've mucked up everything." George stared at him coldly, his gravel voice hissing like hot coals. "Consider yourself lucky, Wickham. It could have been much worse for you. Much, much worse." The second man returned the photographs to George and George looked at them again.

"Of course, we'll keep these. I'm sure you have no need of them."

And the two men left the house withoug another word to either Wickham or his wife. The car was waiting and they entered it. It had stopped sleeting and the night had turned clear and cold; the road to London was covered with icy patches.

Even at this late hour, the planes boomed in and out of Heathrow. The ceiling and visibility were lower than would have been acceptable at an American airport but Heathrow was the vital lifeline between Britain and the rest of the world; it rarely closed, and then only briefly. Heathrow had to be kept open.

The black Rover sat purring in the parking lot nearest the international terminal.

In the back seat, George was speaking to the second man with brown hair and brown eyes and expressionless face.

"The delicacy is compounded because the Russians obviously know that we're onto this business."

"Your lines were tapped," the second man said.

"So it appears, Sparrow." The code name of all agents in the electronics branch of Auntie were names of birds, just as the code names of all agents in the regular branch of Auntie were names of English cities and towns. Only the men called "George" and "Q" were outside the strict security nomenclature.

"Actually, we haven't found the tap."

Sparrow brooded for a moment. "You should have."

"Certainly," George said impatiently.

"Maybe the leak was inside Special Section at Cheltenham."

"That's a possibility too, and that's why we had to get rid of Bluebird. Blundering fool."

"I believe his story."

George looked surprised. "Of course. So do I. But that's not the point, is it?"

"What is the point?"

"There is an agent now in Dublin called Ely. Q sent him out a week ago. Seems the name Crohan has come up there. And now there is an American agent posing as a journalist snooping about the same thing. Her name is Rita Macklin, and, ostensibly, she's a reporter for an American magazine. Obviously, she's with CIA. I can't tell you everything but I can tell you enough. We want the Crohan matter silenced. Maximum silence."

Sparrow stared at the older man with his large, round head and blue eyes and darting white eyebrows.

Maximum silence. The ultimate command within Auntie. Maximum silence was more than a license to kill for the sake of a mission; it was an order to utterly destroy, to utterly wrap up in silence an operation launched either from within the Service or from someone without.

"Max the American woman?"

"That's part of it. That's just part of it. There are too many problems in this and it worries me. Ely is trying to make a liaison with her, get what she knows. The stationmaster in Dublin tumbled to this Tomas Crohan business about three months ago. Another fool," George rasped. "He thinks it has to do with some Soviet submarines he's seen off the western Irish coast."

"You're beginning to lose me," Sparrow said quietly.

George glared at him. "Damn it, I don't understand half of it myself, but I can tell you that someone, somewhere, is starting to build a neat little frame for us. For Auntie. And this is not the time for it."

"What does it have to do with Tomas Crohan? Who the devil is he?"

George was silent for a moment. "He was an Irish national the Americans ran in Austria as their agent in 1944 and 1945. Supposedly, he is still alive inside the Soviet Gulag. And now there are these hints that he is coming out."

"From Dublin?"

"From Helsinki. Three days ago, one of Q's boys was using the name Sims to probe an American agent there. The American was using the name Dixon, staying at the Presidentii. He was making contact with the Opposition and he sent a hurry-up message through the American station in Stockholm that related to bringing out a man named Tomas Crohan. That was the message that Mowbrey accidentally intercepted at Cheltenham and that the damned fool Wickham told me about on the safe line after Seeker turned him down for information."

"What does Sims say?"

"Sims does not speak anymore. He was murdered in a sauna three days ago. For some reason, the Finns have decided not to press the investigation. They were onto the American agent but pulled back."

"That smells, doesn't it?"

"Stinks like a Liverpool whore, Sparrow. Everything about this stinks of trap, of frame, of setup. But what is the trap? And who is it for? And who is setting it?"

"The American in Helsinki?"

"Very tidy. The Dublin stationmaster has been following this female agent from the States named Macklin. She went into American Express on Grafton Street last week and inquired about trips into Leningrad. From Helsinki, of all places."

Sparrow made a face. "I don't like it, George. It gets very curious."

"Curiouser and curiouser," said George. "Seems pretty blatant, doesn't it? As though she's inviting us to follow her along."

"And what about Ely?"

"He's a fool, should have been sacked after he cracked up in Vienna two years ago. He had some pull inside Q's Section, got a file clerk's job. Q put him on the business to keep him out of the way, to draw flies to the honey as it were. We wanted to know what the American game was and we thought someone like Ely was just the man for the job. No one expected the American agent to be bait as well. Two of them out there, each setting a trap that the other is likely to fall into. It has gotten too convoluted, too involved. Q went to the minister last night; we have authorization for maximum silence. That's you, Sparrow."

"Ely?" Sparrow's voice was soft.

George sighed. "He's in the way, isn't he? If you can think of a way to keep him out of it, by all means. But if he becomes part of the accident, then it will have to be."

Sparrow narrowed his eyes, hooding them like a bird of prey working in a sunlit field. "The American girl?"

"Absolutely."

"The one in Helsinki?"

"Yes. That should be an easier busines in any case. They'll figure the Russians double-crossed them—"

"I can take them both out in Helsinki. I don't know about Ely."

"If Ely doesn't follow—"

"Can't you people pull him back?"

"No. He's part of our bait offering to the Americans."

"But what is the trap, George?"

"Tomas Crohan."

"But how can the Americans be using him if he's bloody prisoner in the Soviet Union?"

"That's part of their trap," George said simply.

Sparrow felt disoriented. "But what is he but a bloody Mick and an American agent to boot? Why are we involved?"

For the first time since the interview at Wickham's country house, George glared again, fixing Sparrow with blue eyes that burned in the dim light of the parking lot at Heathrow. Planes boomed overhead into the dense fog of the night sky.

"That is the last question, Sparrow, the one that I cannot answer," George said.

"Cannot? Or will not?"

George blinked. "Either reply would be too much of an

answer. There's a plane at five to Dublin, in case you can take care of the matter there. I don't think the Irish authorities will interfere."

Sparrow realized the answer in George's refusal to speak. The answer was "Will not."

Sparrow felt uncomfortable and did not move for a moment. The car was warm but the wind was rising and it was a cold walk to the terminal from the car. Maximum silence. Well, it didn't matter about the Americans but he felt a kinship with Ely. Just another poor beggar in the field. Maybe he could shove Ely out of the way before it was too late.

As an act of mercy in the bloody business to come.

14

DUBLIN

When the driver made the first wrong turn, Rita Macklin had spoken sharply to him in the voice of a woman who has corrected cab drivers in big cities before. The man with the ginger mustache had merely smiled at her and that had annoyed her all the more. When he made the second wrong turn and actually headed south toward the Ring Road and away from the city center, she spoke again, but with a note of fear in her voice this time.

This time, he produced a small pistol and pointed it at her and then turned it away from her and apologized for it.

"Who are you?"

"You are Rita Macklin, a journalist from the United States."

"What do you want?"

"I want to know what you've found out from Father Cunningham."

"But he's dead—"

"Not silent, however. Otherwise, you would scarcely have spent all this time going through his things. And why do you want to go to Helsinki?"

"Who are you?"

"Well, we can talk about all this in a little bit," Ely said in a gentle voice tinged with sadness. He wore a driver's cap.

Rita Macklin reached for the door handle and gave it a pull.

"I'm afraid those won't work from the inside," Ely said. "Please sit still. We're almost there."

"What are you going to do?"

"Get information, Miss Macklin."

"I don't have any information—"

"You want to go to Leningrad. Why? To see Tomas Crohan?"

Now she could not speak. She rattled the door again.

"What I want to know is what the American game is, actually. You're a journalist? Is it usual for a journalist to lie to acquire information from a dead man's effects?"

"You do what you have to."

"Is that correct? We have very good information, Miss Macklin, to indicate that you are an operative from Central Intelligence Agency. What we wish to know is what it is that you intend to do with Tomas Crohan."

The cab stopped in front of a three-story building in a broken-down section of the city. Some of the windows were boarded up. No one was on the dark street; the lamps had been vandalized and they were enveloped in nearly total darkness.

Ely turned on his flashlight and splashed the light on the stairs of the old building. He opened the rear door and grasped Rita's arm firmly. She struck him across the face, and he was so startled that he dropped the flashlight. Rita began to run down the street.

"My God, what a wallop," Ely said softly and felt blood on his lips. He tasted the salty liquid for a moment, wiped again, and then closed the door of the car carefully. He picked up the flashlight and went to the driver's door and got in. He started the car and flicked on the headlights. He could see Rita running half a block ahead.

He sped up suddenly and pulled the car ahead of her, and then jumped out and crossed the sidewalk.

Rita screamed the only word she could think of: "Rape! Rape!"

A light flashed on in a house down the street and a woman's head peered through a yellow-lit pane of glass.

Ely had the pistol in one hand and the flashlight in the other.

"Miss Macklin, I don't want to do you harm."

"You wouldn't shoot me."

"Of course I would." The voice was utterly calm.

She came close to him and saw the lazy calm in his eyes. She had known one man like that, a man with calm eyes and a quiet voice who could utterly convince her of the violence he was capable of.

She opened the rear door.

"What the hell is going on?" cried a voice from some window in some building somewhere. All the rest was silence in the bitter cold.

He led her up the stairs of the dark abandoned building. There was a flat on the second floor with a table, chairs and a small lamp. He turned on the lamp—it was an oil lamp because the electricity had long been shut off in these houses—and they sat down. The lamp was warm, the only warmth in the place. A large gray rat watched them without curiosity from a ledge that ran along the wall between the boarded windows. Roaches covered the walls in the light of the flickering lamp.

Rita Macklin saw these things but turned her eyes away from them. She forced herself to stare directly into the blue eyes of the man who had kidnapped her.

"Well, Miss Macklin, I apologize for the surroundings but I'm a stranger to this city myself."

"Who are you?"

"That's not important. Let us say I am Ely."

"It sounds made up."

He blinked and stared sadly at her. He spoke with a gentle, calm voice. "I suppose it is in a way. You are with the Central Intelligence Agency and I—"

"I am not a goddamn spook for the CIA," she said harshly.

Ely smiled. "You say. With, I note, some vehemence. Perhaps we were misinformed."

"Why is British Intelligence interested in this?"

Ely looked suprised. "Who spoke of British Intelligence?"

"Who are you then? You don't look Irish."

"And you don't look like an agent for the Americans. But appearances are deceiving at times. We snapped your photograph the first day you arrived—in time for the funeral of the priest."

"You work for Auntie," Rita Macklin said.

"So you do know the little secrets," Ely said with a smile. "Now, the sooner we get this over with, the sooner we can get out of this wretched slum and back to our rooms. I'm quite willing to drop you at your hotel."

"I thought that was your intention from the beginning."

"First, the fare, Miss Macklin."

"Or what?"

Ely stared at Rita for a moment and then smiled sadly.

He still held the pistol in his hand. He looked at it for a moment.

"You're a British agent. Are you going to shoot me?" Rita said defiantly but with a nervous rapidity.

"Would that be absurd?" Ely asked.

"I'm an American."

"Yes. An American agent. And you have some information that I wish to have. So what am I asked to do? Merely to get it, Miss Macklin. Without regard for you."

"So you're threatening me again?"

The smile was gone. Ely's voice was cold. "If you can't help me, I'm afraid I'll turn you in."

"To whom?"

"The Irish authorities. You're a wanted woman, Miss Macklin."

"I've never been in Ireland in my life."

"You're wanted for questioning in connection with a murder that involved a terrorist attack in a Liverpool public house two weeks ago."

She stared at him as though he had suddenly gone mad.

Ely went on, calmly. "You are the suspected liaison between the IRA, which was responsible for the bombing in Liverpool, and the Northern Aid Society front in Washington."

"This is so stupid," she said. "You won't be able to get away with that, I—"

"You'll be held incommunicado in Dublin and transferred to our facilities in Liverpool where you shall be questioned." He stared sadly at her. "Strenous questioning, I should imagine. I won't have anything to do with that."

"You can't do this to me," Rita said. "Goddamnit, I am a newspaperman."

"Yes. A journalist. So you say. I can assure you that you will tell the people in Liverpool everything they want to know. Which would make it so much better for both of us if you would tell me now."

"We're not in Russia—"

"And not in the United States," Ely said. He slipped his pistol in his coat pocket.

Rita did not hesitate. She turned suddenly and ran to the door.

Surprisingly, Ely moved with equal agility. She was a step ahead of him but the door was stuck. He grabbed her thin shoulder and pulled her around. He did not expect her to be swinging as she turned.

The blow caught him on the temple and momentarily staggered him. A second blow fell on his right cheekbone.

Rita turned again to the door but this time he hit her very hard on the side of the head.

The blow made her feel sick for a moment. Again, he turned her toward him. This time he slapped her across her face. And again. And a third time.

"I'll kill you," she said, her face stinging with pain and tears.

"No, you will not, Miss Macklin," Ely said. "You will sit down and you will tell me exactly what I wish to know."

"Then you don't have a fallback position." she said. She smiled. "You either get the information from me or you let me go."

"No, Miss Macklin, not at all," Ely said. "I get what I need to know or I do not let you go. I cannot afford failure."

"My God, you can't—"

"Miss Macklin, I have grown gray in the service and I have no wish to be prematurely retired now because I have failed a rather straight-forward operation to obtain rather unimportant information—"

"So unimportant that you kidnap me and now you threaten to kill me."

Ely stared at her, at the involuntary tears in her green eyes, at her flushed face that bore marks of his hands. He was completely calm, completely without expression.

"All this because of someone who might be dead," she said.

"Our permanent stationmaster at Dublin was a friend of the old priest," Ely began.

"I know that. Parker."

Ely was surprised. "How did you know?"

"More important, how did Father Cunningham know," Rita Macklin said. "He knew Parker was a British agent. The priest wasn't a fool."

"It sounds as though Parker was," Ely said.

"Did you—did your people kill Father Cunningham?"

"Of course not. Why would we want to do that?"

"I don't know, I don't know anything about this—"

"His . . . demise surprised our people," Ely said.

"You know I'm not a spy, that I'm not a terrorist—"

"I know nothing, Miss Macklin. You protest your innocence, which can mean that you are all the more guilty. I don't know."

"Damn you," she said at last. "You hurt me."

Ely said nothing for a moment. Then: "Why do you want to go to Leningrad, Miss Macklin." Softly, insistently.

"Because I think Tomas Crohan is alive. And that he's in Kresty Prison there."

"How brave of you. Will you break him out of prison?"

"I don't know what I'm going to do. I have to go there first."

"Why is Tomas Crohan alive?"

"I just think he is. Instinct."

"No, Miss Macklin. Instinct will take you across the street, not halfway around the world. Let us get down to the matter now, Miss Macklin, so I can let you go home."

For a moment, Rita did not speak. She felt defeated and terrified at the same time. Ely was gentle, almost innocuous. And yet there was some truth in his voice when he said he would not permit himself to fail at this little mission. Even at the expense of her life.

"How do I know you will let me go?"

"Because I would have no reason to hurt you."

"You have no reason now."

"Tell me about the old priest," Ely said softly.

She hesitated.

"And Tomas Crohan," Ely said. "Tell me about him as well."

15

LENINGRAD

They had given him a suit of clothes and he had been examined once again by the doctors. He had shaved closely and he had placed the razor in the little leather packet they provided for him. The last part had involved the private interview with the man called Tartakoff.

He had stood during the interview.

At the beginning, Tartakoff had watched the prisoner in silence with an edge of amusement on his lips. His eyes sparkled in the harsh light. Tomas Crohan felt tired, as though his seventy-one years had become a weight at two in the morning that dragged at him and made him shrink before the gaze of Tartakoff.

"Do you know why you have been given a suit of clothing?"

"No, Commander."

"You are being transferred to the work force at Gorki. I have discovered that you have an ability with languages."

"Yes. I am not as good as I was, Commander."

"Your Russian is very good. Can you speak English?"

"It is my native tongue, sir. But I do not speak it often," Tomas said in English.

"Good. Continue in English for a moment," the Russian said."

"Yes, sir."

"Have you been badly treated here at Kresty?"

"No, sir. I shall be sorry to leave here, sir."

"Yes. Perhaps you shall be sorry," Tartakoff said and again he smiled.

"What shall I do at Gorki?"

"I'm not certain. But it might involve work with languages. We have many prisoners at Gorki, many nationalities."

"The Americans—"

Tartakoff looked sharply at him; his face, genial a moment before, was transformed to ice. "What about the Americans?"

"I'm sorry, sir. There was talk. In the wards. That the Americans were kept in the camp at Gorki."

"Talk is dangerous at times," Tartakoff said. Magically, the mellowness returned to his features as his scowl faded. "In one hour, you will be taken from here and you are to obey all instructions, do you understand?"

"Yes, Commander."

"And you are to speak Russian only."

"Yes, Commander."

"You speak with a Polish accent. I thought that was useful."

"I learned very early from the Poles in my first camp."

"Did you? Well, it is useful. Remember. Only Russian. And one other matter."

He stood still.

"You are Ivan Tiomkin."

Tomas Crohan blinked. He remembered the mad commandant in Siberia. He remembered the men freezing to death because they worked naked in the snow. He stared at Tartakoff but he did not see madness in his eyes. "Yes, Commander." In any case, he must obey the lawful orders of the State. It was a matter of survival; one did not resist the law and one was not punished. It was quite simple.

"Now you will wait in this room." Tartakoff rose. He smiled again and patted Tomas Crohan on one bony shoulder like a child petting a broken bird. "You will wait, Ivan Tiomkin. And then you shall go."

16

WASHINGTON, D.C.

Mrs. Neumann, wearing her customary sweater because she knew Hanley's office would be at sixty degrees Fahrenheit, walked through the open doorway and threw a manila file on his desk. He glanced up at her with an expression of annoyance. It was just after one in the afternoon and it was snowing and Hanley had been forced to work through his lunch hour again.

"There it is," Mrs. Neumann said in her raspy whisper. She towered over the government-issue gray metal desk with something like superiority. This annoyed Hanley further.

"There what is?"

"After the last signal from November. In Helsinki. You remember?"

"Yes. I told him to come out as soon as he could. We don't need problems with the authorities in Finland just now."

"I told you I could get it."

"Get what?"

"The Crohan file."

"How did you accomplish that?"

"I went over and got it," Mrs. Neumann said and she laughed a sudden, short burst like a rusty machine gun cranking up.

Hanley put down his pen very calmly and looked up at the large, handsome woman. He knew that she was prompting questions from him and he had no desire to act as her straight man, but the matter was too fascinating. He did not touch the manila file.

"No wonder they didn't want to let it out," Mrs. Neumann said. "Even to us."

"How did you get this and why is it relevant anymore? The matter of our defector is closed. Devereaux is due out tonight."

"Because I was stubborn. Becuase I was damned if I would let them tell me what files I can see and what files I can't see. We're in the same government—"

"We all have secrets, Mrs. Neumann," Hanley said gently.

"Not secrets because they just say they're secrets. That's not good enough," she said. She decided to sit down on the only straight-back chair provided for guests of the operations director of R Section.

"Besides," she continued. "They only had the case file on this Crohan because they had inherited the paper files of OSS when the outfit was disbanded and the Central Intelligence Agency was set up. They weren't even CIA files."

"And so why did the CIA want to keep them secret?"

"Damned embarrassing stuff."

"For Langley?"

"For all of us for a change, Hanley. For the whole country."

"And you walked over to Langley and got them?"

"To an extent. I told you I would get them. So I made a computer request."

"And they gave them to you," Hanley said with sarcasm.

"Something like that, although it was more complicated. I could tell you all the details, but if you only want the main points—"

"Just the main points, Mrs. Neumann, I'm not very well acquainted with computers—"

"Yes, I know. It involves setting up a Q into the National Security Council and then flashing the Q back to Langley, this time with an NSA identification out of the Council."

"I don't follow that at all."

"I stole the information. They've probably found the leak by now. It can only work for a couple of hours but it was enough. They know it was us, too, Hanley, so you can expect some flack. But I told you I could get them."

Hanley blanched. "My God, Mrs. Neumann, are you crazy?"

"No guts, Hanley?" She was smiling in triumph.

"What will the Central Intelligence director tell the New Man?" Hanley asked, referring to the current head of R Section.

"Not a damned thing, if you ask me. Is CIA going to admit they were stupid enough in security to have the file ripped off right under their noses?"

"But how did you know what to ask for? I mean, in computer language?"

"I didn't. I asked plainspeak," Mrs. Neumann replied, falling into jargon. "And that's the way they gave it to me."

"But it was flagged—"

"Not for the National Security Adviser," Mrs. Neumann said.

"My God, you can't do that."

"Can't?" she rasped. "I just did it, didn't I?"

"But the operation is over—"

"Look at it, Hanley. Knowledge is power."

"You tempt like the serpent, Mrs. Neumann."

She smiled.

He opened the file and began to read it slowly while Mrs. Neumann sat across from him and waited for him.

He read slowly for a long time. It was a strange thing about secrets, he realized; most of them were not important enough to be secrets at all.

And then there were secrets like the case file of an Irish national named Tomas Crohan who had been seduced into a little job for the OSS at the very lowest sort of level and who had been fortunately scooped up by the Red Army marching into Vienna in 1945.

Hanley felt confirmed as he read on. He had told Devereaux nothing. He had temporized; he had kept Devereaux on ice, even after the Soviet named Tartakoff had tempted the agency by offering to bring out Crohan. It didn't matter what his original motive was, to keep Devereaux away, to force Devereaux to see that there was nothing more to be done in the Section. He had done the right thing, even if it was for the wrong reasons.

Crohan must never come out, if he was alive at all.

And Devereaux. Hanley had been right after all to do nothing and finally bring Devereaux back home. The bureaucrat inside him was satisfied with himself.

"Great stuff, isn't it?" Mrs. Neumann said with the interest of a connoisseur.

"You handled this yourself, didn't you?"

"Of course."

"So no one else has seen it?"

"Do you take me for a complete idiot, Hanley?"

"No one must see it."

"I'll shred it in the corridor. I wanted you to read the whole business."

"I find it scarcely credible," Hanley said at last, closing the file.

Mrs. Neumann frowned. "Yes. Who would believe that we knew the Nazis were going to bomb Coventry in the war and did nothing about it for fear that we would be tipping the Germans that we had solved their Enigma code? A lot of people died for the sake of that secret."

"And this one?"

"No one yet, have they?"

"Unless that British agent in Helsinki was murdered because of it."

"Do you think that's what happened?"

"I don't know. I just don't know. In any case, Devereaux should be getting on a plane in the morning. I'm pulling him out."

"And Tartakoff?"

"There was no work at the end. But I'm afraid we will have to leave him dangling."

"Along with Crohan."

Hanley frowned. "If he was still alive at all."

17

HELSINKI

The telephone rang in Devereaux's room. He turned from the packed suitcase and went to the telephone on the built-in desk. He picked up the receiver and waited.

"Mr. Glass," said the voice at the other end of the line.

"No. I'm afraid my name is Dixon."

"I beg your pardon," said the voice. The line was disconnected.

Devereaux replaced the receiver and stared at the black telephone for a moment. Glass. And the previous wrong number two weeks before had been for "Mr. Fellows." It had begun with *A* and was following the Western Alphabet to *Z*. Except there should have been no more contacts from Tartakoff before he departed in the morning for the airport.

Hanley had been plain: "Come home."

"Nothing is resolved."

"Come home. Leave it. Let someone else sweep up the mess."

"Tartakoff?"

"No."

"Crohan?"

"It's not our matter."

"Why did someone kill the British agent?"

"I don't know; I don't care. Come out."

He had felt liberated and a little guilty, like a child sent home from school before the class day was ended. Something had not been finished and yet he was being allowed to escape the trap, escape the city.

And now the call. Mr. Glass.

But there was no way to reach Hanley from here. Not with the police monitoring every call. Including the one from the liaison with Tartakoff.

Devereaux went to the window streaked with reminders of yesterday's snow. The snow had been cleared again. Beneath the window was the construction pit where the police had found the body of Natali.

Two dead and no one understood why. Not Kulak the policeman, not Devereaux.

He touched the glass. It was warm.

Death and death. The policeman had been frustrated. Who had pulled him away from the matter?

Who was Tomas Crohan? And why had Hanley suddenly pulled him back after nearly nine weeks of silence?

This was never meant to be anything. Like the assignment in Jamaica. Devereaux was on ice. Devereaux was locked away in a forgotten closet somewhere because he had embarrassed the administration, because R Section could not afford the truth. And now Tartakoff was making a signal and that meant he was ready to move, perhaps he was already in Helsinki. With a prisoner named Tomas Crohan who had been lost thirty-eight years.

"Damn," Devereaux said.

The choice seemed too strong for him. The tickets for the Finnair plane to New York were on the desk.

And he would go back to the place in Virginia, in the Blue Ridge Mountains, and he would wait for a posting to Asia which would never be approved. Nothing needed to be done; no risk had to be run; time would pass, year into year, and he would still be adrift in the West as he had been.

He suddenly felt kinship with the unseen, unknown prisoner named Crohan. Nothing had been done for him and time had passed and the prisoner had survived only to have this last hope extinguished like church candles put out by altar boys.

Devereaux stared at the construction pit. Why should Natali have been killed in the same way that Sims was killed?

Kulak was right.

It was murder; it was not a game. They had been alive and now they were dead.

Devereaux turned from the window and went to his packed bag and picked it up and put it on the shelf of his wardrobe cabinet. He went to the desk and put the tickets for Finnair in his pocket. He left the room. Now, when he moved about, he carried the ugly .357 Colt Python in his waistclip. There was no need for pretense anymore.

He had not wanted a decision any more than Hanley had. But the lack of action had forced him as much as the telephone call from the liaison. If he did not act, if he went home without finishing this business, then he would have made a choice and taken an action as surely as anything he now planned to do.

He walked down to the lobby instead of taking the elevator. He crossed to the reception desk and spoke to the clerk.

"I will stay a few more days," he said.

"We thought you were leaving in—"

"Yes. I have new business," Devereaux said.

"That will be all right," the woman said. She was calm and methodical. She marked down a note and put it on the register."Thank you, Mr. Dixon. Is everything going all right?"

"Fine," he said.

He turned and crossed the lobby. He would do what had to be done in any case and to hell with Hanley.

He pushed the elevator button and it opened and he did not see the other passenger enter. He had been too lost in his own thoughts.

The doors closed.

The other passenger turned and looked up and spoke: "You." Her voice was low, amazed, soft.

He saw her then and did not believe he saw her. He said nothing. He felt weakened, as though from a blow. He could not move.

"My God," she said.

He did not speak.

And then she crossed the elevator to him and stood in front of him, next to him. He could smell her breath as he had smelled her breath in Florida on that morning they had met and made love. Her breath smelled sweet, without corruption; her breath smelled like a child's milky breath. She stared at him for a long moment and he felt terrified of her, of her touch.

She touched his cheek.

She did not kiss him but only touched his cheek.

And voice was finally wrenched from him: "Rita," he said.

Whom he had never expected to see again.

18

AMSTERDAM

"Everything has been done badly."

"I did my business. I don't need to hear your—"

"Yes, Antonio. You will listen this time. Without cocaine. Without your girlfriends. You killed a woman in Helsinki."

"That was a private matter."

"You were under contract."

"She had to be killed."

The Bulgarian named Penev turned. They were standing in the rain in the town-hall square. Around them were great red buildings painted gray by the rain. Even the hippies who inhabited the square had fled to the porticoes and to the underground bars in the cellars along the side streets and in Kalvertstrasse.

"There is no private matter when you have a contract from us."

"I don't take orders from you."

"No," said the fat man. He made a face and his eyes glistened in the rainlight. "That is obvious."

"You had a job in Dublin."

"I don't know that we can trust you for it."

"I had to kill the whore."

"Why?"

"She had been sleeping with an American. A businessman. I nearly mistook him for my hit. She said he was English. Then I was bothered because this Sims was talking to the businessman. Hell, he was an American. A businessman. I was afraid she would remember something when the police came. Besides, I had hurt her a little. Not too much. The Amsterdam whore never complained."

"Why do your hurt women?"

"Because I want to. It's no business of yours."

"You become too dangerous."

"What do you want? A boy scout?"

"Why did you kill her?"

"I didn't want her to say anything to the police. In case they questioned her about Sims and about the man she thought was an Englishman."

"What was his name?"

"Dixon. Or Nixon. Something like that. It wasn't important."

"Was this the man?"

The Bulgarian held a photograph in his hand and the rain fell on it and streaked it. Antonio looked, his hair matted wet by rain. "Yes. Who is he?"

"That is not important."

"So he wasn't a businessman."

"In a way. You don't want to know too much. My people are not happy. You caused them trouble."

"I don't see why."

"But I do. That's enough."

"What about Dublin? Why can't we get out of the rain?"

"Because I choose to meet here. Do you understand that?"

"Don't threaten me."

"I don't have to. If I lifted a finger, if I farted, you would be blown to dust."

"Sure. I'm terrified. See how I'm shaking."

"Don't go too far, Antonio."

"I'm going back to Paris. You people are playing games."

"Not until you complete the contract."

Antonio was silent. He walked a perimeter around the stolid figure of the Bulgarian. "What do you want now?" He sounded tired but it was not from the killing. The killing had energized him. It was the endless talk from the Bulgarian, the vague threats. It tired him.

"One last figure and then we give you a rest."

Antonio smiled. His dark face did not show mirth. "I have other contractors."

"A man in Dublin. I told you. But the job you did in Helsinki was too complicated."

"I understand your position," Antonio said.

"Do you?"

"Who is the man?"

"Not important. But a professional."

"How do you want it done?"

"This is important. It must be IRA."

"Blow him up?"

"No. But make it IRA. Here is something."

He handed him a card. On it was printed: DEATH FOR THE ENGLISH BASTARDS.

"This is childish. The IRA don't give out cards when they kill someone."

"You call the *Irish Times* after it is done. And you say this."

"I don't speak like the Irish."

"It doesn't matter. Newspapers are newspapers. The death will be real enough."

"And I go home after this?"

"You go to Helsinki, Antonio. One last bit of business after this."

"Always one last bit of business with you people." The man called Antonio shrugged. "It doesn't matter to me. It was damned cold in Helsinki."

The Bulgarian said, "Not too much longer. Did you notice the days are longer?"

Antonio managed another smile that lit his face darkly. "You're an optimist. Days are never longer. It's always the same time. You sound like my father. Long days. Days are days, only the light times can vary. I was in Narvik once, on a job, the sun was up twenty-four hours a day. In June. But it was still the same day."

"I don't understand you."

Antonio shrugged again. "It doesn't matter."

"Don't use the knife. They use a gun."

"That's all right too. I cut him open."

"The man? The woman? In Helsinki."

"The woman. I had a roll of plastic. She bled and bled. I flushed some of her in the toilet. What a mess."

"You didn't have to kill her. It made it a mess."

"She was a mess, I can tell you."

"The business, Antonio." The Bulgarian pulled up his collar. "Stick to the business."

19

HELSINKI

Rita Macklin, her face white and her hands trembling, had gone with Devereaux to his room. She had sat on the chair by the built-in desk where the policeman named Kulak had interrogated him.

For a long time, they did not speak.

"I never thought I would see you again," she said at last, almost sadly, as though it would have been better to have a memory of it than to see him now.

"No," Devereaux said. He went to the window and looked down at the construction pit.

It was nearly three in the afternoon. He should be waiting across from the Alko store for the signal. He felt the press of time after feeling timeless for all those weeks in Helsinki. He was free now but he felt more a prisoner than he had felt during those weeks. He felt her presence in the room.

"Why are you here?"

"I can't tell you."

"The game," she said.

He turned.

"The game," she repeated. "It was always a game."

"Not with you," he said, gently. His voice was flat, uncolored like spring water, still, but it yearned to speak more plainly to her. He could not.

"I had forgotten you."

I had never forgotten you, he thought.

Three years before. She had been a reporter for a second-rate news service working for a man named Kaiser. There had been a priest named Tunney who had come out of Asia after twenty years. He had used her to find Tunney's secret and, in the end, he had saved her life. A simple matter except that when he had used her, he had fallen in love with her. He could not remember having loved anyone in the cold, shallow life he had lived for the past two decades. Yet he had loved her and in the end, he had left her because it could not have been a good thing between them.

He had told himself that.

It didn't matter after a time. After a little while, she only came to him in dreams or nightmares.

"Why are you here, Rita?"

"Vacation."

He turned from the window and smiled. "It's a nice time of year."

"It reminds me of Wisconsin. You remember I came from Wisconsin."

He didn't speak.

"And you. You're here for the game," she said. Her voice was a little too brittle; it betrayed her feeling beneath the cold words.

"You show me yours and I'll show you mine," Devereaux said.

"Sure. That's fair. Will you be fair?"

He waited.

"Fourteen hours ago, in Dublin, I was picked up by a British agent."

"Do you have the right country? I thought Dublin agents were Irish."

"He was British, all right. And he wanted to know about someone named Tomas Crohan."

She watched him for the effect. Her green eyes narrowed shrewdly in the dim light of the afternoon hotel room. The bed still was not made and it bore traces, in the thrown-back sheets, of a restless night.

He did not move a muscle. He waited with seeming patience.

"So I told him what I knew. It was either that or get thrown in the clink. Or maybe something worse, though I don't think they would have killed me over this. Is that why you're here?"

"Why are you here?"

"I'm going into Russia as soon as I get a visa through Finnair tours. I think this guy Crohan is a prisoner in Leningrad."

Again, a cold ghost of a smile crossed Devereaux's face and the gray eyes flashed like winter ice in an Arctic ocean pack.

"Be sure to arrive on visiting day," he said.

"Why would you be interested in this?" she said, ignoring the sarcasm.

"I might be here on vacation, too," he said. He realized that, except for the interrogation by the policeman, it was the first extended conversation he had had in nearly two months. He had never forgotten the low, husky sureness of her voice; never forgotten the slight overbite that gave her mouth an aggressive, sensuous look; never forgotten the presence of her—antithesis of warmth and open life to his thesis of gray, of uncertainty, of frozen indecisions.

She had nearly been murdered twice during the Tunney business and he had saved her life. And then, when she had said she loved him, he had retreated from her openness and certainty back to his own shadow world of muted lights, of grays, of cold.

"I showed you mine," she said and smiled. Conversation had brought back the color to her face. She leaned forward in the chair to see him better outlined against the light streaming through the window. It was always so hard to see him, she realized, even in the same room.

Devereaux decided something.

"You won't have to go to Leningrad," he said slowly, flatly, his voice surging like the lazy ice breaking up in spring.

Now Rita Macklin did not speak and sat perfectly still.

"I don't know what any of this is. A British agent questioned you in Dublin? About this?"

"He kidnapped me. He was nice really."

"Yes. He sounds nice."

"You've done worse things," she said.

He ignored her. "Why were the English interested in him?"

"He didn't say. Your kind of people don't usually reveal their motives easily."

"Not to reporters, anyway."

"He said I was a spy. For CIA."

"Are you?"

"Not very likely."

"There are stranger things."

"I work for—"

"I know who you work for, Rita." The voice was still flat, without emotion, but softness had come to his words and curled up at the edges of them.

"I never expected very much out of this story. I wasn't even sure it was a story," Rita said after a moment of silence in the room.

Devereaux glanced down again at the construction pit where they had found Natali. "Would you believe me if I said there were worse things than being arrested by a British agent?" he said, still staring out the window.

"Like what?"

"A couple of killings. One, a woman. One, another British agent. At least I think he was. And now something is going to happen. This afternoon. I don't know what but I know it is going to happen now. Did this agent in Dublin, did he know about you going to Helsinki?"

"Yes. In fact, he told me. He knew a lot, and a lot of what he knew he got wrong about me."

"Facts and lies, all mixed up," Devereaux said, not to her but to himself. "And who is Tomas Crohan? I'm the only one who doesn't know."

She told him, simply, as much as she knew about the man who had been an American agent behind Nazi lines in 1944 and 1945 and been captured at last by the Soviet army sweeping into Austria. She told him about Mrs. Fitzroy and then about the priest in Dublin who had once been part of the Irish government and who had been hit and killed on a Dublin street the day Rita Macklin came to Ireland to see him.

"What do you think?" she said at the end of her narrative, but he did not speak for a moment.

She stared at him and saw the logic behind the confusing events of the past days. If Devereaux was here waiting, then he was waiting for Crohan; if Devereaux thought something was about to happen, then Crohan must be here. The thought terrified her momentarily, the way a skier feels both exhilaration and terror as the descent begins and all the mundane plodding up the slope to reach this moment is forgotten.

"Is Crohan here?" she asked at last.

"I think so."

"Have you seen him?"

"No. I wouldn't know what he looks like."

"There don't seem to be photos of him. Mrs. Fitzroy had a childhood photo and there was one in Father Cunningham's possessions of someone I guess is Crohan. It was taken about fifty years ago."

"Odd, isn't it?"

"What?"

But he did not answer. He was thinking furiously for the first time in more than two months; he was shaking himself out of the lethargy of routine, of waiting, of enduring day by day without word from the East or the West. No wonder he had felt himself a prisoner; it was exactly like prison, like the nine months he had endured in the St. Charles Reformatory for Boys west of Chicago when he was thirteen, nine months that had seemed like nine years. He had grown up rough on the streets of the South Side of Chicago, had grown up with a sense of survival and brutality, and he had only been rescued, from the reformatory and from the direction of his life, by his Great-aunt Melvina who had suddenly given him a home and by his intellect which had given him a new life away from the streets. Now thought would rescue him again; he felt the thoughts connecting inside him like a string of lights rescued from an old cardboard box and suddenly given light and new life.

"Dev," she said, softly, standing up, walking across the room.

He turned and looked at her. His eyes were ice, his hair patches of white and black mingled, his face rugged and cross-hatched with deep lines that did not reflect age but experience.

"There is some danger in this," he said quietly.

"Of course," she said.

"Will you trust me?"

"Yes," she said.

"I think from their point of view, without knowing who they are, you will have to be killed before it is all over," Devereaux said. She shivered. He did not touch her.

"I think that is the way it will have to be played. Something is wrong at both ends, and I cannot understand the British involvement at all."

"But what is this about?"

"The last thing it's about is an old man coming out of the Soviet Union. There's a trap working here but I don't know against whom and why. I was called home yesterday. I was supposed to go home in the morning. This afternoon, I got my call; I am sure that Crohan is in the city now."

"Are you supposed to do something?"

"Yes," Devereaux said. "I should be out in the plaza on the other side of the hotel right now waiting for a signal. To make contact."

"What are you going to do?"

"Nothing. I have to get a message out."

"Out? Out of where?"

"Helsinki is a sieve for spies," Devereaux said. "Everything can be tapped, everything can be listened to—"

"Some democracy," Rita said.

"It's the only one they can afford sitting next to the Soviet Union," Devereaux replied. He was surprised by his answer; he thought he had no opinion of the Finns at all.

"Why are you waiting instead of making your contact?"

"Because I think they'll give me an extra day," Devereaux said ironically. "I'm sure of it." He went to the desk and opened up a Finnair timetable. "Are you tired?"

"No."

"There's a plane for Paris in two hours. Will you go to Paris, spend the night, send my message and come back in the morning? I will meet you at Stockmann's at ten in the morning."

"I don't know where that is."

"The taxi driver from the airport will know. Go to the fifth floor where the souvenirs are—knives, furs, cloth. I can meet you there."

"Is this all necessary?"

"Getting the message out is necessary. Something is wrong, something is wrong with the signals I've sent from here and from the station in Stockholm. If the English know about you, I'm pretty sure the Soviets don't yet. You'll be safe enough."

She smiled at him. "You want me to be a spy."

"I'm afraid there aren't many choices. Not in this place, not with Crohan. The English think you're an agent."

"Disinformation from someone."

"Yes. But who? And if someone killed the priest deliberately, they did it more for what he knew than for his political beliefs." Again, Devereaux permitted himself a frosty smile. "You, Rita. You are the target again."

"But who do I send this to?"

"I will write it down. There's a number in the States. Call by seven tonight, that'll be one in the afternoon in Washington. Don't answer any questions and don't repeat. Just speak clearly and then hang up and then go and get a good night's sleep and be back in Helsinki in the morning."

"Dev," she began.

He looked at her.

"I never got over you."

He said nothing.

She touched his hand.

"It was easier for you," she said.

No, he thought; but any admission would reveal too much of the truth. What could he tell her that would not lacerate her again, that would not tear the bandages from the dry wounds?

She felt intensely ashamed in that moment, in his silence. He should have said something. He should have comforted her. He had let her speak her heart and he had revealed nothing again. She felt like a schoolgirl. She withdrew her hand and looked away to the window. Why did she speak when he could answer her with silence? But that had always been the agreement between them.

He touched her.

She turned back to him.

He touched his lips with the tip of his finger.

She understood.

He folded his arms around her and held her then and she let her weight sink against him and she felt the warmth of his embrace; for a moment, they held each other without movement, without words, without any sounds.

"There is a lot to be afraid of now," Devereaux said, very close to her, still holding her.

But she only felt his arms around her and buried her face in the shoulder of his jacket. She only held him for a long time.

20
DUBLIN

Sparrow sat on the bed in Ely's hotel room. He had a pistol in his hand. He had been waiting for six hours. In some ways, he hoped Ely would not come; that Ely had left the assignment and the country. He didn't want to kill Ely.

The woman was already flown, to Helsinki. Rita Macklin. It was as George had guessed, Sparrow would max both the woman and the American agent in Helsinki and that would tidy up the business.

Sparrow had thought about a dozen things during the six hours of silence, of waiting.

He agreed with George that Wickham had gotten off lucky. Wickham would keep his mouth shut as well because he knew what George could do to him if he didn't.

The only thing that bothered Sparrow was Crohan. What was it all about except a Mick working for the Yanks in the war? Sometimes these people at the top got all excited over nothing, Sparrow knew, and it was always little fellows like Ely who ended up having to pay for it.

He pitied Ely, he really did.

Sparrow was tough, of course, and he could afford pity. He came from Liverpool and his old da had been half Irish. Liverpool was a tough enough town, then and now, though it didn't have the nigs the way it did now. Sparrow had been a contract employee for the Service for six years before they took him on. Sparrow had been very tough about it: "I got a better offer if you don't want to take me on the rolls permanent like."

"A better offer?" It had been some goddamn supercilious little clerk just like Wickham, all nose and looking down at you and soft hands. They were all the same.

"Yeah. From the IRA," Sparrow had said and that had shaken them and they did one of those conferences they do and they had vetted him back and forth for a month and then they had taken him on. Three years ago, George had come to see his talents. He had come to rely on Sparrow, George had.

Sparrow smiled at that. It was nice to be needed.

He had decided the easiest thing was to wait for Ely in his room. He had not checked out, his bag was still in the wardrobe on the wall away from the single window. Ely lived frugally, Sparrow noted, even on an expense voucher. Maybe he was saving up a little for his old age.

Which would not come in this case, Sparrow thought. At least he didn't have any orders about Parker, the stationmaster. Parker was out of it, filing his little reports about Russian submarine sightings in the western ocean off Ireland. George said he didn't really seem to understand what the Crohan business was all about.

Which was no surprise to Sparrow. He didn't understand it either. He only understood that Ely was going to have to be taken out. A nice clean hit after he got him inside the room.

He heard steps outside the door. He tensed and reached under his jacket for the handle of the Walther.

The door lock tumbled and the handle was turned. The door opened quickly, so quickly that it startled Sparrow who had expected some caution from Ely.

But it wasn't Ely at all.

The man in the doorway was dressed in black, his face was dark and recessive, his black eyes glowed hideously. He was bare-headed and his hair was black, pasted by rain against his scalp.

Sparrow noticed one other thing, the last thing he noticed in his life. The man framed in the door which was banging in that instant against the inner wall held a very large, black pistol in his hand and he was firing it even as the door struck the wall, even before Sparrow could pull down the Walther out of its holster.

The entire action took less than a second but it was so filled with details that Sparrow even had a moment to wonder about the complexities of life. So it would not be Ely after all, he thought slowly, as though he had all eternity to contemplate the matter.

He never heard the shot because his brain exploded as the bullet shattered his face and drove through his skull.

Antonio fired a second time before turning away from the door and the bloody scene. He even brushed past a man with a ginger mustache coming up the stairs but did not pause to beg pardon.

Which is why Ely discovered thy bloody remains of Sparrow seven seconds after the murder.

21

WASHINGTON, D.C.

Mrs. Neumann had been wrong after all.

Hanley sat at the conference table set up in the corner office inside the building in Langley, Virginia, which housed the Central Intelligence Agency. The building was quite ugly and functional and resembled a motel raised on spider legs of concrete supporting the main structure. Unlike the headquarters buildings of Auntie in London which were themselves meant to be a disguise, the Central Intelligence Agency proclaimed its presence boldly in the great seal imbedded in the lobby floor and visible to all who came to the front door.

Hanley had never been inside the building.

He felt uncomfortable as the director of Central Intelligence smoked his sixth Camel of the hour and stared at him silently. Of course they had traced back the stolen data to R

Section, as Mrs. Neumann had expected; but she had not expected confrontation on the matter because it would make the CIA look foolish.

The New Man at R Section was also there. He had replaced Rear Admiral Thomas Galloway (USN Ret.), who had been sacked following the debacle of the Mitterand assassination business nearly two years before. Hanley had served as director for a time, but because he was only a civil servent he was passed over for permanent promotion.

The New Man, as everyone still called him in the Section to separate him in memory from the Old Man who had been Galloway, was David Yackley. Yackley was an intense, dark-browed man of thirty-five who had been the youngest director of a major intelligence agency in the United States. He was a protégé of an old friend of the president and he had come to the job with new enthusiasms and new ideas and new plans of organization. Unfortunately for R Section, he put all his ideas into operation within six months and within a year nearly all of them had proven totally unworkable. Shambles remained, not only in the Section but in the attitude the New Man brought to dealing with other intelligence agencies under the umbrella of the National Security Adviser. He said the mission of R Section, a much smaller agency beside the Central Intelligence Agency, was supportive; when Hanley had explained to him that the Section had been set up by President Kennedy following the Bay of Pigs fiasco when the CIA had botched the operation, the New Man had treated it like ancient history. Hanley had quoted Kennedy: "Who will watch the watchers? Who will spy upon the spies?" as the reason R Section existed—to provide an independent audit of intelligence so that no agency would ever again become so powerful and arrogant that it could mislead the politicians who were supposed to be in charge of the country.

Which now led to the meeting with the director of Central Intelligence.

Hanley was explaining again: "We had need-to-know in this, Mr. Director. We had an agent in place, he had to make a decision. We needed information about Tomas Crohan."

"And so you took it with a cheap computer trick."

Hanley said, "The cheap trick fooled Langley."

The New Man winced. Among things he detested about R Section was the slang rampant in the place. He felt the jargon excluded him, particularly from the club of old-timers that existed in the establishment of the agency. He had begun, carefully, to weed out the old-timers, to separate them from their fiefdoms, to break down power. He had not even neglected the field though he had learned from the lesson of Stansfield Turner when Turner had thrown the CIA into a tailspin with his wholesale retirements of agents in the field.

The New Man named Yackley did not move so dramatically. He moved slowly on the sources of his discontent. Slowest of all was his move on Hanley. He would hate to admit to anyone that he still needed Hanley; Hanley had the secrets, Hanley still had the power. But even that would change in time with careful chipping at the secrets; like now. Hanley had stubbed his toe.

"Who is the man in Helsinki?" The director said at last.

"We have no one there now," Hanley said.

"It was one of our old-time hands," the New Man interjected and Hanley was plainly shocked. *This is the Langley Firm. They are not our friends. They cannot share our operations secrets.*

But Hanley said nothing.

"Hanley put him there on ice, to cool him down for a long winter's night in Finland," the New Man said with pleasure. There was an essential streak of sadism in him which those who admired him called ruthless efficiency.

"There turned out to be more to the business—"

"Yes. Director Yackley informed me. So you've seen the file on Tomas Crohan. Now do you understand why it must be kept secret?" the director of Central Intelligence said.

"We are hardly the enemy," Hanley said with dignity. "Under Section Three of our charter, we are to have free and open access to all records predating the establishment of the Central Intelligence Agency under the act of 1947."

The New Man turned to him."Why didn't you tell me that before?"

"Because you never asked me," Hanley said with some petulance.

"Never mind," the CIA director said. "This is not a law court. What I need to know is what is being done now with the information?"

"Nothing. I destroyed it in the shredder after I read it."

"But what is your operative in Helsinki intending to do?"

"He has been recalled as of two days ago," Hanley said.

"And where is he?"

"I don't know."

"You don't know?"

"It is difficult to get a safe message out of Finland. You know that."

"But two days ago? Is he taking a ship home?"

"There was no need to hurry."

"No need to hurry? What is his normal assignment?"

Hanley turned to the New Man and refused to answer. The New Man said, "He has been waiting for an assignment. He was on standby."

"Is there any chance he might . . . well . . . not have received the order?"

"No," said Hanley.

"Do you understand? This would be an embarrassment to us. If he came out of the Soviet Union."

"It happened a long time ago."

"Damn it, it's important now," the CIA director said.

"Why?"

The New Man had been looking at Hanley and now he turned to the CIA director. "Yes. Why now?"

"I'm afraid that's classified information."

"Is it?" For the first time at the meeting, an icy note was sounded in Yackley's thin voice. "Then there is nothing more to discuss, is there?"

"This is a delicate matter," the director of Central Intelligence continued. "It does not involve R Section."

"But apparently the Section is intruding upon it. Is that correct?"

"In a simple way, yes."

"Then let us cooperate."

The director frowned at Yackley. Yackley was a fool, a puppy. The director felt comfortable with him because he felt certain he could always manipulate him. Not so Hanley. Hanley was an old hand in the Section; Hanley had dealt with the CIA before.

The director, who was short and fat and had white hair and mottled red skin, lit another Camel and gave his customary cough at the first puff.

He decided something.

"Did it occur to either of you to wonder why someone in the Soviet Union would let out a prisoner like Crohan just now?"

"Yes," Hanley said, though it was a lie.

"Good. What conclusion did you reach?"

What conclusion have you reached?" Hanley continued the defense.

"Ireland."

"I don't understand," said the New Man.

"The Irish are cash poor and resources poor and the Irish currency is tumbling."

"So it says in the newspapers," Hanley said.

The director ignored the remark. "For six months, there has been Soviet submarine activity off the Blasket Islands in the Atlantic off the western coast."

Hanley did not speak.

"The Soviets want very much to acquire a lease to one of those islands. As a refueling station."

Hanley was silent but the New Man spoke up. "And why would that involve releasing a prisoner held forty years in the Gulag? That would be rather stupid of them, wouldn't it? I mean, if our information is correct, wouldn't the release of Tomas Crohan go against them in the public favor?"

"Eire is a neutral country. Not part of NATO. The Soviet Navy would love just a small toehold for its fleet in the North Atlantic."

"You didn't answer my question," Yackley said.

"Yes he did," Hanley said dully.

The director smiled. Yackley merely gaped.

God, Hanley thought. What a mess, what a dirty tangle it had become. But now he understood.

"We used Crohan," Hanley said. "We promised him things. In exchange for his doing some dirty work for us."

"In Austria," prompted the director.

"And if he comes out, he can be expected to be less than grateful to us."

"Yes," the director continued. "And tell the world about the dirty Americans. More particularly, tell the Irish."

"At the same time the Irish government announces a leasing arrangement for a worthless island with the Soviets which will provide jobs—"

"I think they are also arranging a grain and cattle importation deal," the director said.

The New Man understood vaguely and, at such moments, found silence a useful retreat.

"Would it work?" Hanley said.

"Like all of the best plans, it depends on timing. It's not terribly sophisticated but it might. At the very least, they can claim some propaganda value in the business. The more we push the Irish, the less they like to be pushed."

"That's why the British agent was killed in Helsinki."

"Yes. We knew about that, listening in at Cheltenham. We're allies, you know."

"And we're working for the same government," Hanley said bitterly. "You could have solved this earlier by telling us—"

"Secrecy," the director said, stubbing out the cigarette in an overloaded ashtray. "Everything is a secret. We got inquiries from a journalist who had worked with you. Three months ago."

Hanley looked up.

"Rita Macklin. Ring a bell?"

"She doesn't work with us."

"She did a good imitation of it on that Tunney business."

"What did she want to know?"

"About Tomas Crohan," the director said. "And you don't need to tell me the name of your agent in Helsinki. I know it already. The same man involved in the Tunney matter. How coincidental, Hanley."

"It was a coincidence," Hanley said sharply. "We inquired because we were afraid we were being set up." He dug it in. "As you were, last year, on that cipher clerk. If you had cooperated."

"That's water over the dam. The point is, secrets must remain secrets."

"I don't understand," the New Man said.

"Your man has to come out. And Crohan has to be refused. Beware Russians bearing gifts."

Silence filled the office. Thin sunlight streamed through the double windows and covered the book-lined walls. There were photographs everywhere of the director with the president, the director with various generals, the director with senators. He was a man of some influence.

"This is all the fault of November," the New Man said at last, trying to reestablish himself in the two-way dialogue.

Hanley shuddered. Never speak the name of an agent. Never.

The director frowned. "He is coming out, isn't he?"

"As far as we know," the New Man said. "Hanley?"

"I sent the message openly."

"You talked to him."

"Yes."

"There was no misunderstanding."

Hanley shook his head. He felt miserable and terribly isolated. Two days had passed. Where was Devereaux?

"He understood his orders?"

Hanley glared at the New Man. Damn him. Devereaux was the best man of the old crew left. Damn him and his plans and his reorganizations and his determination to break down the old order in the Section.

And now this. If only they had found out earlier about Crohan and about the Soviet talks with the Irish government.

Because he could not tell them the message he had received two hours before.

A woman's voice, speaking clearly, saying the message only once over the transatlantic line and then breaking the connection. Hanley had taken it alone in his bare office hidden deep in the Agriculture Building on Fourteenth Street.

"Mr. Hanley?"

"Yes?"

"From Helsinki. We are coming out, all of us."

And nothing more.

Could he not tell them this?

But the director said there had to be secrets.

Hanley sat and stared at them and felt nothing but cold seeping into him though the pale sunlight had lightened the room.

22

PARIS

Rita Macklin stared out the circular port as the plane arched lazily up through the clouds covering Belgium below. She did not see the clouds or the patches of land that appeared between them; she was staring only at the thought of what she had done. Of what he had made her.

Are you a spy, now?

Rita closed her green eyes for a moment. The silent question might have been asked by Kaiser in his mocking gravelly tone.

No, she would answer. And it would be a lie.

None of them would have understood her or why she had agreed to the mission for Devereaux.

She was a journalist, not an agent for her country. She had no causes but the truth—

She smiled because she heard Kaiser's laughter at that answer. It isn't good enough to retreat to principles, little Rita, he would have said. Principles are thin reeds to hide behind.

"Do you see anything?"

For a moment, the voice confused her—it might have come from her thoughts. Rita turned in her seat and saw the dark man sitting next to her. The seat had been empty at takeoff. He had chosen to sit next to her. She stared at him.

"Do you see anything?" The Italian accent was not very thick but she understood what it was. "No," she said in icy politeness and turned back to the window. Her thoughts had been scattered by the intrusion of the stranger's inquiry and now they crept back to her like cautious forest animals.

I did what he wanted me to do because it was him, she said in her mind to Kaiser, to Mac, to the professor at the University of Wisconsin who had led her first to the idea of journalism and who had given her her first principles. Principles didn't count now.

No rational argument could have persuaded her to help Devereaux; patriotism had nothing to do with it.

"My name is Antonio," the dark man intruded. "Do you mind if I smoke?"

Annoyed, she glanced at him. "Don't bother me, please."

His dark face darkened; the dark eyes turned mean. "I thought to be polite."

She didn't answer.

He shrugged and lit a cigarette. The smoke curled in the thin air of the cabin and was sucked up into the vents.

Three winters ago. He had used her, made love to her, and then saved her life when no one could have helped her. She had been fascinated by him at first and then repulsed when she realized he was an agent, when she realized that he had used her as cynically as he had used anyone.

Why had she gone to that retreat he had on a mountain near Front Royal? It had been dead winter in the mountains, the roads had been slippery, the sky gray as a field of tombstones.

Three winters ago.

She closed her eyes. When he had touched her, his touch had not seemed sure at first, as though she had stepped outside the cold world he lived in to come to that place in the mountains and she might not be real to him.

"Don't touch me like that," she had said to him and she had pressed her body against him as they stood in the doorway of the house he had on the mountain. She had held him fiercely and he had known she was real, she was not a fragile shadow, that in or out of his own world, she had decided to love him.

They had loved but without words. He was immersed in silences in that place, in that season; it was like the time she had gone on a women's retreat to a place in Minnesota and spent a curiously peaceful weekend in contemplation, in silence, in a world inhabited only by thoughts and prayers. She had been sixteen years old then.

When she had slept, he stroked her hair; she knew that even though she had not awakened.

Once she said, "I love you," to tell him the truth. He had not replied; he had only stared at her, his gray eyes quiet and even a little sad, as though remembering a pleasant time past and never to be had again.

She lived with him for five days that winter in the silent, snow-deep mountains. She realized at last it was an idyll and that it was ending and that nothing would be decided at all between them.

Rita had wanted to ask if he loved her but she could not

form the words. She was afraid there would only be silence as an answer or, worse, a spoken lie.

When she left him that morning, she had known she would never see him again.

"Damn you," she had said to him as he stared at her on the path in the snow three winters ago.

He had touched her hand then, as shyly as he had touched her five mornings before. His gray features were hard and unyielding but in the touch was something like a child's groping. He had understood and there was nothing they could do about it.

"I happened to you, Rita, that's all," he had said finally.

"It doesn't have to be that way."

"No. You know that it does."

And she had agreed with the same silence he had rendered her when she had said she loved him. What was he but an incident in her life, an accidental lover? Devereaux. He was alone, from choice or necessity; perhaps it was only the manifestation of survival for him. There was no other way. She had known it when she had driven to him from Washington five days before but she had ignored reason because all love defies logic in the end.

She blinked now in the plane and found her eyes glazed with tears. Damn, she thought, and opened her purse and wiped at her eyes with a tissue.

"Are you upset?"

The dark man's dark voice hissed next to her.

"Your smoke," she said curtly.

"Oh. My pardon. I will put out the cigarettte. I did ask you, didn't I?"

"It doesn't matter."

"Are you staying in Helsinki? Or are you going on to Leningrad?"

"Yes. I'm going on."

Antonio smiled. "Too bad. We could have such a good time, Miss Macklin."

The sound of her name chilled her. She turned back to him.

"Who are you?"

"My name is Antonio," he said. "I told you."

His eyes became flat, like a cat's. His cheeks were hollow, the ridge of bones beneath his black eyes too prominent. His head seemed a death's head to her; the skin pressed too tautly over the skull.

"How do you know my name?"

"Did I say your name?"

She stared with hard eyes at him but she felt afraid. She wanted to jump up, run out of this place. The plane began a slow dip to the right over Germany and the clouds broke. The shimmering half-frozen waters of the Baltic were in view. She glanced out the window and felt like a child who wants an interminable journey to end.

Was she now a spy? Did he feel this way all the time? Had this driven him to silence, to isolation, to a coldness that could not accept human feelings from her?

In a day she had betrayed her ideals and even her job to help him. The betrayal burned in her now. This is what he did all the time, betrayals and little lies until, over the years, the shadows had closed around his life and left him nothing, left nothing true or good in words or deeds, only in the slim grasp he kept on his own survival. He was using her now.

Why did the dark man know her name? What would Devereaux do?

Rita turned in her seat to stare at him again. The dark man smiled lazily, unpleasantly, as though he knew exactly what he was doing to her.

23

HELSINKI

He saw the city from the window of the old hotel where they had put him.

He had watched it from the first light of morning, when the first buses began streaking in from the Helsinki suburbs, when the first people had emerged onto the brick-covered streets, and when the first schoolchildren skipped along to their classes. He saw automobiles as though he had never seen them before. He touched the coverlet of the bed, and that amazed him as well. In a small refrigerator below the desk in the room, he found orange juice. He drank it and made a face and then found it quite wonderful. The room was warm. He took off all his clothes and went into the bath and took a long private shower until his skin was itchy and dry. A private shower. He soaped himself again and again. He rubbed his old body with the towel until it was red. He turned on the television set but there was nothing. He turned on the radio and he understood only a little of the language because he had never met many Finns in the Gulag. The Finns always seemed to want to kill themselves instead of being prisoners. He found writing paper in the desk drawer. He made designs. He wrote words in English:

Tomas Crohan.

Liverpool.

Dublin.

Tomas Crohan.

Michael Brent.

The last name he had not written for a long time.

The pen felt stiff in his hands.

He went to the window. It was a sunny morning. After a while, the streets were clotted with people. He smiled down at them as if he were God. He saw the streetcars and delighted in them as a child delights in an electric train. He saw trucks moving into the streets.

He saw a drunken man stagger, fall down and rise again.

He saw a blue police car at a corner waiting for the traffic signal to change. A young man crossed in front of it.

He smiled at everything he saw.

Naked, he climbed back into the bed and pulled the coverlet over his clean body. He snuggled beneath the clean sheets.

He closed his eyes but a thousand images flooded his mind and he could not sleep. He awoke and touched his hair. His body smelled of the light perfume of the soap.

He climbed out of bed and stood in front of a mirror. He touched his penis and pulled at it until he felt warm.

He went to the closet and looked at the clothes hanging there. He went back to the bathroom and turned on the shower again and climbed inside and let the water fall on him. He opened his mouth and drank the water. He got out and selected a new towel and rubbed his body again with it until his skin hurt. He sat down on the toilet and made it flush. He moved his bowels and wiped himself with the soft paper. He took another shower and washed his private parts and rubbed himself with the towel again.

He opened the refrigerator and took another orange juice from the cabinet and then he saw the bottle of beer.

He pulled it out clumsily and knocked over another bottle. He opened the beer and drank it.

The beer warmed him and he felt like crying. He cried and let the tears fall down on his cheeks and onto his pale, flat belly.

When he was finished, he washed his face in the bathroom again. He smiled to himself. Two teeth were blackened, one was made of stainless steel. Places for three teeth grinned empty in the mirror.

And no one disturbed him.

24

LONDON

George picked up a cigar and considered it and put it down. After a moment of silence, he picked it up again. It was a Dutch cigar of a make called Panter Mignon and came in a yellow tin package. He lit it at last.

Q sat beside him on the leather chair in the room that was behind the room where Q normally held his audiences. This room was not bare; the walls were covered with rosewood cases filled with books. There were carpets on the floor and two fireplaces tended by young men who were positively vetted every three months. Q was a great believer in positive vetting.

"I like Dutch cigars," George said at last. His face was in repose. His blue eyes appeared lazy, which was their most dangerous perspective.

"I had to quit," Q said. "Abnormal heart rhythms."

"Doctors," George said. "We're getting old."

"I don't mind that as much as I mind deprivation. Even of such little pleasures. On the other hand, when they come in the night, the heart palpitations frighten me. I realize I don't want to die."

"Well, dying is not much concern to me," George said.

More silence.

The little room contained a striking clock with a German Jauch movement hanging on the far wall. Every hour, Westminster chimes rang and the hour was struck with firm, resounding notes. Every quarter-hour, an incomplete tune was rung. The music of the clock never intruded. The room was completely soundproof and therefore silent save for the striking of the clock and the ticking of the minutes.

"What happened?" Q said quietly.

"I don't know. Ely found the body in his room. He found identification. That was careless of Sparrow."

"Yes."

"Who killed him, I wonder?"

"Ely?"

"Ely didn't have the guts for it. And he had no reason. Sparrow was a fellow agent. Two dead men on our hands, Q."

"The minister is wrought up a bit."

"I daresay he would be."

"What did you do?"

"I sent Ely to Helsinki. I didn't want to involve anyone else at this stage. Besides, it may be too late. He wanted to go in any case. To follow the American agent. The girl."

"Yes. I got his report. She knew quite a bit."

"Why do you s'pose they're leading us on like this?"

"The Russians?"

"Americans."

"Trap."

"Exactly. But why the squeeze?"

"They want control of Cheltenham. Been hinting at it with the foreign office for more than a year since the scandals. They feel that our security arrangements are less than satisfactory. And now they propose to spring . . . spring Tomas Crohan. Damn Cheltenham. That was the business with the phony Russians and Wickham. They want to take over, call us incompetent to handle security."

"The P.M. would never stand for it."

"The P.M. can stand for quite a lot. It's our necks," George said.

"And the P.M.'s neck. The spy scandals haven't helped."

More silence. The clock struck the quarter-hour.

"What can Ely do?"

"Extricate us. He was a fixer in the old days."

"That was before Vienna. He lost his nerve."

"The Americans were onto Ely from the start. Damned reports that Parker was sending from Dublin station through

Cheltenham to us. About his fictitious Russian submarines lurking off the Blasket Islands. Nonsense. And the Americans knew it and fed us."

"I hate to be played for the fool."

"What will Ely do?"

"Max."

"Will he do it?"

"Up to Ely, then."

"Well, it depends on him, doesn't it?"

"Unfortunately."

"Damn it. He was all I could think of. Before I can get another hitter to Helsinki, it will all be over. I think this matter is coming very quickly to the end."

"I don't quite see how the Americans arranged to get Crohan away from the Russians."

"It must have been part of a trade. They brought out that Soviet cipher clerk last year, the one who turned out to be a double. Maybe it was that."

25

HELSINKI

When the plane stopped at the terminal of Vantaa Airport, half the passengers were already out of their seats, pulling down bags from the overhead compartments, stretching their arms through the sleeves of overcoats and furs.

Rita Macklin got up and held her little bag close to her breast. Antonio remained seated next to her, his lazy legs blocking the passage.

"Excuse me," she said and pushed past him. Her legs rubbed against his legs as she edged into the aisle. She knew the contact was deliberate on his part. He touched her, not gently, on her behind as she moved past. Her face flushed angrily but she said nothing. She had to get away from this man; he was part of the new game she had joined so willingly when Devereaux asked her.

Forty minutes to meeting Devereaux.

Then it would be safe.

Antonio rose behind her and pressed against her in the crowded aisle as the passengers shuffled to the exits slowly. He was smiling and Rita Macklin knew it but she would not turn around, she would not say a word to him.

"*Merci, madame,*" said the Air France hostess at the exit door. Rita mumbled a *merci* in return and started quickly down the rampway to the main terminal corridor. She went through the sign marked CUSTOMS and then to PASSPORTS.

Seemingly without effort, Antonio was always visible if she looked for him. He was just a doorway behind. He moved slowly, like a cat stalking in the high grass; his eyes never left her.

She almost ran out of the terminal building into the bitter cold of Helsinki. The wind stung her cheeks red. She shuffled into another line for a taxi and slipped into the rear seat. She locked the door as she entered and again looked around for him; but Antonio could not be seen.

"Stockmann's Department store," she said quickly.

The dark driver grunted some sort of reply and pulled the meter. The car surged forward across the ice-streaked roadway for the long pull into the center of Helsinki.

Rita breathed deeply, once, twice. She felt afraid as she had felt three years ago, when she had met Devereaux, when her life had been endangered. Did he feel like this all the time? Was this the price she said she was willing to pay?

Who was he?

Why had he known her name?

Why did she feel such menace?

The next thought terrified her and she realized she was sweating and her eyes were wide: Devereaux. Had he set her up?

My God, that's paranoia, Rita.

The idea would not go away. Devereaux killed; he knew how to kill and he killed as a surgeon slices a tumor; Devereaux had killed a man on the sidewalk in Green Bay when she had been pursued three years before. Even if there was no proof of it, she knew Devereaux had killed the banker in New York after that. She knew it and said nothing and when he had held her, gently, in the retreat in the mountains, she had nearly forgottten what he was.

And then how could you love him if you didn't trust him?

She closed her eyes. The thought burned her like the impure thoughts that had come to her as a child, each thought carrying the pain of mortal sin and eternal Hell if she were to die; the thoughts tumbled one after the other into her consciousness as a child, each thought more sensual, more depraved than the one before as she struggled between sleep and wakefulness to wash her mind as clean as the nuns said it should be. The thoughts, on spring nights in the old house in Wisconsin, would never leave her and she would finally sink into them, sink into the guilty pleasure of them, let them touch her and caress her, let them open her and fill her. So now this nagging thought about Devereaux, this thought that all was a sham in his world of shadows, that there was no trust, no truth, no moment of decency, no ideals, no right, no wrong. Only survival; only to have existed and to exist tomorrow.

Antonio saw her leave the cab and walk across busy Mannerheimintie Street to the imposing bulk of Stockmann's department store. Antonio thought it was such a pity not to have a little more time to play with her but there was no time left; they had been quite certain about that; the female agent, they had said, had to be eliminated quickly to avoid complications.

His masters had become convinced in the past few days that Rita Macklin was not a journalist but one of the Opposition, a deep-cover member of R Section. It was the only satisfactory explanation for her second mission with the agent called November. Rather than abort the operation using November, the second agent called Macklin would have to be dealt with so no counter-operation would be mounted.

So they explained to him, and the explanation bored him. Antonio did not care for motives or details. He was a simple man who wanted a target and then wanted to be left alone to effect the operation the best way he could.

Rita Macklin strode with wide steps across the sidewalk.

Antonio was seventy-five feet behind her. He felt the edge of the knife along the skin of his right arm.

The knife was simple, working on a mechanical trigger pull fitted into his half-clenched right hand like a ring. It had been concealed as part of the brasswork on the briefcase he carried through the electronic security apparatus in Paris. He had fitted the knife to his arm in the lavatory on the plane and then sat next to Rita to play with her as a child plays with a doll.

Games were over. He would clench his fist and the knife would fall into his hand and lock at the wrist. It was an effective weapon. He had used it on the whore, Natali, when he was finished with her. Natali had pleaded at the end, which he had expected, and it pleased him to pretend to listen to her pleadings. She had kissed his naked feet. They were in the bathroom; Natali had kissed his body while she remained on her knees on the cold tile floor. When he had finished his amusement, he had said her name and she had looked up at him, holding him around his hips with her hands, tears in her eyes. He had sliced her open from throat to belly in one swift, shallow movement.

Antonio had a surgeon's eye; he had once studied *Gray's Anatomy* and reviewed the remains of corpses in the morgue at Reggio Calabria under the guise of being a medical student. He knew which parts of the body meant instant death and which parts meant slow death.

Natali had not felt pain but surprise. She had said, in English, "You promised me." It had been absurd. He could have let her die slowly but she had pleased him and so he finished her then with a quick thrust into the heart. Her blood washed over him, over the floor. He had put her in the shower and let the water wash the blood from her and then he had wrapped her naked body in plastic and dumped it in the excavation lot behind the Presidentii Hotel.

Rita Macklin would die differently.

He pushed through the doors of the department store and started up the steps to the second floor. He would not cut her deeply. She would die in agonizing minutes, writhing on the floor in this department store, horrified people gathering at the sound of her screams, her intestines spilling from her, the screams finally drowning in blood coming from her mouth and nose. She had chosen this way to die because she had not spoken to him, because she had not seen that her fate was decided anyway and that it was as well to play the game Antonio wanted to play. The thought of her murder—of the act and of the agony that would follow—excited Antonio and his eyes grew wide as he continued his careful track up the steps.

The store was nearly empty. The cold sun and bitter wind were unrelenting in winter, though the ice on the shoreline was already broken and spring was very close.

He followed Rita Macklin from floor to floor.

Two sales clerks—girls in fancy blouses and plain skirts—stood speaking to each other near a display of Russian chess pieces in a far corner of the fourth floor. Rita Macklin turned from the escalator and looked around the nearly empty floor. She glanced for a moment at a display of traditional Lapp hunting knives. The handles were of bone and leather; the blades of the knives were carved with intricate patterns and with scenes of reindeer roundups. In another corner, Finnish glassware sparkled in the bright lights. Fifteen minutes until her meeting with Devereaux. She glanced around and saw Antonio at the stairs. He was smiling.

Her face went white. She stumbled back a moment and steadied her hand on the counter. She looked toward the two sales clerks but they had disappeared into a back room.

Antonio walked toward her without any wasted motion.

Rita made a sound that was half a cry and turned and grabbed an enormous Lapp knife from the display counter. She ran behind the display with the knife in her hand and around a second corner. The floors were shaped around the stairs like spokes in a wheel.

FINLAND WELCOMES YOU exulted a poster on a wall. She ducked into an aisle between racks of fur coats. She pushed to the end of the aisle and turned and realized she had trapped herself at a dead end.

Antonio's form darkened the entrance of the dead end.

"Miss Macklin," he said.

Her nostrils were wide, her eyes were wide, her face was flushed with blood; her breathing was heavy, as though she were fighting or running. She held the knife in front of her, the handle against her belly.

"Absurd," said Antonio and he clenched his fist and opened it. The knife fell with a rasp into the lock around his wrist. It was thin and pointed like a dagger or stiletto; the angles of the knife glistened in the light of the store.

"I'll kill you," Rita said. Antonio took a step toward her. She braced herself and smelled the fear of death; once she thought of Devereaux but the image of him was piled under with a thousand sudden images from a thousand days of her life, not passing in review but screaming in her mind for attention and then drowning in the tide of other memories. This is death, she thought and she waited.

Antonio slashed once, a lazy cutting slash that tore neatly through her coat and grazed her hand with a bright red cut. She dropped the knife with a clatter on the tile floor. She pushed back but there was no place to go. A glass angel on a shelf above the furs fell to the floor and shattered on the tile. There was no other sound.

Rita felt no pain but saw the blood on her hand.

Now I lay me down to sleep/I pray the Lord my soul to keep.

Rita kicked out sharply with her shoe and caught his shin with the edge of her toe. Antonio winced for a moment and then his hand arced down and Rita, off balance, fell toward him and accidentally muffled the blow. The knife sliced into a fur on the rack and momentarily became entangled.

Rita stepped back again.

"When you are dying, you whore, you will scream and then the screaming will stop, not because you do not feel pain but because you will choke in your own blood," Antonio said. She saw his eyes fill with pleasure.

She pulled against the rack and a bolt came loose and the furs suddenly were dumped on the aisle between them.

Antonio stepped back. They were six feet apart.

"You stupid fucking whore," he said and took a step and slipped on a blue fox fur. He took a second step.

He grasped her bloody right hand. "Get on your knees."

She was stunned; she could not speak or move; terror had turned to a sleepy stupor. She was like an animal suddenly shaken to death in the jaws of a lion; in the moment before death, sleep and calm overwhelm. Her hand had not strength left in it.

The second man filled the aisle behind them; Antonio raised his hand.

Kulak fired twice and the shots were muffled by the furs so that the clerks in the back room did not hear them.

Each bullet kicked into Antonio's outstretched back; the first broke his spine and killed him and the second lodged in his right lung.

Antonio was off-balance and fell back and Kulak fired a third time, sending the bullet surging into his skull. Antonio's eyes widened; he turned, the locked knife tearing into furs; he fell against a shelf above the furs and sent a case of glass angels and gargoyles crashing to the floor. He fell in the broken glass. The pieces were around him like flakes of ice; shards of glass cut the flesh of his dead body.

Rita said nothing. She stood and stared at the body and the furs and the broken angels. Silence after the shattering glass.

Kulak stepped into the aisle between the rows of furs and stepped over the body. He took Rita's bloody hand and wiped at it with a handkerchief.

"This is not so great," he said gruffly. "It is a little cut."

"He was going to kill me," she said without emotion; her face was pale and her voice was quiet.

"Yes. Do you know why?"

"I don't know," she said, staring at the handkerchief-wrapped around her hand. "He was on an airplane—"

"Yes. You came from Paris this morning."

She paused and her eyes widened and she looked at Kulak for the first time. "Who are you?"

"I am the police, madam. I am Chief Inspector Kulak."

"I don't—"

"Please, don't say anything now. Come out of this place. I will take you to a place where we can sit down and talk."

"I'm a tourist—"

Kulak's cold eyes narrowed. "Madam, you are a journalist. At least, you say this. You are also a spy, too, I think. I know this one now; this is the one who killed Natali. I wish I could have cut him and skinned him the way he cut her. The way he would have cut you."

"I'm on vacation, I—"

"You are lying to me, madam, but I expect that. I do not want murder in Helsinki. I do not want you . . . people here. Am I clear? But now I must examine you, myself. First, we will take you to the hospital for your little cut and then we will go to the police headquarters for a talk. You and me, madam."

"But, I—" and she could say nothing. Devereaux would come and she would be gone. She would extricate herself from the police station eventually but everything depended on timing, Devereaux had said.

For the second time that morning, she thought of the dead man and Devereaux in twin thoughts. No, she would not believe he could betray her; he had saved her life.

But then she understood suddenly. It was what he had meant in Virginia three years ago when he would not accept her because he could not offer her this world of betrayal and shadows. Every thought was suspect now; every alliance was temporary; every truth was only a reformed lie. No matter what they vowed in words, no matter what they gave to each other, there would always be the nagging edge of doubt about him, like an infection that lasts for years, that never kills but slowly poisons every good thing.

One P.M. Melted snow ran down the gutters outside the plaza. Devereaux stood across the way from the Alko store in the shadow of a building full of shops that sold everything from coffee to Marimekko prints.

Something had gone wrong at the rendezvous. The store was filled with policemen. Devereaux had turned away from Stockmann's and spent the next nervous hour waiting across the wide avenue from the store for any glimpse of her. She had emerged at eleven with Kulak. He had not followed her. They would meet again, later, in the hotel. The fall-back position was routine but he had not thought they would need it.

A large man with glittering, arrogant eyes entered the Alko state store at precisely one ten and emerged ninety seconds later with a bottle wrapped in brown paper. He looked around him and opened the wrapper and removed a precious bottle of Finlandia vodka.

He placed the vodka on the walk next to the door of the store and then walked away.

An amazed derelict who, moments before, had pressed his eyes against the window of the Alko store like a child viewing a Christmas window, gaped at the bottle standing naked on the walkway. He looked after the departing stranger and then at the bottle and then looked all around him.

Without a further moment of hesitation, he crossed the walk, snatched up the bottle and shoved it in his pocket. He hurried away with shambling steps.

Devereaux followed the large man who had purchased the vodka as a signal. It was Tartakoff.

Tartakoff crossed through the bus terminal parking lot and then went into the terminal itself and then out again across the street and down the block to the train station. He descended the stairs outside the red granite station building to the underground plaza.

Devereaux followed loosely behind. He kept looking around him, not so much concerned at losing Tartakoff but at being followed himself. But no one seemed to take more interest in him than in anyone else. He felt the cold grip of the .357 Colt Python in the pocket of his drab brown wool overcoat. He had worn sweaters mostly in Helsinki through the long winter's wait and today wore a brown turtleneck sweater that was really too warm for the afternoon. But Devereaux was not discomforted by the warmth; it seemed he had been cold too long to ever be too warm.

Tartakoff took a turn toward the department-store entrance in the underground mall. The corridor was not crowded but it was populated and Tartakoff had arranged it long before as the prime meeting site, so it could not be changed. He turned and saw Devereaux approach him. He was smiling.

"You did not meet me yesterday; I thought you had gone," Tartakoff said in his heavy accent.

"Do you have the prisoner?"

"So. He was important to you after all."

"Do you have him?"

"He is safe."

Devereaux stared coldly at the other man. Something was wrong, something had been wrong from the beginning. Why were there policemen today in Stockmann's?

"There's no time for games," Devereaux said.

"It was not a game to me," Tartakoff replied with disdain. "It is you, Messenger, who put off this contact for too long."

"Where is he?"

"Safe."

"That could mean inside the Soviet Union as well."

Tartakoff shook his head. "Here. In Helsinki now. We are ready. We were ready yesterday."

Yes, Devereaux thought. You were ready yesterday and you had the luxury of waiting. You are not terrified, Tartakoff. It is I who should be afraid.

"Everything has been arranged," Devereaux said slowly. "We will separate the two of you—"

"No."

"Yes," Devereaux said in a flat, calm voice while his eyes tried to probe the reactions of the other man. "It is the only way. The old man will go to Stockholm. Silja Line tonight. You are going to fly to New York directly this afternoon by Finnair. You have an hour."

"No," Tartakoff said suddenly, backing up. "This is too soon. It does not suit me."

"Too soon?" Devereaux felt the trigger beneath his index finger. He had chosen the coat because of the unusual size of the pockets and the fact that they were not covered with flaps. The pistol could be removed very quickly and replaced just as quickly.

"Too soon. I must show you where the old man is—"

"I trust you. Tell me and here is your ticket and your identity." He reached inside his vest pocket.

"But I expected to go with you—"

"Look. You'll be in the air before the old man gets aboard the *Finlandia* at six tonight." Devereaux spoke slowly, flatly. "There is no way we can double-cross you. Unless, of course, you are double-crossing us. Is that it?"

"Do you think that? I will take you to the old man myself."

"Your plane leaves in an hour," Devereaux said.

"There is no great hurry," Tartakoff said. "There is a second plane to the United States at four. I know this thing. I study all the timetables of Finnair—"

"All right. Take me to the old man."

"You know how important he is?"

"Not really."

Tartakoff looked surprised.

Devereaux smiled. "But then, I'm just the messenger."

26

AMSTERDAM

"Accounting," said the Russian, and Penev, the Bulgarian, opened the large accounting book.

They sat in the back room of the shuttered offices of the Balkan tourist authority which Penev ran. It was raining again in Amsterdam but the day was warm and the windows were steaming. Slowly, almost reluctantly, the first signs of thaw and spring were breaking across the European continent.

Penev had never seen the Russian before. He usually dealt with the Soviet KGB station chief in Rotterdam but this man was from Moscow. It must have been an important matter and Penev had had no idea of the importance of it.

In the accounting book were names and times and places, all rendered in a neat hand.

The names might have been names of customers of the travel service. In fact, there were six legitimate names and departure schedules on a page and then one name and schedule involving another part of Penev's business. The part that had to do with assassination.

"Should I speak aloud?" Penev said.

"Do you thing it is safe?" The Russian was mocking him. "Of course speak aloud or I will not be able to hear you."

"I do not know what procedures you wanted followed, comrade; that is all," Penev said, somewhat annoyed. After all, he had upheld his end of the matter. He had never failed. Even if there had been mistakes made along the way.

Penev felt warm and clammy. Sweat spread a stain under his arms.

"As I was instructed," Penev began.

The Russian waited across the table from him without speaking.

"I contracted Antonio from Reggio Calabria. We have used him before with satisfaction. He is somewhat . . . odd . . . in his habits. Cocaine user. I had no reason, based on what he had done for us in the past, to think he would have fouled the operation. I said she was a spy. He never failed before."

"But he did this time."

"First, he killed the priest in Dublin."

"That was satisfactory."

"I did not understand that part—"

"The priest knew the mission of Crohan in the war. That is all. He was too talkative. He corresponded with the old woman in Chicago. It was better to get rid of him from the first."

"From there he went to Helsinki. That's where the mistake was made."

"Two mistakes," said the Russian slowly. He removed a cigarette and fitted it into a holder and placed the holder in his mouth. The Bulgarian lit the tip of the cigarette for him.

"He panicked over the whore. So he killed her and he stupidly left the body near the hotel. And then he arranged the murder of the agent so that this American agent, Devereaux, would find him. That was not what he was told to do."

"I didn't know about the American agent. I was not instructed," Penev said.

"No, comrade. But it was a mistake nonetheless. Continue."

"The third mistake. He was to eliminate Ely, the British agent in Dublin. Ely had the assignment to investigate the matter of the priest. The death of Ely would only frighten the British into thinking the Americans were behind this. Instead, he killed the wrong man. An agent named Sparrow."

"And so you sent him to Helsinki to kill the American journalist. The fourth mistake. He might have killed her if the Finnish police had not been waiting for him at the airport.

"The police were the problem." Penev agreed. "Kulak had to be pulled from the American agent, Devereaux. He might have arrested him. But it was clumsy."

The Russian saw criticism in this and he frowned. "It was direct. Direct action was needed. Kulak had to be kept away from Devereaux. He was the messenger."

"Antonio had made too many mistakes," Penev continued. "Let the police have him in Helsinki for the two murders there."

"We did not expect the American journalist to be in Helsinki. This was fortunate for us. It allows the disinformation to be applied quickly, before the British can move to stop it. Crohan will tell her the truth once he is certain he is safe."

Penev glanced up from the book.

"What is the truth, comrade?"

The Russian smiled. "Very simple. The British made a signal to the SS in Vienna four months before we liberated the city. We found the records of it. The Germans save everything, even secrets. The Germans were told the identity of Crohan by the British. It is that simple. It is the reason we could arrest Crohan."

"But what reason—"

"The American OSS had sent Crohan into Vienna as a spy to save Jews there from transportation to the concentration camps. But he was a spy, nonetheless. And the English were terrified when they found out what the OSS had done. Crohan would have emerged as a national hero in Ireland after the war. He was an agitator against the British; he was a socialist. He would have caused Britain great harm after the war. So the British wanted the Germans to kill him. They betrayed him. That is the great secret."

Penev frowned. "But this is tied to the submarine base for refueling?"

"There is no such plan," the Russian said.

"I don't understand."

"Let the British worry about the submarine base while the threat comes from another place. The threat comes from the mouth of Tomas Crohan who will reveal that he was betrayed by the British when he was working for the Americans behind the Nazi lines."

Penev understood at last and a slow smile spread across his face. "An old man held prisoner was made prisoner because the British betrayed him to protect their own selfish interests."

"And then, after the war, when we said to the British that we would release this man, they gave us evidence of his anti-Soviet activity on behalf of the Nazis. Until this last moment, we were convinced the evidence against him was genuine."

The two men were smiling. "And where did we get the evidence? The false evidence?"

"From our mole inside British Intelligence. Very, very important man. I cannot say his name."

"And the matter is closed now?"

"Yes. Tonight, the American will take the Irish prisoner back to his home and the journalist will reveal all that Crohan has been told—"

"It will finally break the American trust of the British—"

"Of course. They will demand separation from British liaison. Even at Cheltenham. Which will make our work much easier."

"But Tartakoff?"

"Oh. He will be back in Leningrad tonight, I think. Unless something has gone wrong. He has one option he did not have before, before the American journalist came into the picture."

"What?"

"If he is suspected, he will be able to kill the messenger."

27

WASHINGTON, D.C.

"I don't have any time," Devereaux said.

"Where are you?"

"Just where you think."

"My God." Hanley paused. "There are difficulties."

"Our people are out."

"You were supposed to come home."

Devereaux did not speak.

"You know the lines from Helsinki aren't safe," Hanley said.

"That seems to be the last consideration of anyone here. Why didn't you answer all those weeks?"

"There was nothing to say," Hanley said. "You defied your orders."

"No, goddamn it, now you listen." Devereaux spoke low and harsh, an undercurrent of anger in his flat voice like the undertow of a placid sea. "For nine weeks you let me dangle because nothing was supposed to come of this. You thought Tartakoff was a trap and it was convenient to get rid of me for a while."

Silence crackled on the international line; the silence confirmed everything Devereaux said and both men knew it.

"But mention Tomas Crohan and everything began to change suddenly. Hanley finds a voice at last, just to cover this thing up. 'Get out, November.' But now I can't get out."

"Where is Tartakoff?"

"Ten feet away from me. I'm watching him drink a glass of beer."

"My God. Where are you?"

"In the Helsinki train station."

"It . . . It's a public place.—"

"Everything has changed, I told you that. There were two murders here. One was the British agent, Sims. I think the other one was a mistake, but the point is, I was set up. I'm being set up now—"

"You know it's a trap—"

"I'm not a fool, Hanley," Devereaux replied. "But I need some backing from your end."

I can't do anything. The New Man—"

"Fuck the New Man," Devereaux said.

"I have my orders."

"And I have Tomas Crohan," Devereaux said. "And Tartakoff."

"Leave. Leave now. Walk away from it and get on the first plane back home."

"I can't do that."

"That's an order."

"No. Not this time." Softly now, with an edge of menace. "Do you remember a woman named Rita Macklin?"

"What? You mean that reporter? In the Tunney matter?"

"Yes."

A long silence followed. "What about her?"

"She's here."

"What did you say?"

"She's here. She wants to know about Tomas Crohan." Devereaux paused. "So do I, Hanley."

"I don't know anything." Hanley considered the lie and revised it. "The information is not . . ." Again, the lie was altered. "Information is not germane to your mission now that your mission is terminated. You have no need-to-know."

"You aren't listening to me, Hanley."

Indignation sputtered on the international line but Hanley's tone was too tinny to carry it off: "Damn it. Are you blackmailing me now, November? Have you lost your senses? This is the Section—"

"Fuck the Section," Devereaux said. His voice was calm, low. "And fuck you, Hanley."

It was suddenly open between them; loyalty had cracked.

Devereaux spoke again in the same calm, surging voice; his voice was like a river in flood, inexorably spreading across barriers. "You let me dangle for the past two years, since the business in Paris. I wanted to wait you out; I didn't see any other way. But I won't be the dead puppet anymore, not for you, not for the New Man. It comes down to my survival now, Hanley, and you don't really have any choice but to help me."

Silence on the line.

"November," Hanley began. But Devereaux interrupted:

"I want to know about Tomas Crohan and I want to know what has been going on from the beginning. . . ."

Hanley's voice was suddenly tired. "We don't know that. Not all of it. Can't you get rid of them, even now?"

"I'm not your hitter, Hanley," Devereaux said. His voice had become weary in that moment as well; the two voices, like two old friends meeting at the end of a long day. Or two old enemies. "I won't hit Tartakoff for you."

"An attack of morality?" Hanley probed.

That would be a joke, Devereaux thought. He saw all the killings in all the years, hits seen and unseen, and he had gradually frozen his soul until the little deaths around him did not touch him. But he was not a hitter, not for Hanley, not for the Section, not for a little game they were playing which he did not understand. He stared out the telephone booth at Tartakoff sitting calmly at a table, sipping beer, staring back at him.

"I'm not talking about the journalist," Hanley said. "But she is a major part of the problem."

"Not of my making," Devereaux said.

"Things have gotten out of hand."

"You want Tartakoff hit and then the old man and then Rita Macklin—"

"I didn't say that."

"You make vague suggestions and shuffle away. You don't want to know the details."

Hanley's voice was cold. "Exactly."

"The details can't be taken care of so easily this time."

"You are not in a position to make bargains with us, November; we can forget this conversation occurred. Walk away from it. We can send in . . . someone . . . to solve the problem of the Russians."

"And 'solve' the problem of Rita Macklin."

"We're not barbarians, November. She is an American citizen."

"A small protection. Will she show her blue passport to the hitter?"

"Get out, November. Walk away from this."

"Why? Why is that important?"

"We can't be involved."

Devereaux sighed. There were never any answers, never facts, never connections of logic. Classified material in the government was even called Sensitive Compartmented Information to emphasize that each secret must not be connected to the secret that came before or the lie that would come after. He could not argue with Hanley anymore.

"Who called you on the special phone, Hanley?"

Hanley, nearly five thousand miles west, held the phone tightly and did not speak.

"Was it a woman? Who said, 'We are coming out'?"

"The call came from Paris."

"I know," Devereaux said.

"My God, what have you done? This cracks security, this—"

"There is no security left in this, Hanley."

"It was that woman, Macklin. You've opened up our operation to a . . . to a goddamn journalist."

"She went to the CIA two months ago to look up files on Tomas Crohan and she wasn't allowed to see them. The newspaper morgues had been stripped of references to him. She tracked the matter to an old priest in Dublin but he was killed before she got to him. Does it surprise you that she became curious about Tomas Crohan?"

"Sarcasm," Hanley identified.

"What are you going to do?"

"What is she going to do?"

"The secrets are safe with me," Devereaux said gently, irony coloring the words.

Hanley thought then of the humiliating interview with the New Man the previous afternoon. Yackley said the Section would cooperate with the CIA, that the trust would all be placed on one side. But he couldn't trust his own agent dangling in Helsinki for one long winter.

"Mrs. Neumann got the file from CIA. On Crohan."

Devereaux smiled. "If anyone could, she could."

"I saw it. I destroyed the copy after I saw it."

"Where is the original?"

"In the OSS Section. At Langley."

"Why are they involved?"

"I don't know." Hanley paused and then rushed ahead as though the words washed away some stain that had nagged him. "The New Man is sucking up to Langley." The slang surprised them both. "I don't like any of it."

"But it doesn't matter now," Devereaux said.

"No. No, I don't suppose so. Not if you're unwilling to come out alone—"

"I couldn't walk away from it from the moment I sent Rita to Paris."

"That was very unwise," Hanley said with dejection.

"Any action would have been."

"Yes. I suppose you're right." He paused. "I will tell you, November. Now. I'm sorry." The apology surprised him as much as the slang, as though he no longer controlled his words. He had done nothing wrong but he felt shame, deep and heavy, inside himself.

"Tomas Crohan was a Fascist sympathizer to the point of forming a neo-Nazi splinter of Fianna Fail in the late 1930s in Ireland. He came from wealth, mostly in land. He and his father visited Hitler in 1938 before Czechoslovakia. You understand the position of the Irish government in those years . . .

new state, somewhat shaky, depression, determined to steer a course away from British domination. Lots of admiration for the Nazis in Ireland simply because they were anti-English—"

"I understand."

"When the war came, Ireland opted to be neutral. Both sides used the country to their advantage. Nazi spies in Dublin, just as they were in Portugal and Sweden and Switzerland during the war. The OSS came in with a scheme to turn Crohan, use him behind the Nazi lines, promise him some great reward after the war."

"What was the promise?"

"The usual thing we offer dictators in Latin America. We said we would give him the country after the war. He would become Taoiseach of Eire."

"Could we reasonably promise that?"

"That is the wrong question. Could Crohan believe it was in our power to do it? He was already in government, was wealthy, was well known and admired in the country for his anti-British stance. The British had a positive paranoia about him, feared he might become prime minister in Ireland—"

"What did he do for us in Austria during the war?"

"How do you know that?"

"Rita Macklin told me."

"A journalist? Are you sure that's all she is? How did she know—"

"I'm not sure of her, of you, of any of this."

"You have to be careful."

"No, Hanley. It's time for you to be careful. The puppet cut the strings, Hanley. You tell the New Man that."

"If you release any of this, you've breached security at the highest level. I can cover the use of the special phone by that journalist. She could be in trouble if she revealed information about internal security . . . not to mention you, November. But any of this about Crohan is classified—"

"You stole it from the CIA."

"Damn you—"

"No more threats, Hanley. Threats and promises don't mean very much to me anymore."

Another pause. "We needed British cooperation. After all, they had the Senior Intelligence service and part of it was keeping an eye on Ireland, even during the war. We got their permission to put Crohan into a black job for us; we told the Brits he would arrange passports and passage out of Vienna for a group of Jews we were interested in saving."

"Not cleaning women or peasants," Devereaux said.

"There are always priorities. Scientists mostly—"

"Go ahead."

"That's what we told the Brits, as I said. But Crohan wouldn't have lifted a finger to save Jews. Besides, we knew the Jews had been killed already in the camps, the ones we named. We knew that."

"Then what did we want from Crohan in Austria?"

"An incident," Hanley said vaguely.

"What sort?"

"To push Ireland into our arms, out of neutrality. We set him up to kill Hitler."

Devereaux blinked. The line crackled but there was no other sound. Tartakoff still stared at him. He was in the present, in Helsinki, waiting to get out and yet he felt disoriented, as though half of him were now in wartime Austria with Crohan, setting up a hit. An impossible assignment.

"That's absurd. We wouldn't have sent in an amateur to set up a hit like that."

"Even if we contemplated such a hit," Hanley said. "Once the war had started, Hitler was his own worst enemy. We never wanted him dead until the war was over and won."

Devereaux felt burdened by Hanley's revelations; it was too much dirty knowledge, too cynical to want to know, too true to keep from haunting his unconscious thoughts at night, too awful not to be the stuff of nightmares.

"We wanted the Abwehr to seize him in good time, try him and kill him. The charges against him would be fantastic. No one would believe them."

"That's madness. Why not tell the Brits what we were doing?"

"Security," Hanley said, as though that explained everything.

"It couldn't have worked."

"Madder plots worked. Remember the pilotless gliders bringing saboteurs into Norway in the war?"

"They crashed; the men died for nothing."

"And a woman called Madeleine who was dropped into France and who unconsciously betrayed one network before she was picked up by the Nazis and killed?"

"So your scheme didn't work."

"It wasn't mine; it was OSS and it was a long time ago. Unfortunately, our Irish Fascist went into Austria just before the generals decided to kill Hitler and blew up his meeting room. Crohan was trapped in Vienna and tried to survive the war. We left him dangling. He might have survived it, too."

Devereaux understood. "Which would have been embarrassing to us. In case he blamed us for his predicament."

"He was certain to blame us."

"So we betrayed him."

"We told our allies, the Russians, by circuitous means, that he was a spy working for us."

Devereaux felt so tired. He closed his eyes a moment. He opened them and nothing had changed. Tartakoff stared at him still.

"We let the Russians get rid of Crohan," Devereaux said.

"But they didn't get rid of him, did they, November? And now you have him and what are you going to do with him?"

"He is still an embarrassment."

"Yes. We have our leverage with the Irish Republic. We have certain . . . needs. Oil off the coast. And now this business of the Russians negotiating for use of a naval refueling base."

"Is that true?"

"We don't think so; but paranoia demands we believe it sometimes."

"So this was a trap after all," Devereaux said.

"Yes. It appears so."

"You could have avoided the problem from the beginning."

"Damn it, November, we didn't know what the problem was. Langley told us nothing. There is too much security sometimes."

"We have to work our way out of this."

"I don't see how."

"The New Man wanted me out of Helsinki."

"Yes."

"You told him I was out."

"I thought you were."

"No," Devereaux said. "You knew I was still inside. You knew it and you lied to him, deliberately."

Hanley gasped. "I did not."

"This time, you did. This time, you're going to have to save my neck to save your own." The voice had changed again; it was low and harsh, like the growl of a hidden animal on a dark night. "You're going to have to take the heat on this."

"Why would I?"

"Because I can't go back on any of this. Because I have Rita Macklin and I have Crohan and I have Tartakoff. Your solution is to walk away from it. What do you think Rita will do then? This is a story and even if she doesn't have all the answers, she has the questions. And she knows about Crohan."

"And you," Hanley said. "She knows about the Section and she knows about you. She knows too damned much."

"So hit her? And Crohan? And Tartakoff? And then who should be next, Hanley? Me?"

Hanley said nothing; the possibility had occurred to him and he was not certain he had rejected it.

"If I work out of this, I'm through," Devereaux said. "If I don't, I'm dead.

"Yes," Hanley said. "Those might be the only choices."

"I'm sick of you," Devereaux said. "I'm sick of the Section. I'll work out of this and you'll take the heat from the New Man and you'll figure out how to survive; you've been figuring that out for a long time."

"And you will quit."

"We call it retirement, Hanley, with maximum points and payoffs like medical care." Devereaux smiled. "All the mundane pleasures of the middle-class servant. I want you to fix it."

Hanley did not speak for a moment and then continued in a soft voice: "I can fix it."

"I want everything cleaned up after this," Devereaux said. "I want the break total."

"I understand."

Devereaux said coldly, "No hitters after me, after Rita."

"What are you going to do with her?"

"That's not your problem anymore. Listen to what I said. No late hits after I cut myself off from the Section."

"You'll have a safe-conduct pass," Hanley said.

"I trust you because you have to trust me. If there is any foul-up after I walk away from the Section, everyone will regret it."

"There won't be anything from us, November."

"Not from you, not from Langley, not from the policemen at NSA. You will have to fix it. For me. And for the woman."

Devereaux said the words slowly, as though he had thought about them for a long time; in fact, the thought came as the words were spoken. It was the only way out for them, the only safe way to escape the trap. She would have to agree with him to be safe; he needed her to be safe. Neither could survive the matter alone.

"Can you guarantee her?"

"Trust me," Devereaux said.

Yes, thought Hanley suddenly. It was the only option left to him.

* * *

Two hours later, Hanley sat across from Mrs. Neumann in her office in Computer Analysis Section. For a long time, he sat silently and then, with slow and careful words, he told her of the conversation with Devereaux in Helsinki.

Mrs. Neumann did not speak.

Once she got up from her desk and went to the closed door of the small windowless office and opened it as though making certain there was still an outside world and that there were still concerns beyond this time and place and the story that Hanley was telling her.

All was calm outside; women were at rows of video display terminals, punching in endless series of code numbers, creating records and retrieving them, upgrading documents and destroying them at the push of the "permanent delete" series of buttons. All was usual; all was in order.

Mrs. Neumann closed the door and looked around her windowless cell. On the back wall was a sampler done in needlework by one of the women in Comp An and presented to her at a Christmas party five years ago. In archaic lettering, the sampler said, GARBAGE IN; GARBAGE OUT.

The sentiment made her frown now. All the information about Helsinki and the prisoner had contained elements of garbage, right from the first lies told the British during the war about the nature of Crohan's mission. Who was lying now?

"Devereaux is right, in a peculiar way," she said at last.

"About what?"

"There's no choice for him. You let him dangle along too long, Hanley—you know that as well as he does. When you were finally ready to tell him what to do, it was too late. He couldn't leave Crohan or whoever that is or the Russian. It was a trap; you thought he was the only one who might be trapped by it. Now he's got you."

"For all I know now, he set up this business with the Macklin woman."

"Do you think so?" Her eyes were sharp and her voice growled. "She did make request for information under the Freedom of Information Act at CIA and they turned her down. Devereaux was already in Helsinki then."

Hanley sighed. "Mere paranoia, Mrs. Neumann, I suppose this problem has too many facets to it."

"There is a moral point," she said.

"Morality? At this late date?"

"Don't be indignant, Hanley. We set up Mr. Crohan during the war and essentially condemned him to death. Now he has a chance to come out and we want to kill him again because he is an embarrassment to an organization long since disbanded—the OSS. We want to kill him to save the reputations of a bunch of ghosts. The moral choice seems clear to me."

"Mrs. Neumann, we are not speaking of morality or ethics; we are talking of practical things."

"Shoes and ships and sealing wax," she said.

"This is not a matter of levity. I will have to cover for him, put my neck under the New Man's ax."

"Everyone is expected to make sacrifices," Mrs. Neumann said.

Hanley was annoyed by her words and her tone. "I don't know what I am going to do."

"Bullshit," she said in her hoarse whisper. "You know exactly what you're going to do and so does November. He's got you, Hanley, and you just want to talk to me about it, have me talk you into doing what you're going to have to do anyway."

"It is still a trap, a Russian trap."

"Not anymore," she said. "A trap only works when it is unexpected."

"I wish this wasn't happening," Hanley said, a child caught in a bad dream.

"You made it happen."

He seemed surprised. "Me? But I never wanted to do anything," Hanley said.

Mrs. Neumann nodded. "Exactly, Hanley. And you waited too long."

28

MOSCOW

Stolinaya knocked at the door of the third director of the Committee for External Observation and Resolution and waited for a response. It was usual for visitors to go through the elaborate security gauntlet through the main entrance but Stolinaya—and a few other privileged bureaucrats inside the Committee—could reach the third director through the back door, as it were.

Stolinaya was director of classification and identification of foreign agents for the Committee. His job was the most creative inside the vast records department because he was the man who decided at last what the enemy was and who he was.

Or, in the present case, who she was.

Stolinaya was a tall, thin man with a bristling black mustache and large, luminous eyes. He was a perfect bureaucrat and a perfect Muscovite: the former description suited his careful, cautious way of dealing in an area where too much creativity could pull suspicion upon him; the latter description suited his easy arrogance, a sense that the Soviet peoples were damned lucky to have Muscovites at all, lest they disintegrate as a union.

There was a muffled response to his knock.

He opened the door and entered the room. The steam pipes were banging up heat; the single window in the large room rattled with the wind and the rhythm of traffic beyond the window.

He sat down at the secretary desk next to the large desk assigned to the third director and opened his files without preliminary remarks. It was the weekly updating of the lists of enemies and a formality in a sense because Stolinaya was a trusted man. Still, the third director took some pleasure in altering the status of the unseen people contained on Stolinaya's list.

"The first is Abdul Raj-Hassadi of Sudan," began Stolinaya in a perfect Moscow accent. He continued the description and then precisely explained why the second deputy of the Ministry of Transport in Sudan was now to be considered a paid espionage agent of Colonel Khaddafi of Libya. The third director listened and then nodded and Stolinaya entered the change of order in the files. Thereafter, until another status change, Abdul Raj-Hassadi would be elevated from the rank of "Bureaucrat/Foreign/No Political Status" to the rank of "Bureacrat/Mole/Intelligence Agent 4th class/Political Status Questioned." Stolinaya had devised the elaborate coding system of the four hundred thousand names of foreign agents and politicians contained in the vast computer files of the Committee; he was proud of them.

"Rita Catherine Macklin," he continued. "Ostensibly an American journalist since 1975. Age thirty. Former employee of the Green Bay Wisconsin *Press-Gazette*, Universal Press Service, Washington, free lance for the *Washington Post* newspaper. During that period, she served as liaison to R Section, American, in the matter of Leo Tunney Case File thirty-four dash nine-nine-eight-two dash seventy-nine C."

"What was that?" the third director said.

Stolinaya handed him a précis of the case printed on a single sheet of paper. For a long moment, the third director read silently and then returned the paper to Stolinaya.

He continued the summary, listing her current employer, and detailing the observation and attempted resolution of her in Helsinki.

"She is working for the American R Section again?" said the third director.

"That is obvious beyond all question," Stolinaya said. "She has access to their secret codes. She telephoned their headquarters from Paris on the instruction of the agent November. She had worked with November three years before. We choose to upgrade her status to 'Journalist/American/Intelligence Agent in deep cover.'"

"That seems reasonable."

Stolinaya frowned. "There is one other matter here and I wish you would consider it."

"Yes?"

"She and the agent November have been *agents provocateurs* twice now, and they have exceeded their normal and expected briefs within R Section. In addition, the agent November has been responsible for the unwilling defection of our agent, Tiomkin, three years ago as well as the uncovering of our mole inside R Section. I request that you consider his name for assasssination."

"And the woman?"

"No, not yet. Her effectiveness seems tied to her operation with him. She is a propagandist at worst; a nuisance."

"But an assassination invites retaliation in kind," the third director said with a frown.

"Two years ago, he retired from the R Section and then rejoined the service. We do not quite understand all the matters but perhaps he will detach himself from the Section again. And its protection."

The third director sighed. He took the paper proferred and placed it face down on his neat, empty desk top. He sighed again. "These matters must be decided at the highest level," he began.

"I understand, Comrade Director."

"For the moment, though, this November is still under the protection of the Service?"

"Yes, Comrade Director."

"Then let us tread carefully," the third director said. "Let us wait and decide if it is worth the retaliation to us to eliminate him."

29

HELSINKI

George had met Ely at the airport in London and given him a final verbal instruction. Ely was frightened of the order.

"I'm certain she's merely a journalist," Ely said.

"Are you really?" George had smiled in his superior way. "My dear Ely, we have made other determinations. She is fouling up our operation, things going on you know nothing about."

"Then why not use someone who understands the reason to max the woman?" Ely said at last.

"Ely, you are existing on sufferance inside Auntie. I hope you understand that plainly. This is not a matter of discussion."

"She's a civilian, George. She told us everything."

"She set up Sparrow in your bedroom, your bloody girlfriend did. You saw him there, Ely, with the top of his head blown off. Who do you suppose arranged that?"

Of course he had to max her. There was never a choice in these matters, not after you received the L Order in your career at Auntie, permitting you to kill in situations other than self-defense. He had killed before, justly or not; he was convinced that killing Rita Macklin was not just. But then, Ely had no choice.

He touched the small Beretta automatic in the pocket of his coat. His hands were cold, the pistol was cold. He had felt depressed on the flight from London to Helsinki, thinking of the woman, thinking of what had happened in Vienna two years before. He had lost his nerve once; this was a second chance and there would not be a third.

He tried to hate Rita Macklin for killing Sparrow but realized he had no feelings of hate or disgust or righteousness. Everything in him was empty.

He rode the silent elevator to the sixth floor. She was registered in a room on the sixth floor of the Presidentii Hotel. He walked down the silent corridor and placed his fingers around the grip of the pistol in his pocket.

George was right, of course; the service could not permit the murder of Sparrow to be unanswered. Yet was she the one who had set up Sparrow? Was she a spy? George was right again. Everything indicated it.

Ely had worn a light coat and it was too cold. His face was blotchy red with the cold. His pale blue eyes were tired. His ginger mustache was not fierce anymore; the ends drooped around his thin mouth. He felt so terribly tired, even sick of the game.

But it was the only game he played.

He flicked off the safety of the automatic and knocked at her door.

Quickly.

He pulled the pistol from his pocket.

The corridor was empty and light.

Maybe she had fled, he thought suddenly. Maybe there was nothing he could do.

The chain rattled on the other side of the door. The handle turned.

He brought the pistol up to the level of his chest.

Quickly. Without pain for her; with only a lingering horror in the aftermath for him.

Rita Macklin opened the door wide. Her face was drawn, pale. She stared at him and the pistol with green, fearful eyes. She trembled.

"I'm sorry, Miss Macklin," he said with politeness that struck him as terribly absurd. He wanted to speak again but she shrank back from him into the narrow hall of the room. He held his pistol in front of him and saw that it trembled.

"My God," she said.

"I'm sorry," he repeated inanely. "I am so sorry."

"You're not sorry yet." The harsh, surging voice came from the side of the hall. He was abreast of the bathroom door and yet Ely could not turn to face the voice because the barrel of a large gun was stuck in his ear. The cold of the metal shocked him.

Without a command, he lowered the pistol even as Rita took another stumbling step back into the room.

"Him," she said with a shaking voice. "The British agent."

"Close the door," Devereaux said. Rita edged around them and pushed the door shut and locked it.

"Why did you come here?" Devereaux said.

"I had to see—"

"No more lies," Devereaux said. "Speak the truth."

"Really. I cannot say anything."

"I'll blow your head off."

"That's melodramatic—"

"Merely true."

"Yes, I suppose so," Ely said sadly, still staring ahead of him, unable to turn toward Devereaux. "It was the method you used in Dublin with Sparrow. You and Miss Macklin. George was right."

"Who is Sparrow?"

"Come now. He's the one you killed in Dublin. In my room."

"So you came to kill Rita."

Ely felt very tired. It was over at least. He was calm. They would kill him in a moment, without words or regret. It was better to die than to have to kill again; better to end this sordid life at the hands of another than to stumble on through with it.

"Yes," he said softly. "I came to kill her. She had killed one of our agents. We can't permit that."

Ely closed his eyes and waited for death.

But the pistol muzzle was pulled away from his ear. He

opened his eyes and blinked. He turned his head and saw the winter-hard face of the man with gray eyes in the doorway of the bathroom.

"Go into the bedroom," Devereaux said. "And sit down. I want to talk to you now, Ely. About Sparrow. And George."

They spoke a long time and the three of them in the small bedroom sat still as they talked and listened. After an hour, Devereaux went to the telephone and made a local call.

Ely sat fascinated as Devereaux spoke first with the operator and then with a second person in stilted Swedish. Devereaux was one of those persons who never forgot a language and acquired basic languages easily; he had been in Sweden nearly fifteen years before, out of Vietnam, on a matter involving a traitor who had taken refuge there. Devereaux spoke nine languages and dialects with more or less fluency—his best was French, acquired in Vietnam, and Vietnamese patois. In his long winter of isolation in Helsinki, Devereaux had learned that nearly all Finns could speak Swedish, though some reluctantly.

When the call was finished, he turned back to Rita and Ely.

"The old man is here." It was the last secret revealed among the three of them; they were spies stripped of secrets now because their own survivals required an alliance.

"You saw him," Rita said.

"Yes. As long as I have Tartakoff on hold, there probably won't be a problem. I think they wanted the old man out in any case." He wrote something down on a sheet of paper. "This is where they put the old man." He gave it to Rita.

She stared at the paper and then at Devereaux. She did not speak but her eyes held the question.

"Ely and I will have to wait here now."

"What am I supposed to do?" she said.

"Get out of Helsinki now. Quickly. Don't use the airport. It's become a shuttle for spies in the past few days. The *Finlan-*

dia sails tonight at six for Stockholm. You and the old man will be on board. He's an American now; here's his passport. Get on board and stay away from the public rooms until the ship sails."

"Are you going to meet us?"

He smiled at her. "I suppose so. If everything works."

"Why do you have to stay?"

"Tartakoff is in my room at the moment. That's part of the deal. I'm the messenger boy and I take him out when everything is set with the old man. Our British friend here has complicated the matter somewhat but I can use him now."

Ely said nothing.

"And if it doesn't work out?"

"Oh, you of little faith," Devereaux said, and he was smiling. Rita glared at him but the mocking smile played lightly on his thin lips and doused her anger in a moment.

"Will he come with me?"

"If not, hit him."

"Dev."

"Rita, he's a prisoner, a lifer." His words turned easily into rougher usage. "If you said squat to him, he'd ask you how many times. He has nowhere to go unless he is told to go somewhere. Get him now while I occupy Tartakoff. Before other matters interrupt us."

"What about him?" she said.

"Tartakoff? He'll be taken care of."

Ely suddenly exploded: "Why are you saying these things in front of me?"

"Because the only way you are going to survive is to do what I tell you," Devereaux said. "You have to understand the game and the trap. When you get to Stockholm—" He turned to Rita. "Here is a name and address. Use it the second day, if I don't arrive. It's a safe house."

"She is a spy," Ely said.

"No, Ely. You were wrong and George was wrong." He turned to look at Rita sitting on the edge of the bed. "She was caught in the trap." He spoke softly as though he did not see her in that moment. "Like you, Ely. Nothing was as it seemed." He glanced up. "Get going."

"I don't understand why you have to stay if I have the old man," she said.

"To close the back door," Devereaux said. "I have to wash the dishes and lock the place. The hall was only rented for the night."

Nine minutes later, Ely and Devereaux entered Devereaux's room on the fourth floor. Ely had the sense of a drama rushing to a conclusion; it was the last act.

Devereaux felt only a sense of release. The room had been his tomb for a long, dead winter and now it was opened.

Ely had been relieved of his Beretta; trust did not extend to weapons between them.

Tartakoff was at the window staring into the cavity of the construction pit across the street where Natali's naked, frozen body had been found. He turned as they entered. His eyes widened angrily when he saw Ely in front of Devereaux.

And then he saw the pistol in Devereaux's hand.

He started to make a move and then stopped.

"What do you mean by this, Messenger?"

"Sit down, Tartakoff. There. Take that chair."

"It is after five. The ship leaves for Stockholm in—"

"Sit down."

Devereaux took a step past Ely. He stood in front of Tartakoff and saw the flicker of a movement of Tartakoff's hand. Without seeming effort, Devereaux slapped the Russian across the cheek with the pistol barrel. The blow cut a line of blood across his face. The Russian took a step back and Devereaux pushed him into the chair. The muzzle of the pistol was pressed against his cheek.

Devereaux reached down into the Russian's coat pocket and pulled out a large automatic weapon which was a sort of pistol modified from a Uzi submachine gun.

"Rather large to get through Customs," Devereaux said. "How did you manage it?" He smiled and pulled out the banana clip and threw both pieces on the floor. "Sit there, Ely."

"We are going to miss the boat," Tartakoff said, his voice rising.

"Exactly," Devereaux said.

"Messenger, you have no authority."

Devereaux pressed the pistol muzzle against the hollow of Tartakoff's cheek until it rested against his teeth, insulated by the Russian's skin.

"You are a dead man, Russian. How did you get the pistol through Customs? Why did you need it here?"

"I smuggled—"

"You are a liar, Russian. You are a fucking dirty liar." Each word dropped slowly, like stones in a still pond. "You lied from the first meeting."

Tartakoff did not speak. His eyes stared wildly at the gray man in front of him.

"It was a trap, Russian."

"I am a defector. How is this a trap?"

"You were a triple. One of them who would become one of us but still be one of them. A matter of disinformation to begin with; then, later, you would become a mole."

"This is not true."

"Russians play a clumsy game because there are always killings," Devereaux said in the same slow voice. "Everyone who would interfere with me was taken care of. The messenger had to be protected, had to be left alone. Your people killed the prostitute because she had slept with me and with the British agent. You were afraid of her because you could not believe she was only a simple prostitute. But it was all she was. Your people killed the British agent in the sauna. When the cop, Kulak, came to arrest me because of your clumsy killings, he was called off. You people can do that in Finland, can't you? You killed the priest in Ireland because he knew too much about Tomas Crohan; maybe he would contradict whatever your candidate for Tomas Crohan wants to say. Killing and killing and killing and all of it wrong, all of it clumsy, all of it making no sense. You probably killed the British agent Sparrow because he was the wrong man. Maybe you wanted to kill Ely. Nothing could interfere with me or with the trap or with getting Tomas Crohan out of your country. And now, this morning, a dirty little dago named Antonio was going to kill Rita Macklin in Stockmann's because you were afraid that she was a spy, not a journalist, and that she would spring the trap the wrong way. You were afraid that we would eliminate Tomas Crohan before he said whatever he was supposed to say. That makes me angry because up to that moment, she was not involved in the game at all. She wasn't an agent but you made her an agent and now she has to play like we play our games. Do you understand why you're a dead man, Russian?"

Sweat beaded on Tartakoff's flushed face. "You cannot kill me. I am still a defector, I have many things I can tell you—"

"Tell me."

"You promise me sanctuary—"

"Promises are past. Tell me things."

"Please, the pistol hurts me—"

"Only for a moment, Russian. The bullets contain soft, crossed heads. They will explode on impact and part of them will tear the roof of your mouth away and explode your brain. Others will blow out the back of your neck and your skull. You understand me, Russian; you've killed a few people in your time."

Devereaux's face had become absolute winter, absolute ice and cold. His eyes were clear Arctic fields of ice; his lined face was the terror of a white winter sky.

Ely did not move; no one moved for a moment.

"I was not to defect," Tartakoff said.

"That's a lie. You were a triple and you have a fall-back if you see the trap won't work.

"I know about the old man."

"Tell me."

"I cannot tell you. I need an assurance."

"I can only assure you that you are a dead man, Russian."

"Tomas Crohan is the man you sent to Austria in the war. An American spy," said the Russian.

"I know that."

Tartakoff's eyes widened. "Then why do you not say this before?"

"I'm tired of you, Russian."

Devereaux pulled the trigger.

Click.

The Russian shuddered. "One empty chamber. It is a precaution. The next chamber is live. You know it is live."

"My God, you are going to kill me."

"You are dead already."

"What can I tell you?"

"The truth."

"I—"

"Tell me about the British. Tell me how you manipulated them so well."

"I don't know what you're saying."

"The mole," Devereaux said softly. Ely's eyes widened now in fascination. He sat bolt upright on the edge of the chair.

"The mole."

"Don't repeat what I said, Russian. Tell me what I don't know. It is the only part I don't understand. How did you manipulate the British? How did they keep dogging my steps? Why did this British agent think that Rita Macklin was part of our operation? Why was there a Brit in Helsinki in the first place? I can understand the killings of the British agents if I can believe there is a mole. Somehow, you and Crohan and whatever story you're putting together is supposed to drive some wedge between us. Mutual mistrust. Your disinformation is supposed to accomplish it."

"I don't know of a mole—"

"That is a lie, Russian. There has to be one. None of this could work if someone on the inside in British Intelligence had not set it all in motion. How did the British suddenly, randomly, tap into our message center in Stockholm when I made an inquiry about Crohan? I didn't know who Crohan was, but you people did. And you made certain the British knew as well. Who is the mole?"

But the Russian did not answer; it was Ely. In a surprised voice, he blurted a name: "George."

The Russian paled. He shook his head suddenly.

"George," said Ely again. "That's it, isn't it?"

Devereaux stared at Tartakoff. "Speak for the last time in your life."

"Yes," Tartakoff said at last. "George."

Tension exploded out of the room like a burst balloon. Devereaux removed the pistol from Tartakoff's cheek; it left an impression against the skin, angry and red.

"Who is George really?" Devereaux said, not to the Russian.

"It's the only thing that makes sense," Ely said in a wondering tone. "He told me Rita Macklin was the agent who had set up Sparrow. You and her. He used me."

"He used everyone."

"But he must have known I would fail."

Devereaux did not speak.

"Used like that," Ely said.

"Crohan was the important link then, wasn't he, Russian?"

The Russian only stared at Devereaux's gun and did not speak.

"What were you?"

"I was not important," Tartakoff said.

"Crohan was not the bait for the trap. You were the bait. Crohan was going to make the trap work."

"Yes."

"And then you were going to kill him. Or see the job done. So that the story would not be confused in anyone's mind. Crohan would say whatever he was going to say and then you'd see him dead. Or me. Or Rita. Or all of us. And then you would still have the option to play the defector or return to the Soviet Union."

The Russian shrugged; something like a smile returned to the arrogant features. The pistol in Devereaux's hand did not frighten him now.

"Who is George?" Devereaux asked Ely again.

"The man in charge of computer division in Auntie. He is the British commander at Cheltenham."

"A nice base for traitors," Devereaux said.

Tartakoff made a sudden move for the pistol. Devereaux waited for it almost as a cat waits for the mouse to dart across the floor. He slapped him lazily with the pistol through a high arc that cracked against his cheek again. Tartakoff slumped back in the chair.

"Be still, Russian," Devereaux said. "George. Now do you see, Ely?"

"Yes," Ely replied. "Not all of it, but I see enough."

"And now we take care of the Russian."

"What are you going to do?" Tartakoff said.

"Should I send you back to Russia? That wouldn't be pleasant for you."

Tartakoff did not speak. He saw the horror of his choices; there were no choices left to him. The careful trap had been handled clumsily and now it had sprung on him.

"Or you can defect," said Devereaux.

There was a knock at the door.

Devereaux said "enter" in Swedish.

A short man with a bull neck and black eyes stood in the hall. He came into the room.

"Inspector Kulak," Devereaux said to the Russian and Ely.

"Well, Mr. Devereaux, are you at last going to tell me what has really happened?"

"Of course," Devereaux said. "Sit down. It makes a good story. All about spies and killings and mistakes made. You had your murderer today, but this is the man behind the murderer. Sit down. It's a long story and you might get lost in it, but we have time now to make everything clear."

30

LONDON

The man who was called George entered the apartment building located three blocks off Trafalgar Square in the noisy, brassy heart of the West End. He had followed all the usual precautions, including the routine double-back with two cabs, the aimless Underground trip on the Baker-Loo Line and the final walk from the station at Piccadilly Circus down the crowded streets to Trafalgar.

George was a man at home with subterfuge because he had been successful at the game during a sometimes-brilliant twenty-seven-year career with British Intelligence.

Not to mention his fifteen-year career as an "exterior officer" with the rank of colonel in the Soviet Committee for State Security.

The two roles had never seemed at odds to him and he had not been discomforted by them until the new spy scandals of the past two years. The belated discovery of a double agent at Cheltenham—under his nose, as it were—in 1982 had troubled him. Not because he was unaware that the traitor named Prine was also passing secrets to the Soviet Union but because the discovery had focused too much attention on what had always been a secure little fiefdom where he could routinely pass on information to Moscow or tap into the Americans who also utilized the center and still enjoy the comfortable respect of his colleagues without fear that any of them would tumble to his secret. A secret life was best lived openly, George had always felt.

"What is it you finally want from us, George?" he had once been asked by a high-ranking member of the KGB who later became an undersecretary to Andropov.

"Nothing. Nothing at all."

The answer had troubled the Russian; George's charming vagueness had always troubled them. They felt they had trapped George into working for them fifteen years before but, in fact, it had not been their trap at all. George had gladly become a mole inside Auntie for a simple reason the Russians would not have understood: Boredom.

He had been bored all his life.

He had been born to privilege. Privilege had eased his life, though ease had not been comfortable to him. From the nursery with the mothering care of Nanny and the servants through a brilliant and lackadaisical career at Oxford, George had expected doors to be opened to him by faceless people, and it had always been so.

He had never married because sex was a relief from boredom and marriage would have smothered that. He had experimented with homosexuality and found it wanting because it was too respectable to be a homosexual in his class. He had developed several affairs over the years and enjoyed balancing the women in his life against each other, making certain each was contained in a compartment of his own making; he enjoyed the thought that someday he might be caught out by one or another of his mistresses.

He felt contempt for his class, for its indolence and arrogance and leisure; but he had felt the same measure of contempt for the little strivers who by dint of examination and hard work and good luck were his colleagues at Oxford. "Napoleon was right," he once said on a late evening, drinking brandy and smoking cigars with those school chums he permitted to be intimate with him: "We are a nation of shopkeepers, but the description does not go far enough. The baseness of the middle class has been bred into our class and we now are forced to admire the shopkeeper for his industry and thrift even when we, and the shopkeeper, know both values to be fraudulent. There is nothing left to strive for, but we make a great show of striving; there is no goal worthy of the sacrifice, but we regularly parade our rededication to those goals."

No. The Russians could not understand him and they were always uncomfortable with him. Though George did not know it, an investigation had been held ten years previously to determine if George were actually a triple agent—one who worked for the British, seemed to work for the Russians as a double, but actually remained on the British payroll. If George had known it, he would have been amused. The game was all that mattered to him, the few moments of terror at the thought of being caught, the sense of thrills.

"Will you come to Moscow at the end of the game?" the Russian had asked.

"No, my God, man, I couldn't stand it. London is my home and I'm comfortable with it. In five years' time, I shall retire from Her Majesty's Service—and I suppose, from your service—and be settled in my ancestral estate near Canterbury. That will be my crisis; to live out the remainder of my days in the perfect peace of absolute boredom."

"What will you do?"

"I shall probably go out some morning to shoot birds and find it convenient to place the muzzle of the shotgun in my mouth and blow my head off," George had said pleasantly.

George had somewhat enjoyed the previous forty-eight hours because the game had become very dangerous now, very filled with the terror that energized him. Matters had come unglued and that is why he had been summoned to the house three blocks off Trafalgar Square.

The man who waited for him inside the safe house—for that is what it was—was called Latvia (though that was only a false name) and he had met the man called George twice before—in Nice, during the previous summer, and once in Liverpool, during the hastily called conference when George had been fully briefed on the KGB plan to move Tomas Crohan out of the Soviet Union.

George was the key to the success of the plan and far too intelligent to take part in it without understanding all the elements of the scheme.

But the scheme now had apparently failed. The only option left was to save George at any cost. He was too valuable as a mole.

George knew this; he had not feared the summons.

He was also arrogantly certain he would survive this latest flap.

"Why?" asked the Russian named Latvia as they sat down at a bare table in a bare room over cups of steaming tea. "Why will this not affect you?"

"Affect me?" George raised his eyebrows, his fierce blue eyes glaring triumphantly at the sullen face of the Russian. "Of course it will affect me. But it shall not deter me, and that is all the difference."

"Tartakoff has defected."

"I doubt that very much. I believe he was forced to the defection by the American agents at Helsinki, this Macklin woman and November. You people have made too many blunders in this matter. This man, Antonio, for example; wherever did you drag him up?"

"Loyalty and precision are the requisites of a hit man," the Russian said, slipping into a mix of English and American argot. "One hardly expects a hit man to be normal in all other respects."

"Yes, but he was dreadful. I suspect that Tartakoff was moved out of Helsinki with special help, probably from that police inspector who became involved in the murders."

"So we all suspect," the Russian said. "There is no proof of this. You cannot push the Finns too far."

"As your people have learned," George said, smiling, and lighting a Panter Mignon. "But—to cases. What is it you expect to happen?"

"Tartakoff has told them everything."

"And that includes telling them about me?"

"Yes."

"That was careless of you, old fellow." He inhaled the mild cigar and let the smoke filter slowly into the still, damp air of the room.

"Tartakoff was as essential as you were, George. He was in on the planning from the beginning of the operation." The Russian frowned and picked up his cup and took a sip of the scalding liquid.

"How can you drink that without milk?"

"I do not like milk," the Russian said.

"So the problem is: What will we do with George?"

"That is the problem," the Russian said.

"You will do nothing with me, old fellow, because nothing will happen to me."

"But the Americans have Tomas Crohan—"

"They shall do nothing," George said with a smile. "You see, Latvia, none of us understood at first that we were really double-crossing each other. From the beginning, in the war. And I doubt seriously that we need to drag up this matter at this late date."

"What do you mean?"

"Forty-eight hours have elapsed since Tartakoff was packed off to America. Accompanied, I might add, by our former British agent, Ely. I wonder what they will make of him? The trouble with the Americans is they can clean up the loose ends because they have so damned much money. Ely will doubtless find a new and sensible life as an orange-grower in California or some other equally dreadful place. But Tartakoff. Now he is an important defector, albeit a reluctant one. He alleges that I am a mole and he alleges that I was part of this plan to drive the wedge between ourselves and our American cousins. Particularly at Cheltenham. Very well. What will the Americans do with this information?"

"They have Tomas Crohan."

"You keep insisting on that and they do not. He has not reappeared since the American woman took him out of Helsinki."

The Russian seemed puzzled; he stared at his teacup.

George smiled again and waved the cigar in illustration of what he was saying. "We sent in Michael Brent to murder Tomas Crohan in Vienna in 1945. Crohan had been abandoned by the Americans, though God knows he may still have clung to the tired promise that the Americans would give him the Irish government after the war. We could not tolerate Crohan from the standpoint of our own security. So Brent was sent to kill him, which Brent did quite well."

He paused and puffed the little cigar. "How unfortunate for Brent. He really became quite expendable after that. Not that he wasn't loyal, but we do not make the same mistakes in hiring our assassins that you do. We sent the Russians a message that Tomas Crohan—who had a new life in the guise of Michael Brent—was an American spy and your admirable army did the rest for us when they entered Austria."

The Russian frowned again, by way of concentration. George was enjoying himself.

"Let us look at the American problem, old man. It seems certain they did not want to see Crohan emerge from Austria after the war either, after allowing him to dangle there for two years. They were quite relieved the Russians arrested him."

"We discovered that he was an American spy."

"Did they let you discover that?" He waved the cigar again. "Let it go. In any event, there were protests after the war from Ireland, from the Crohan family, from some of the State Department people in the United States who had arranged the fiasco. Some in the OSS were upset as well because everyone thought that Crohan was alive.

"Well, darling, what could we tell our American cousins? That we had solved their problem by killing Crohan ourselves?

"So the OSS did a quite clever thing, or so they thought. They let leak to you evidence that Crohan was a Nazi collaborator. Pictures of him with Hitler before the war; faked documents to show that he had been working hand-in-glove with the Nazis during the war. That is why he was in Vienna. But the evidence was puzzling because the man you had was obviously not Crohan. So you waited and the Americans thought you had fallen for their trick and we, of course, were satisfied to hear the last of the matter. My God, we thought we were all fooling each other." George laughed then, a deep, rumbling chuckle that ended in a fit of coughing. He put down the cigar and reached for the cup of tea laced with milk.

"We did not know who this man was, not for two years after the war."

"Of course. He was a bloody British agent. If he kept silent, assumed still Crohan's identity, he thought he had a chance of being released eventually. He was an Irish neutral, after all. A British agent would never have gotten out of your admirable prison network."

"In 1947, he identified himself. He protested that he was Michael Brent."

"And by that time, you didn't believe him."

"No."

"Aided by the fact that we sent unofficial word to you that we had no agent named Michael Brent. His file was expunged. It wasn't so terribly difficult; unlike Crohan, he had no family and no one mourned his disappearance."

Silence filled the bare room for a moment like a third person. The two men waited for words to return.

"Tartakoff was to accompany the prisoner long enough to tell his story to the American journalist—"

"His story of being Tomas Crohan—"

"And then Tartakoff would have killed him."

"And the American agent if necessary, the messenger in Helsinki."

"And Ely was going to be held responsible for the murder."

"Yes. As the Americans say so colorfully, framed. Because Her Majesty's government knew the truth about Michael Brent."

"We conditioned Crohan for a year at Kresty Hospital. He could not live without the pills."

"After forty years, we call him Crohan when we know he is not. I suppose he actually believes at times that he is Crohan. He has lived in that dead man's skin for so long."

"But the trap is sprung and empty."

"Yes. Too bad." Again, he reached for the cigar. It had gone out. He fumbled for his lighter. "A lot of work, that. Too bad. But do you see, my dear fellow? Even if I am implicated by the Russian, what good is his charge? If I am vetted by Auntie, I shall come through with flying colors. I am in charge of Computer Section, after all; I am the man who controls Seeker and I know what my records say about me. They are spotless, full of commendations. If it is necessary, we will bring up the matter of Bluebird to the P.M. We handled that rather well, it reflects well on me, considering our people kidnapped the poor darling themselves." George smiled again. "Poor old Wickham. But when we have thrown Wickham to the wolves, they will be satisfied and, in a half year's time, I shall be as unassailable as I have always been inside Auntie. Don't forget the case of American cooperation with us—the Yanks want us to handle their missile bases, they need British support to keep NATO from collapsing. It is not in their best interest to raise doubts of Her Majesty's Secret Service based on the ramblings of a Soviet defector who may or may not have any solid information. Even if the old man makes it back to the U.S., which I seriously doubt, who is he and why will his voice be heard?"

"The journalist?"

"This Macklin woman? She's a spy, Latvia, for the love of God; she's under her own orders."

"Can we be certain?"

"Nothing is certain." George paused. "Uncertainty is the only interesting proposition left to us."

"But the Americans will suspect you."

"The Americans suspected Philby from 1948 on and not a damned thing was done about it. The Americans suspect a lot of people but getting proof is something else, and Tartakoff is no proof. Her Majesty's government is rather prickly on the subject of internal affairs; we do not wish to be told how to manage our affairs by the Americans. No, Latvia, nothing will happen because no one wants the embarrassment of the secrets of Tomas Crohan or Michael Brent—not you, not us, not the Americans. None of us."

And George was absolutely right.

31

STOCKHOLM

The sun lay low in the west. The light of the sun danced on the copper steeples poking above the massive buildings huddled on the islands of the city. The city lay in a frozen mosaic of stone that stretched clearly into the gray Baltic beyond.

Devereaux and Rita Macklin made love.

The blinds were thrown up to catch the last of the light falling gently into the large, quiet hotel room. Next door, in a locked room, the old man slept. As the ferry from Finland had approached Stockholm harbor, the old man suddenly in tears had confessed to Rita that he was Michael Brent, not Tomas Crohan. The story had thrilled her but depressed Devereaux.

The old man's story seemed to doom them, Devereaux thought. Every side would be turned against them. But Devereaux said none of these things to Rita when they were finally alone. He still had silences but she had shattered his coldness. Devereaux realized he loved her. It was absurd but but it was true.

He kissed her breasts gently. He licked them. He kissed her mouth. He held her in the hollow of his body and arms. He warmed her as he felt the warmth of holding her seep slowly into the icy crevices of his own feeling. He made love to her as though she were as fragile as a glass angel; he loved her slowly; when she spoke, once, he held his hand over her mouth because he hated words. Words glossed every real thing with brittle artifice and deceit. Words were always lies, always intended to deceive even when they held the truth; the truth of things was in not speaking, was in touching and not telling.

When they were finished, they lay back on the bed, side by side, their arms extended and their hands touching but their bodies apart from each other. They were like exhausted survivors of some shipwreck washed up on a foreign shore. They stared at the ceiling and the last light of afternoon colored the room with shades of gold.

"What are we going to do?" she asked at last. She might have been asking the question for herself or for the sake of the old man in the next room; the question might have had many answers due it.

"I don't know. Wait."

"This is a helluva story in case I haven't mentioned that."

He did not look at her. He stared at a spot on the ceiling that was not like any other spot. He stared until he actually did not see the spot but was in a trance; he had the trick of travelers and spies to induce a trance to escape the constraints of time passing. It was also the trick of prisoners who survived.

"Is it?"

"When I first met you, Dev, you pretended to be a newspaperman. At least pretend now to see the possibility that someone named Michael Brent went in from British Intelligence to kill one of our agents who happened to be an Irishman named Crohan. You haven't heard that story lately."

"There's no proof,"

"I'm not a lawyer, I'm a journalist. Besides, isn't that old man proof sitting there in that room?"

"No." The cold eyes did not see; the cold voice fell flatly between them. "The only thing he can prove is how to get us killed. He's a loose cannon, Rita. The British must want him dead, the Russians certainly want him dead. For all I know, so do we."

"Why did they let him out?"

"It was a trap from the beginning. I don't have proof either, but there has to be some logic to this. The priest in Dublin; he must have been prodded into making contact with the old woman in Chicago. Maybe a letter or photograph or something dropped on him by the Opposition. She contacts a journalist and that is not coincidence either; she was a friend of the publisher of your magazine. You pursue the story and become intrigued when the old priest is killed. All of it was so subtle and yet so clumsy."

"What are you talking about?"

He turned and looked at her. They were naked. Her body was lean and unmarked; his was lean and pale and marked with wounds. Her face was soft, he thought, though it was not; he merely saw the golden light falling on it. Her red hair framed the paleness of her face and he thought she seemed so young it was only that he felt himself so old. Her green eyes held his simply and without aversion. He touched her hair with a clumsy hand, unaccustomed to caresses. "Rita Macklin would write an investigative piece of journalism that would thumb its nose at the evil and corruption in the American espionage establishment. At the same time, the government would be embarrassed and would ask embarrassing questions of the British when it was discovered the old man was not Tomas Crohan. Perhaps they were going to kill him after he talked to you; perhaps the Russians were playing the British side at the same time, exciting their suspicions of an American plot to discredit them. Paranoia is the coin of the business; it could be spent both ways. What did they want with all this? To destroy Cheltenham, I suppose, to make it too difficult for the Americans and the English to work with each other in trust anymore. Maybe that's why Sims was in Helsinki and maybe that is why the prostitute was killed. She didn't know she was a danger to the Russians because she had slept with me and with Sims."

Rita turned away from his touch. She stared at the wall opposite him.

"Why did you sleep with her?"

He stared at her back and smiled at her, with affection and yet with a sort of mocking look in his gray eyes. "Because I was tired. Because I wanted to make love."

"That wasn't love."

"Rita, be still."

"No. I love you. I told you. You never needed anyone else."

He said nothing.

She turned suddenly and looked at him. Her green eyes were burning bright in the sunlight low in the sky. "Did you hear what I said?"

"Is this a test?" Gently, mocking.

"No, goddamn you, there isn't any test. Fuck you."

He said nothing.

"Damn you. What moves you? What makes you feel? What makes you cry or get mad or anything?"

"You."

"What?"

The trance was broken, he realized. What he had said to Hanley would now come true. He did not feel any emotion but release, as though everything he felt had been dammed up by his silence.

"I love you, Rita," Devereaux said for the first time and they both knew that was all they had waited for, that a few words had committed both of them to some uncertain future. He had meant it when he told Hanley he would quit this time and he had mentioned Rita as part of it only to protect her from the wrath of the Section; at least, that is what he thought at the time.

She reached for him then. She held his face in her soft hands and kissed him softly and they moved together, touching and holding each other. The light finally fell away beneath the buildings and the sky turned purple; clouds streaked across the horizon of the Baltic but they did not see them. In the dusk, they held each other. "I would do anything for you," she said. He knew it was true and it frightened him.

What could he say to her now?

"I was afraid," she said. "When that man followed me . . . when he tried to kill me. I was afraid for a moment that you had sent him. I have to tell you that."

"No," he said. "You don't have to tell me anything. I won't tell you anything. I have secrets and you will never know them. I don't want your secrets."

"Don't we have to understand each other?"

"No." He kissed her to silence. "No. No words. No secrets. No betrayals. I didn't want you, Rita. I didn't want to see you again. Once I could send you away; I can't send you away again."

"What are you going to do?"

"Get rid of this thing. I have a promise from Hanley. I'm quitting the Section."

"I thought it was the only thing that kept you alive."

"It was."

"Will he do it? Will he let you quit?"

"Yes."

"Why do you believe him?"

"Because the alternative isn't acceptable, to him or to me."

"How can you resolve this?"

"Do nothing," he said. "You will tell the story of Tomas Crohan and it won't be a secret anymore. There is one other matter."

"What?"

"George."

"The British agent?"

"Yes. That's part of the story you can't tell."

"Why not?"

"Because then they could never let us alone," Devereaux said. "Tell what you have with the old man and let the rest of it alone."

"I'm a newspaperman," she said. "I'm not a goddamn spook. I don't start changing the way the story is told to suit myself. . . ." She paused in her outburst as suddenly as she had started speaking. *My God, it isn't true anymore, is it? This changes all the rules for me as well as him.*

"You are what people think you are, Rita," he said with gentleness. "George thinks you're a spy, by now, I'm sure of it. Who else does? Antonio did."

"I would do anything for you."

He smiled. "Even betray all your journalism ethics."

Her face was grave. "I would do anything. Lie or steal or even kill for you."

"How fierce you are," he said, again in a voice of peculiar gentleness. His tone was still flat, his words were without emphasis, and yet he spoke as a child speaks describing a wonderful thing and uncertain how to frame it in words. "I love you." And they suddenly came together without any more words between them. She touched his body and let her fingers follow down his belly and when she bent to kiss him there and there, he touched her hair again and held her head in his hands and said her name again. He opened her legs and lay in her lap and they made love again as dusk turned into the cold night of Stockholm beyond their windows.

Rita slept next to him, on her belly, her head buried in pillows. She slept like a child, deeply and trustingly. She was naked and he could see the ribs of her back as her body rose and fell, rose and fell with heavy breaths. For a long time, in the glitter of moonlight pouring through the window, Devereaux sat in bed and watched her sleeping.

He had always counted on his own survival as the goal of life, from Vietnam to here. There had been a thousand hotel rooms in the twenty years, a thousand places like this one. He had known women when he wanted them and taken little pleasures like a priest sipping brandy on Sunday; but he had stayed apart from the world, from its attachments. He had chosen to be a stranger because it was the only way to survive.

"*I know what you are. You're a goddamn spook, a spy.*" She had said it to him once in her curious tough, little-girl way, her slight overbite making her aggressive face seem more threatening but, at the same time, not really a threat; she was a make-believe bully who might be tough.

Yes, he thought, Was she tough enough?

Did he believe Hanley?

No. Not at all. But the time to survive was over for him, he realized. It meant nothing to him if there was nothing left to survive for. Devereaux realized that he was afraid of Rita Macklin because she had offered herself to him a second time and if he had refused her again, then it would all be ended for him. An odd fate had given him a second chance and he had instinctively seized it, enmeshing her in the assignment until she could no longer be extricated. Until she could no longer leave him.

But what would happen a month from now or a year from now, when she had lived with him and slept with him and found that it was not enough for her? He was afraid of that as well. But then, he had been afraid before and he had lived with the fear without reward, except for survival. This was something more.

Devereaux watched the old man eat. It was morning and Rita still slept in her room, but Devereaux had taken the old man downstairs to a restaurant in the hotel. The restaurant was decorated with green plants and with its huge windows it resembled a sort of greenhouse shut down by winter. A blustery morning buffeted the solemn city beyond the large plate-glass windows. The windows were coated with frost.

Again, the old man ate eggs as he had on the *Finlandia*, but this time, he had reduced their numbers because he had eaten too many before. He ate two eggs and ate them with relish, as though eggs were not a common thing.

"What story are you going to tell Rita Macklin?" Devereaux said. A cup of coffee smoldered in front of him but he did not eat. Devereaux ate only for fuel and only when his body demanded it; he took no pleasure in food.

"About Tomas Crohan?"

Devereaux waited.

The old man had egg yolk on his lips. He sucked his lips and the smear disappeared. He licked his lips with his thin tongue. His thin throat was all movement as he ate—adam's apple bobbing, lines of muscles quivering as he swallowed.

"I was supposed to tell you the truth as though I were Tomas Crohan. Those were my instructions. The truth in any case, except I am not Tomas Crohan."

"And what will you do now?"

"Do you think I should eat another egg?"

Devereaux stared at him and did not speak.

"Cheese," the old man said. "I could have cheese and fruit. Even in winter, look at this fruit."

The old man snatched an apple and bit into it. He reached for a plate of cheese on the table and shoved a piece in his mouth even as he slowly injested the apple. His eyes were sad suddenly, misted as the windows misted.

"A man could kill for a meal such as this in the camps. In Siberia. Do you know that?"

"Is it the truth?"

"Yes. We are all beasts if survival demands it."

Devereaux stared at the plate of food and tried to comprehend the idea of starving men fighting each other to death for these scraps.

"When I was a young man, Citizen Comrade, I thought the world contained at least a few absolutes. There was good somewhere and evil, certainly. And there was freedom. But now I am old and very wise." The old man smiled.

"You are free now," Devereaux said.

"No. You do not mind if I contradict you." The old man tore a piece of black bread with his yellow teeth. "I am not free and you know it. The prison has just gotten larger. You want to take me to Dublin where I will be put in another jail because I am Michael Brent who killed their Tomas Crohan in 1944. Why did I kill him? Because I was so certain of good and evil. I was an agent and I would kill for King and Country and Crohan must be killed for the safety of the nation. Hah." He dropped the bread and reached for a second apple.

His eyes glistened. "I would kill a man for a piece of bread in Siberia and that was more important than killing a man to save my native land. Do you see what a fraud everything is?"

Devereaux waited without prodding. His hands rested on the table in front of him. The coffee was not touched.

"Such a waste of life. Look at my life, sir. My whole life is gone. You see, there are tears in my eyes. I can still cry for myself because who else will cry for me? My whole life is nearly ended and I was a prisoner for so long; and now there is still no freedom for me or peace."

"Who are you?" Devereaux said at last. The old man seemed surprised.

"I told you, sir. I am Michael Brent."

"No," Devereaux said.

The old man stared at him.

"You are Tomas Crohan."

"I killed him."

"No. For thirty-eight years, you have been Tomas Crohan. You have lived the life you took."

"But who will believe that?"

"I do. Who won't believe it? It is mostly the truth except for the first fact; it is probably more of the truth than most stories have. The English will believe it because they cannot contradict it. The Russians will believe it. Anyone who could contradict it is dead, even the old woman in America who is so sure you are alive will believe you are alive if you tell her it's true. There was no British double cross; you were Tomas Crohan who went on a mission of mercy for the Americans in the war. You went into Vienna to save Jews and when you found they were dead, you were trapped in Vienna and eventually imprisoned by the Russians."

"Why did they release me?"

Devereaux smiled. The old man was smart enough to want to grasp the lie Devereaux told him. It would work out.

"I don't know," Devereaux said. "Perhaps you escaped."

"I could not escape."

"We can suggest that Tartakoff took you out when he defected. Maybe that would be the best way."

"Where is he?"

"In Washington now, getting the first debriefing from the Section. He will agree with anything you tell the reporter, believe me."

"But you know the truth. And Miss Macklin, she knows the truth."

"Yes. Some secrets can't be helped."

The old man tore another piece of bread. "It is a secret then?"

"Yes."

"And the woman agrees with you?"

Devereaux did not hesitate: "Yes."

"Why?"

"That is my secret."

"What did my country do to me? Should I not take revenge on them if this is so important?"

"Do you feel the need for revenge?"

"For a long time I did." He paused. "It kept me alive. They abandoned me."

"No. They betrayed you."

"Yes. There is a difference, I suppose. It took me a long time to understand what they did to me. Why shouldn't I take revenge now on them and tell the truth about what they did to me?"

"Who cares?"

The old man looked up sharply at the man with the wintery face across the table from him.

"I care. I bled. I suffered."

"And now you will die if you want to take revenge. Your 'truth' leads to death or more prison for you; my 'truth' will set you free."

"But I feel it, sir. I am a man. I am a man."

"All right." Devereaux finally tasted the coffee and made a face. He put the cup down. "I'll take care of your revenge. You take care of your survival."

"I do not understand all of this," the old man said. "Should I choose to trust you, sir?"

The old man looked up slyly; it was the sidelong look of the eternal prisoner, always under scrutiny and yet surviving because he kept his strength hidden from those would make him weak.

"Yes, Tomas. This matter was not of my making or yours, and now we are both in the middle of it. And Rita Macklin as well. I don't have any choice and neither do you."

"Then we are both prisoners, sir," the old man said.

Devereaux did not speak.

"But it is a larger prison than the one I came from," the old man said. "Yes. I will do as you say."

32

MOSCOW

Stolinaya was not accustomed to being summoned by the man who was Gogol, the operations officer in charge of that section of the KGB called the Committee for External Observation and Resolution. It had never happened before in these circumstances.

Gogol was a small man with Asian features and he sat behind an immense desk in a windowless room framed with immense General Electric air conditioners. They were operating at the moment though the temperature outside the building was twenty-two degrees; the heating system was so erratic that the air conditioners were needed to offset the steady rush of heat that permeated the building.

Gogol had been given Stolinaya's reports on the Helsinki incident and on the classification of a new spy in the logs of the KGB central computer.

Stolinaya was very nervous. Gogol was the highest-ranking member of the bureaucracy that Stolinaya had ever dealt with. All the time he awaited the hour of the summons he had fretted about the report and evaluation he had turned in on Rita Macklin and the spy whose name was November. Perhaps he had overstated the case; worse, perhaps he had understated it. He sweated now as he waited on Gogol, who was rereading the reports arrayed on his massive desk.

"Why is the woman important?"

"I beg your pardon, Comrade Director?"

"Why is the woman important?"

"Sir, because she is a spy. She must be reevaluated in the light of her work with the R Section in the United States three years ago and her work as the agent of this November in Helsinki. In both cases, sir"—and here he paused to cough—"in both cases, it resulted in the defection of one of our agents. This is not the work of a journalist; it is the work of an agent."

Gogol smiled thinly, his brown lips pulling back to reveal yellowed teeth, like a serpent smiling the moment before striking.

"I do not think so."

"Comrade," said Stolinaya stoically and automatically.

"But you make a clear case for November. His name is Devereaux."

"Yes."

"He has annoyed me on occasion before. The woman is used by him, certainly, but he is the *agent provocateur*. He is not a spy but a counterinsurgent to our operations. And now he is to leave the Section."

Stolinaya only stared.

"We have that information, I can assure you. He will leave the Section at the conclusion of this matter. I think it would be worthwhile then to consider a change in his position. Yes, a considerable change." And Gogol smiled because he had spoken English at the end to enjoy the English pun and the man across the desk from him was puzzled.

"Sir?"

"The woman Macklin is not important to us. We have no evidence against her. But the man. He is going to be our target."

"Will you upgrade the agent Macklin?"

"Yes, of course. Your work is essential to us, Stolinaya. But Macklin is not important to us. Unless she is in the way. We have to deal with November not only because of his success against us but because of his insolence. Twice he has kidnapped our agents, once in the United States, now in Finland. He is a bad example. He operates outside the orders of his own section. I do not feel there will be reprisals against us when he is finished with."

"Why, Comrade Director?"

"We operate in constraints, their side and ours. He is beyond our control and their control. He does not follow their orders but he has been lucky in defying them. No, the time of November is over now, I think."

"What do you want me to do?"

"Recall these files on November and on the Macklin woman. They will need adjustment, I think, in the light of what is going to happen."

"What adjustment, sir?"

Gogol stared hard at Stolinaya. "We need some pretext and I am certain you will find it. When November was in Ireland five years ago on that matter with the IRA, do you suppose he stole money and guns while working for his government? He was in France two years ago; I believe he was dealing cocaine on the black market."

Stolinaya stared at the printout in front of him. He shook his head. "I do not see this in his files."

"Yes, because it is not in his files yet. It will be. So that when November is taken care of and there is a mild inquiry from the Opposition, we will just as mildly return the files to them that you have prepared. On November and, in the event it is necessay on the journalist. Do you understand now?"

And Stolinaya, who arranged files and was proud of his scrupulous work, realized he was to use the computer to justify a killing. He nodded at the small, yellow man in front of him. Yes, he understood and he felt sick at the understanding.

33

WASHINGTON, D.C.

Hanley picked up the black phone connected to the double-scrambler box and held it to his ear without speaking.

"What happened?" came the voice from the other end of the line. Because of the antitapping precautions built into the phone system, the voices were not true, especially over long distances; but even without resonance, Hanley recognized Devereaux's flat, even speech.

"Where are you?" Hanley leaned back in his chair. Washington was in the drab throes of an early spring; the sky was sullen and streaked with vertical dark clouds; the wind was warm; the grounds of the Mall around the Reflecting Pool were wet and spongelike. Hanley reflected the sullen mood of the city.

"It doesn't matter where I am at the moment. Did you take care of those matters?"

"This is a damnable gift you've sent us. A British agent on the run and a reluctant Russian defector. How did you get them out of Finland?"

"I helped a Helsinki policeman and he helped me. We're supposed to cooperate with the local authorities in these matters," Devereaux said, mocking Hanley and the primary manual for intelligence officers distributed to new recruits in the Section.

"Damn you, November. You've put me in the middle."

"It's a rare experience for you," Devereaux admittted. "Welcome to the club."

"Tartakoff puts us in some difficulty."

"I supposed he would."

"The problem is George."

"So Tartakoff says."

"Damn you, this is not a time for levity."

"What does the New Man say?"

"Yackley is hopping mad and he's taking it out on me. He's angry with you."

"Fuck him."

"Yes, that's very well for you, you're getting out—"

"Have you arranged those retirement matters?"

"They're proceeding, if you're serious."

"Did you think I would change my mind?"

Yes, Hanley thought. It was the thing he had counted on. Despite the dangerous nature of the man, Hanley had hoped for two years he might slip Devereaux back into some front-line operation, but Yackley's dislike for November had never abated. Yackley did not see what Hanley saw too clearly: the Section had grown flabby; it needed some life, some thought, some bold stroke to renew itself. If he had to admit it to anyone, Hanley would have said the Section could not afford to let Devereaux go.

"What about this Crohan?"

"He's safe."

"But where is he?"

"I suppose he must be arriving in Dublin at the moment," Devereaux said. "With Rita Macklin."

"My God, you've lost your senses."

"He's safe."

"Safe? You keep saying that, but safe from what?"

"From you, for one thing. Or the people at Langley. Or the Russians. I suppose by now that Tartakoff has told you that Crohan is really Michael Brent—well, don't worry about that. We are in the process of revising history again. It'll work out, Hanley; I don't know why you're upset or the New Man—you've got a nice little defector in your hands."

"And a nice little British agent who can't go home again."

Devereaux's voice carried the trace of a smile behind it: "We have a large country, Hanley. Be a generous man. One more spy in California retirement won't break the bank for us."

Hanley's voice was full of controlled fury, as though the outlet of mere words was not enough to convey his feeling: "You have blackmailed me with this matter, November; you have blackmailed the Section with the presence of this Macklin woman. The Section is not going to be held hostage to you. You are a goddamn agent in the field and we are the government of the United States—"

"Fuck you, Hanley, and listen to me: You called all this on yourself and the Section. If you wanted me out of Helsinki, I was willing to go weeks ago but you were playing a fishing game and I was bait; you wanted to see what the Russians were up to. Well, when the trap was sprung, I wasn't in it and now we've turned it on the Russians and you can't stand success."

"But we have the problem of George," Hanley insisted.

"Is he our problem? Or a problem for the British?"

"Both. What can we tell the Brits? We need Cheltenham, believe me, and the only way to have that listening post is with British cooperation. If we have another spy scandal now, it will kill us. Especially when the scandal breaks from our side of the water; it's bad enough when the Brits find their traitors by themselves. Besides, we only have the word of a defector to go on. Trapping George will take time—months, years. And what if George chooses not to fall into the traps? This is a delicate matter."

"Is it? I don't understand politics," Devereaux said. "You're going to do what you have to do—"

"No, not this time. This time you're going to have to help us out, I'm afraid—"

"Doing what?"

There was a pause. Hanley began chewing the nail of his left thumb. He would have to make the pitch effectively; thank God he wasn't facing November in person.

"I can clear everything for you . . . even for the woman . . . make certain that neither of you are chased by our people after your early retirement from the Section. . . ." Hanley paused.

Devereaux did not speak and for a moment, the line was silent. Then Hanley resumed: "We need to take care of George in some way."

"What are you going to do?"

"Not me, November; it will be up to you."

"I'm not a hitter. You have hitters in the Section."

"No, you're not a hitter but you're about to become one."

"I won't kill someone for you, Hanley."

"I'm afraid you'll have to. You want out of the Section, you want protection for your girlfriend, I'm afraid you'll have to see this matter my way."

"Why can't you use a hitter?"

"November, this is not a usual target, is it?" Hanley's voice was cold now, as cold as Devereaux's, two ice storms meeting on a dull, starless night in a frozen land far from any comfort or warmth. Hanley closed his eyes and Washington was gone from sight and he might be existing on a dead planet now, talking across the darkness to the only other survivor of the end of the world.

"We don't have any proofs on George but we are suspicious enough to want him out of the way. I talked to the New Man last night; this is the only way out of it. We can't go to the National Security Adviser to get positive approval and initials for action; nobody would agree to it. But we can't have George doing his dirty work—"

"If George is a mole," Devereaux said.

"There is every probability that he is," Hanley said. "We have questioned the Russian as well as Ely; this Macklin woman walked into a nasty nest of spies, didn't she? No wonder you're concerned for her safety. I would think her life might be in great danger."

Devereaux accepted the threat in Hanley's cold terms; there was nothing to say to him. He waited.

"November, you are the man for the job quite simply because you are involved in the matter up to your ears. We don't need to pull in a hitter and explain to him why he has to kill a high-ranking member of British Intelligence; you know the reason already. You have foxed us on the old man but you are now in a box of your own making. You want to come home again to Uncle with your girlfriend and you want Uncle not to take unkindly anything that you have done; well, Uncle is quite willing to forgive and forget, but you are going to have to do Uncle a favor."

"And if I hit him, you have something on me," Devereaux said. "You have something to keep me in line five or ten years from now. You see why I won't do it? I won't be able to walk away from you."

"You've killed men."

"Yes but not a hit. The killings were line of duty." The killings were for survival, Devereaux thought.

"This is line of duty because it is an order—"

"Don't be stupid, Hanley. There are no orders to kill; it is against the charter of the Section just as it is against the charters of all the intelligence organizations. You will merely tell me to kill someone and if it is convenient for you, you will remember to bring it up the next time you want to use me. It's not going to happen, Hanley."

"You killed that banker in New York three years ago in the Tunney matter."

"If you thought that, you would have to prove it."

"All right. You want something from us and you won't give us anything in return."

"We'll go back to the status quo," Devereaux said. "I'll be back tomorrow."

Hanley smiled. It was exactly what he wanted. He had played the card neatly and it had worked; he had never expected the death of George in the first place, certainly not from Devereaux. "Fine, fine. You see, you couldn't leave us until we wanted to let you go."

There was a dull pause now and when Devereaux spoke again, there was a hollow weariness in his voice. "What about Rita?"

"I'm sure she'll be all right. I can't speak for the Russians but I can assure you we have no further interest in her." Hanley was suddenly pleased. "When you get back, we can arrange a leave for you so that you can . . . 'date' her or however you would say it."

"You're scum, Hanley."

Hanley's face went white. "And you are a goddamn agent, November, not God. You are going to have to follow orders like everyone else; you are going to march when we say march and dangle when we want you to dangle. And when you're used up and we don't need you anymore, we'll get rid of you."

"And you'd let me go if I took care of George," Devereaux said.

"That's the only way, I'm afraid. You would have something on us and we would have something on you."

Again, there was silence on the line.

"But I have Tomas Crohan."

"An embarrassment, as you pointed out, but we can survive it. It all happened a long time ago. . . ."

"You weren't so sanguine about it before."

"That was before we found out he was Michael Brent. Our Russian defector had an interesting story. It seems we have something on the British as well. We might have crossed Crohan but the British double-crossed everyone when they sent in Brent to kill him. And that's who you have now, nothing; you have a goddamn English killer."

"You're mistaken, Hanley," Devereaux said then.

"What?"

"We have Tomas Crohan."

"But that's a lie," Hanley said.

"Are you going to prove it isn't true? Are you going to parade Tartakoff off to a press conference to explain that the man they kept in prison for thirty-eight years was really a British spy sent to kill an American agent behind Nazi lines? What kind of questions do you suppose the Section would get after saying something like that?" Now it was Devereaux's turn to slash and cut with words like shards of ice. "You have your game and I have mine and if it's stalemated right now, it isn't over."

"Damn you, we work on the same side."

"Do we?"

"Yes, damn you," Hanley said fiercely.

But he was met with a voice like an ice field: "When you're in the middle, all the sides look the same after a while, don't they?"

34

DUBLIN

In Stephen's Green in the center of the city a tinker woman with a dirty child in her arms stood begging coins from the passers-by. Only a few stopped to drop a shilling into her outstretched hand. Her face was dirty and her head was covered with a black and dirty shawl; her eyes were dark and they appeared in pain, but it was a trick of begging and it had been passed on to the tinker woman from her mother before her and her mother before that; she would pass it on to the child she held now in her arms. It was not that the woman was not truly poor; she was and it was a way of life passed on by generations of tinkers and their kin.

Rita Macklin passed her without looking at her and then stopped and turned back and dropped a coin into her hand. The grief on the face of the beggar woman never changed, did not lessen or become greater. Rita Macklin turned away from her and walked back through the park. He was late and she felt afraid and alone.

Her hands were thrust in the pockets of her tan raincoat. It was bitterly cold and damp but the gray skies had not yielded any rain since the night before. She paced down one walk and turned and tried another; Stephen's Green was not a large square but there were many paths and many trees and perhaps she had missed him.

She could not escape her thoughts and each time she turned one over, it made her feel sick until she felt trapped in this foreign city, in this dirty gray world.

She did not see Devereaux until he was beside her, walking with her suddenly step by step.

She took his arm and buried her face against his chest.

He held her in the middle of Stephen's Green for a moment and realized she was shaking.

When she pulled away and looked at him, he asked her, "Did everything work?"

"The way you said," she replied.

"Where is he now?"

"The priests took him in at the rectory. He did everything he was supposed to do. I filed the story this morning. In two days, the world is going to know about Tomas Crohan."

Devereaux held her arms and did not speak.

"Damn it, Dev. I feel sick all the time. I lied to the M.E., I coached the old man in his lie. . . ."

"It wasn't a lie," Devereaux said softly.

"Of course it was. He's Michael Brent—"

"No. He's an old man who served thirty-eight years in prison and now he's free."

"He's a killer. He's a hit man, that's all he ever was," Rita Macklin said. "You forget that Tomas Crohan was supposed to murder someone and Michael Brent was supposed to murder someone. It doesn't matter who the old man was; he's a killer, just a killer."

"He's an old man," Devereaux said. "He's just a bit of history that washed up one day. We can forget about him."

"I can't," she said. "And what are we going to do now?" Her green eyes stared mockingly at him. "Got the next chapter figured out yet?"

"I did," he said and his voice was leaden and dull like the color of the sky.

They stood apart from each other on a quiet path on the green where no one trod.

"What happened?" she asked him.

I wouldn't kill a man, he thought but he said nothing for a moment. "I can't leave the Section yet."

"Damn you, damn you," she said.

"I was . . ." He chose the word. "Forced. To remain a while longer."

"They can't force you to do anything. It still is a free country—"

"No. Only a larger prison," Devereaux said, remembering the old man's words.

"What are we going to do?"

"I don't know, Rita."

"You said you loved me—"

"Yes," he said and he said it so softly it was as though he were affirming a truth too immense to speak of but in whispers.

"Oh, Dev. What are we going to do?"

"You'll be safe. I had them promise that. Nothing that happened has changed. You can go back to the magazine and—"

"And we can have little rendezvous when you're back in the country, is that it?" She doubled her fist and her face was flushed; her small overbite was suddenly prominent.

"No," he said, again gently.

"No? Then what did you have in mind for me? I mean, you've used me to get out of this mess and now it's kiss-off for little Rita, right? Love 'em and leave 'em. Up to the mountains for a little piece of ass and then send them back home, right?"

"Shut up, Rita," he said with flat, dull words.

"Goddamn you, Devereaux, I love you and I would do anything for you, I told you—hell, I did it all for you—"

"And I did it for you," Devereaux said at last.

"What?"

"Stay in the Section. It wasn't safe any other way—"

"Why wouldn't it be?"

"I can't explain it all. There was something I was supposed to do and I couldn't and the only way I could make sure you would be safe was to remain in the Section—"

"What couldn't you do for me? What couldn't you do for me, Dev?"

"Kill a man."

It was so quiet for a moment in the park that neither could breathe for fear of disturbing the quiet. And then all the color went out of Rita's face and she was shaking again and she came and held him tightly, wrapping her arms around him, burying her face on his chest. There was nothing more to say and they both knew it and the sadness enveloped them like the silence.

35

LONDON ❖❖❖❖❖❖❖❖❖❖❖❖❖❖❖❖❖❖❖❖❖❖❖❖❖❖❖❖❖❖

What happened next was not expected by anyone involved in the affair, least of all the man called George.

In reality he was Sir Adrian Hugh-Fuller, KCB and KCE, and fourth in line to the barony of Giles.

George had survived, though it had taken some fancy footwork in the past few days; the Americans had botched the matter from the beginning and George had been amused by their clumsiness.

It had begun cleverly. The R Section in America had sent a long coded telegram to Q with a copy to the prime minister. The telegram thanked the British in strong but unofficial terms for their cooperation in the seizure of the KGB officer Tartakoff and regretted in unofficial terms the loss of a British agent named Sims who had been part of Operation Helsinki.

The prime minister expressed her interest in the matter. She was given full background on the operation at a private meeting the following day; the background was given by Q and George personally. The meeting had been delayed because Q had not the faintest idea of what Operation Helsinki was until the Americans gave him background notes on it and again piled on their congratulations for the help provided by Ely, a British agent who had been generously loaned to the American section as a liaison officer.

"I wasn't up on any of this, George," Q said grumpily and George had to convince the old fool that George had been aware of the operation from the start and could not divulge too much in case it became necessary to "compartmentalize severe reactions." The gobbledegook suited everyone from the P.M. to George.

But George was still afraid of an end run by the Americans and pushed his probe for the whereabouts of the British agent, Michael Brent. Unfortunately, Michael Brent surfaced four days later on the cover of an American newsmagazine as Tomas Crohan. He had been hidden safe in a priest's house in Dublin until the long, bizarre story of his arrest and imprisonment was broken.

"It is the American agent again," Latvia said to George on the day the story was screaming on front pages in the British papers. "Both of them."

"Yes. But there's very little to be done about Miss Macklin now. Or for that matter, about our Michael Brent. At least he can hardly go back on his new-fashioned lie, unless he wants to face a charge of murder."

Tomas Crohan became a national hero overnight in Ireland and the *Irish People* dutifully recorded on Sunday that Tomas Crohan preferred eggs for breakfast and apples as well.

George felt at last he was safe because the Americans had been unable to follow up their first telegram with a probe about the man called George. The story by Rita Macklin had boxed them in as well as the British; neither side could contradict the lies of Tomas Crohan and the woman journalist without revealing more about their own sordid operations than was good for them.

Nothing had changed, George thought; not for him, not for either of the people he worked for. He only regretted the boredom of being safe again in his dual role as computer director and Soviet agent.

Which is why George was the last person in the world to credit what would happen six days after the story broke about Tomas Crohan and three days after George was mentioned in the *Times* as receiving personal congratulations from the queen for a recently completed Anglo-American operation that emphasized the friendship and cooperation of the two peoples. Naturally, nothing about the operation itself could be mentioned in the paper.

It was a windy and wet night in London where theater goers scurried along the streets of the West End with their faces flushed by fresh, stinging breezes that smelled of the River Thames. It was a strange, invigorating evening full of lightning flashes and sudden downpours and then, sudden periods of immense calm.

The man called George stepped out of the rear door to his black Rover in front of his graystone residence at 29 Gloucester Road and waited a moment for the chauffeur to close the door behind him. He left instructions to be picked up the following morning at seven; he had to fly to Brussels for the day, first for a conversation with the Americans at NATO and later, for a reporting session to the European Theater Soviet control officer who lived in Liège.

George started up the stone stairs as the car pulled away. He paused a moment at the top of the stairs to regard the face of the red-tinged London sky. Lightning broke sullenly over the old houses and he thought the feeling of the evening was quite enough to rid him of his boredom—at least for a few minutes. George actually smiled as the sky broke again and again with lightning that was, nonetheless, followed only now and then by muted thunder.

Thunder, he thought then; the slow and faithful servant to the brilliant messenger of the gods.

The sentence framed in his thoughts pleased him as well and the smile did not fade as he stood at the top of his stairs and surveyed the world.

"George."

He glanced down to the walk and saw the figure huddled against the stone banister on the street. He blinked in the dim light to better see the man just as a bolt of lightning broke like crazed glass across the sky.

"Why . . . Bluebird. What on earth do you want?" George asked with mild interest. He had not seen Wickham from the moment he had been sacked nearly six weeks before. Poor old Wickham, he looked dreadful.

"George, I had to see you, they wouldn't admit me at the ministry—"

"Of course not, Bluebird. You're not secure."

"But I got in anyway," Wickham said and smiled strangely. "Not through the doors but through the computers. I got in through the computers at Cheltenham. All I needed was a small home computer and a telephone. And George, I went back through the records in Seeker and this time I used your code name—"

George stood perfectly still. He had nothing to fear but it was obvious that Bluebird was insane. His eyes glittered in the strange light of the strange evening and he smiled too much.

"You've changed the files, George. You're the only one who could change them. About me. About the kidnapping. You knew I was going to be kidnapped."

"You're talking utter nonsense, Wickham. Are you drunk or mad?"

"Both, George. You set me up, George; my God, George, for no reason at all, you've ruined my life." Wickham sobbed then but made no attempt to climb the stone steps to the place where George stood watching him with faint fascination.

"I thought it was for no reason," Wickham continued suddenly in an altered voice, one that was too calm for his words. "George. You're not what you seem to be, are you?"

"I'm afraid I don't follow you, Bluebird, and I am afraid I do not wish to continue this conversation—"

George turned on the landing.

"No, George," Wickham said. He held a metal object in his right hand; it had not been there a moment before. George felt energized suddenly. He turned to face the man at the bottom of the steps.

"Is that a knife, Wickham?"

"No, George. It's a pistol."

"Where on earth did you purchase a pistol?" George asked with sudden curiosity. What an odd question, he thought dreamily, as soon as he had uttered it.

"It doesn't matter, George. George, I want my position restored, I want to be reinstated—"

"I'm afraid you'd better go home and sleep it off—"

"My wife has left me. Do you understand what you have done to me?"

"I've done nothing at all to you."

"Damn you, George—"

"But I will do something if you don't leave immediately. You are threatening an official of—"

"Shut up, George, I don't care." The calm was replaced by a sob again. "I don't care about anything."

"My God, Bluebird, act your age," said George in a gruff voice. He took a step down and Bluebird did not react. He reached the bottom step and saw that Bluebird was crying copiously.

No guts, George thought. They never had any guts.

He took the barrel of the pistol and began to remove it gently from Wickham's right hand.

Wickham, inexpertly, had wrapped his first finger too tightly inside the trigger housing. The fleshy part of the first third of the finger became caught as George removed the pistol. No one meant what happened; it was a small act of fate, similar to the fate that caused lightning to strike and destroy a four-hundred-year-old oak that night in Hyde Park to the west.

The bullet exploded almost quietly, the roar muffled by George's heavy coat. If the bullet had been anything but a .45—

caliber shell, George might have survived it. The bullet tore into his liver and then struck the edge of a rib and ricocheted up into the lungs and had enough velocity left to tear across the left ventricle of the heart.

George was alive for about four seconds. His last image on earth was of Wickham standing very close to him, his eyes wide in horror, his face covered with a stubble of beard.

And George thought, the moment before he fell, that the absurdity of his death fit well the absurdity of his life.

36

WASHINGTON, D.C.

"I told you, Hanley, I wanted to see him."

"Yes," Hanley said distractedly. He had been staring at the same spot on the top of his government-issue desk for the past five minutes. He had looked up only once when the New Man, Yackley, entered his windowless office without knocking. The New Man had taken the uncomfortable straight steel chair across the desk from the director of operations.

"My God, he doesn't own this place," Yackley said. "He can't just waltz in and out—"

"Devereaux resigned thirty minutes ago."

"I thought you told me he wasn't going to resign," Yackley said.

"So I thought. We all make miscalculations."

"After you convince me he's valuable to us, how could he walk out on us?"

"It's a free country," Hanley said with a bitter smile. "At least it is some of the time."

"But he needs us—"

"No. Not anymore. And we don't have any way to stop him."

"We didn't have any way to stop him before," the New Man said with a puzzled tone. He felt uncomfortable, in the chair, in the little molelike office, uncomfortable dealing at all with Hanley who never said exactly what he meant.

On the desk between them was a copy of the *New York Times* with a photograph of Sir Adrian Hugh-Fuller above a story noting that the famous director of intelligence at Cheltenham in England had been shot to death by a disgruntled employee the day before on the steps of his home. It was a slow news day, otherwise the murder would not have been given prominence; the story hinted that the killer might have been in the employ of one or another terrorist groups, including the groups used by the Soviet KGB. Nowhere in the story did it mention that a four-hundred-year-old oak in Hyde Park had been struck by lightning on the same night and destroyed by fire.

It was the last hold Hanley had on Devereaux and they had both known it.

"Now I will be left alone," Devereaux had said.

"Yes. And what are you going to do with her?"

"That's none of your business. Don't involve yourself in my life anymore," Devereaux had said. He had removed the plastic card without photograph or identifying mark on it from his pocket. He had placed it on Hanley's desk. Then, as though giving it a second thought, he had broken the card in half and then again in quarters and thrown the pieces on the floor.

"I suppose I should apologize about Helsinki," Hanley had managed.

And Devereaux had only stared at him for a moment, without expression, the cold eyes boring into the pasty features of the little clerk. He had said nothing. He had walked out the door of the office and said nothing.

"Lucky for us, about this killing," the New Man said suddenly, changing the point. Hanley glanced up at the newspaper on his desk. Lucky, he thought dully.

"Now you won't have to proceed with that . . . little plan," the New Man said.

"The plan was completed four days ago. We had the highest-level code access to Seeker and Mrs. Neumann put in the incriminating information herself," Hanley said in the same flat voice.

"Do you think this was intended then? I mean, by British Intelligence?"

"No. The information we inserted into the Cheltenham computer against George is useless now, but there's no point in retrieving it. George is dead and he'll get a very nice state funeral out of it and this poor wretch who murdered him will get life at Wormwood Scrubs." Hanley paused and thought mundanely of the best-laid schemes of men; a stupid little accident by a stupid little nobody who hadn't the faintest idea of what George really was and who by killing George had stripped Hanley of his last hold over an agent called November.

Well, Hanley sighed. It was over at least.

At the same moment, as another cold, clear night wrapped itself around the city of Moscow, in an operations briefing room inside the Committee for External Observation and Resolution—which was the passively named section of the KGB in charge of foreign operations against American Intelligence—a Red Army colonel passed a briefing paper across a wooden table to two men who studied the Cyrillic letters for a moment and then asked two questions in bad Russian. Both men were Bulgarians.

"Will the woman be with him?"

"We don't know. It is not relevant to us."

"If she is with him, what do we do with her?"

"Obviously, you must judge that for yourself," said the Russian colonel. The matter was not routine but it did not interest him greatly; he was only a messenger from Gogol's office to the subsection of the agency in which the assassination bureau was housed. He had never heard of Rita Macklin or this man Devereaux. He was only following orders even as he contemplated a late supper that evening with a woman he knew who had arrived that morning from Leningrad and was now patiently waiting for him in bed in his apartment on the south side of the city.

The next morning, while Hanley worked on a new plan to revise the code names of field agents and to change the control system used in eastern Europe and a Russian army colonel slept naked in a rumpled bed next to a woman he had known all night, the M.E. strolled down the carpeted hall from his office to the cubicle where Rita Macklin was cleaning out the last drawer of her desk.

Rita closed the door and dropped the keys for the desk and the office on the desktop. "That's it," she said.

"You sound like you're going away forever," Mac smiled.

"Just three months, just to write the book about the old man," Rita said, and her returning smile was too quick and they both thought she had lied.

"I'd hate to lose you, Rita. I get the feeling you're really not coming back."

The M.E. stood like a little boy with his hands in his pockets, staring at the blank screen of the word processor at the side of her empty desk. She had piled her junk in a cardboard carton that had once contained laundry soap boxes.

"Thanks, Mac, but I'll keep my word."

"Okay, kid," Mac said in an awkward voice. "Don't forget we always need fast writers."

"Sure. I've got most of the transcripts from the old man. It's hard to believe you can remember so many horrible things so clearly."

"Ghosts," the M.E. said. "You never forget ghosts or bad dreams."

"You can try," Rita said.

"Sure. But the ghosts are always waiting for you. The old man has ghosts and he can't get rid of them."

"Maybe he's too old."

"It's not a matter of age," the M.E. said and he realized Rita was not looking at him but looking somewhere in her own memory. He smiled again and said something neither of them heard and shuffled back down the silent corridor to his office.

Rita left the building before eleven o'clock. The sun was shining but it didn't matter; she didn't need sunlight to add to the feeling that had come over her in the past few hours. Since he had talked to her; since he had told her what he had done.

37

FRONT ROYAL, VIRGINIA

The mountains were green again and the morning fogs burned off by midday so that you could see the top of Skyline Drive that ran along the Blue Ridge Mountains down the central spine of Virginia, down to the Tennessee line.

In the mornings, they would go into the woods together and find the trees that had fallen in the winter and they would drag them back to the cabin where he would cut them with a chain saw. If the fallen trees were too large, he would cut them on the spot where they had fallen and drag them back to the cabin in pieces.

It was hard work but she saw that it seemed to please him and that the longer he was in the cabin, in the mountains, the more he seemed to be content with himself. He still dreamed, violently, and the dreams he would not speak of frightened her most of all. She would shake him and say his name over and over until he would awaken and realize she had witnessed him dreaming. That had made him ashamed at first, as though he had revealed a weakness to her that they should never speak of. He would not tell her of the demons or ghosts of dead men who inhabited the violent dreams.

In those dreaded moments, in the middle of the black night, he was most frightened. Not because of the dreams that he had learned to live with but because of the fear that he could never break away from the past of his life, even with her help, even with her body next to him, even away from everything on this mountain in the middle of the Shenandoah.

"I love you," Rita would say then as though she could read his thoughts and he would let himself be comforted; he would hold her as a child will hold its mother, with trust and yearning.

Because all words lied, he never spoke to her of what he felt for her now except to say her name. She would understand that after a time.

They would work now in the heat of the day. Sometimes they would walk together in the woods, along unmarked trails shared with bears and deer, with possums and badgers and the other creatures who had come alive after the long winter and had survived it.

At evening, they would build a fire inside the old cabin, in the stone hearth, and they would eat together simply and talk.

She never tired of him. She would wake first and see him sleeping next to her. She would trace the scars on his body but when she would ask him where the scars had come from, he would not say.

She pried at his secrets but he would not reveal them.

"Nothing I did was so important or so secret," he said once to her. "It's just that it's an old life and I don't want to go back to it. Like Crohan talking about the life in Russia. He is frightened to talk about it."

"But he tells me."

"But not me. I can't do it. I can't mix you up in my mind with what it was in the past. Just bury it, Rita."

"I want all of you."

And so that he would not have to speak to her anymore, he would hold her instead and kiss her and touch her in places she opened to him. "Rita," he would say. And it would be enough.

"I bought food and they told me at the grocery."

She looked frightened. Her face was pale. Devereaux paused in his work as she threaded her way up the slightly-sloping ground to the place by the cabin where he was splitting wood.

He put down the metal splitter and took the bags from her arms and led her inside the cabin. He put the bags of food on the kitchen table and turned to her. His face was red from the sun, his gray eyes did not appear as icy fields anymore to her; he wore a checkered shirt and his hands had become rough again with the hard work.

"Who told you?"

"Mrs. Gibbons in the grocery. She said a couple of men were asking about you."

"What kind of men?"

"Foreign men. That's what she said."

"Men in suits?"

"Yes. Suits. Two days ago. Who is it?"

"What else did she tell you?"

"That's all. Just two men in suits, asking where you lived."

"Did she tell them?"

"She lies to them. Said you lived west of town, on the other side of the river."

"You can't lie to them," Devereaux said.

She held his arm. Her face was white, as though a sudden illness had struck her. "My God. That's what I thought all the way coming back here. I was so scared I had the boy put the bags in the trunk just to have company in the parking lot. I drove like hell getting out of town. I didn't care if I was stopped. I just wanted to get back here. I'm so scared."

"Yes."

She looked at him and saw that the flatness had come back to his eyes in that moment, that the arctic grayness had not gone away but had just been altered for a time in her company.

I'll be back in three months after I finish the book.

But it had been a lie, just a convenient lie for Mac. She never intended to be back.

And he had never intended to return either. They would run away from their worlds together for as long as they could; they would have no pasts, no tomorrows, make no promises, tell each other no lies.

She heard the ugly metal snap. She turned.

He had opened the shotgun. He filled the double barrels with two shells and closed it. He reached for the pistol and spun the chamber. He shoved the pistol in his belt. He took extra shells for the shotgun and put them in his shirt pocket.

"Who are they?"

"I don't know."

"What can we do?"

"Nothing. Not until they come."

"My God, Dev, let's get out of here."

"You don't lie to them, you don't run from them."

"But this is America. This is Virginia."

"Sometimes they have to step outside the rules. They draw up the rules after all. I'm outside the service now; so are you. Maybe that's the reason."

"But they can't do this."

He stared at her. "They can do anything they want unless you're ready to stop them."

"What are we going to do?"

"It didn't work out, did it?" he said.

"Don't say that. Please."

"Get out, Rita. Get back to D.C. Just go like hell and—"

"No, goddamn it. You don't get me in this thing and then tell me to take off like a movie heroine. Besides, I'm afraid. I don't want to be alone. Not now. Not ever."

He looked out the window. "I suppose we did it too easy. Maybe we should have waited."

"Dev. I love you no matter what," she said. "No matter what." Her voice was stubborn but on the verge of breaking and they both knew it.

They went out into the sunlight and there was nothing to see all the way down to the hairpin turnaround where a car could go back if it had wandered onto the trail by mistake. But at the foot of the mountain where the trail led to the asphalt highway, there was a gray car that had not been there before.

He took her hand and led her across the clearing to the edge of the woods. They plunged quietly into the woods for about a hundred feet, to a natural culvert formed by the passing of an old melting creek from the mountaintop. He helped her down into the culvert. Mud clung to them. He held the shotgun against the rim of the culvert.

She did not speak.

They waited a long time.

The two men had edged along the roadway up the mountain. He saw them and Rita nearly gasped but held her mouth with her right hand. She felt sick and cold.

She realized it must be the way he felt all of the time, but mostly at night, when the dreams came to him, and he was naked in sleep, too weak to fight against them.

One man whispered loudly to the other and the other nodded.

Bulgarians, Devereaux thought.

He turned to Rita. She was staring at him. She knew what it was as well as he. For a moment, they could only gaze at each other, in silence, wanting to say one true thing to each other which would wipe all this away, which would make the fact of the two men stalking the trail not a fact at all. He quietly pulled back both hammers of the shotgun.

The two men in suits passed fifty feet from them, at the edge of the woods, outlined in the clearing by the bright sun.

Devereaux held the shotgun level at the edge of the culvert like a soldier in a trench. The two men were apart from each other by about ten feet if faced from the house. But at this angle, they were together. Close enough for a shotgun in any case, Devereaux decided.

The shotgun kicked against his shoulder and the boom tore into the silence of the forest.

Both men were down and blood was on the trail, on their clothing, on the trees around them.

Devereaux climbed out of the culvert and loped forward, reloading the shotgun as he ran.

Rita made a strangled sound that was half a cry, half a scream. She put her hands to her ears as though to stop the sound of the shotgun long after the echo of it ceased to reverberate in the sudden still of the forest.

When he reached the place where they had fallen, he stood over them. The first one was short and dark and plainly dead.

The second man was alive.

He moaned. His belly was open.

Devereaux reached into his coat and pulled out the Czech pistol and threw it aside. He reached for identification cards.

Balkan Export Company.

He threw the cards aside and the dying man spoke, slowly, as Rita ran to the scene. She was sick and turned and vomited away from the bloody bodies, into the woods.

Devereaux listened to the dying man.

Then he stood up and pulled the black Colt Python from his belt. His face showed nothing.

She spoke: "Dev."

"Death to spies," he said quietly. "He said it in Russian." He stared at her for a moment but he could not say her name even, not now. And then he fired point-blank into the face of the dying man.

"My God, my God," she said.

But he did not speak. He only felt the heaviness of the pistol in his hand, felt it hold him like a chain.

They buried the two men in the woods. When the horror of it was over, they could not speak to each other.

They sat in the large room of the cabin before the roaring fire and felt cold, felt apart from each other.

"I can take you back in the morning," he said.

"Yes," she said dully. She stared at the fire and saw the bodies of two men. She saw Devereaux standing over a man with a pistol, firing into his face. She saw a man at the end of a corridor in a department store with a long, thin knife blocking her way.

"We have to go in two cars. I'll take the rental car and dump it in Fairfax on the way in. You can follow me and pick me up."

"Yes," she said, without tone.

"You saw the way it was," he said.

"I can . . ." And then she couldn't speak. She began to cry. He did not move toward her.

"Dev, help me."

And then he touched her.

"I feel so cold," she said. "I feel so cold."

Cold and cold, he thought, until you can feel nothing again.

"I don't want to leave you," she sobbed against him. "I love you, I love you, but I'm so frightened."

Cold and cold, he thought, it would never end. Hell was not fire; hell was a frozen place. Hell was darkness and separation and emptiness.

"I love you," she said.

"Rita," he replied. They held each other then against the night that enveloped the mountain, that blackened the forest on the mountain until the shadow and substance of the woods were the same thing, that permeated the house, that was held back only by the flickering flames that gave them a momentary warmth before the cold enveloped them.

Begun in Paris, 1982

Finished in Chicago, 1983